PON

✓

LIMITED TIME

By Robert Greer

Limited Time
The Devil's Backbone
The Devil's Red Nickel
The Devil's Hatband

Robert Greer

LIMITED TIME

THE MYSTERIOUS PRESS

Published by Warner Books

A Time Warner Company

Mysterious Press books are published by Warner Books, Inc., 1271
Avenue of the Americas, New York, NY 10020.

Visit our Web site at www.twbookmark.com

A Time Warner Company

The Mysterious Press name and logo are registered trademarks of Warner
Books, Inc.

Printed in the United States of America

First Printing: January 2000

10 9 8 7 6 5 4 3 2 1

Library of Congress Cataloging-in-Publication Data

Greer, Robert O.
    Limited time / Robert Greer.
      p.   cm.
    ISBN 0-89296-684-X
    I. Title.
PS3557.R3997L56   2000
813'.54—dc21   99-29484
                                                   CIP

Robert Greer

LIMITED TIME

THE MYSTERIOUS PRESS

Published by Warner Books

A Time Warner Company

Mysterious Press books are published by Warner Books, Inc., 1271
Avenue of the Americas, New York, NY 10020.

Visit our Web site at www.twbookmark.com

 A Time Warner Company

The Mysterious Press name and logo are registered trademarks of Warner
Books, Inc.

Printed in the United States of America

First Printing: January 2000

10 9 8 7 6 5 4 3 2 1

Library of Congress Cataloging-in-Publication Data

Greer, Robert O.
    Limited time / Robert Greer.
        p.   cm.
    ISBN 0-89296-684-X
    I. Title.
PS3557.R3997L56   2000
813'.54—dc21   99-29484
                                                            CIP

Dedication

Again, for Phyllis

Acknowledgments

I owe a debt of thanks to my editor, Sara Ann Freed, and publicist, Susan Richman, for their continued support and friendship. Special thanks to my agent, Nat Sobel, for guiding me along the bridge that unites mystery and suspense. As always, special thanks to my tremendously hardworking secretary, Kathleen Hoernig, and the most skilled of copy editors, Connie Oehring. For the Spanish included in this novel and the translations, I thank Roberta Alvarez-Villa, Virginia Ontervieros, and Abigail Jacquez. Thanks to Tony Sanchez of the Santa Fe Cigar Company for his tobacco expertise.

And finally, for my wife, Phyllis, thank you for putting up with the lengthy gestation period required to pen *Limited Time*.

Author's Note

The characters, events, and places that are depicted in *Limited Time* are spawned from the author's imagination. Certain Denver and Western locales are used fictitiously, and any resemblance between the novel's fictional inhabitants and actual persons living or dead is purely coincidental.

LIMITED
TIME

That it will never come again
is what makes life so sweet.

—Emily Dickinson

Chapter 1

Whenever Leah Tanner felt exceptionally nervous, the fine blond hairs between her eyebrows stood on end. As she walked toward the starter's block to take her mark in the finals of the hundred-yard butterfly, the downy hairs were fully erect. Aware of the idiosyncrasy, she stopped momentarily, ran her hands across her eyebrows, and looked out into the packed three-thousand-seat University of Colorado aquatic center until her gaze stopped on her father. Nathan Tanner was seated in the same front-row seat he had occupied during the three days of the U.S. Olympic team's swimming and diving trials. Anthony Rontella, Leah's boyfriend, was seated next to him. Watching Anthony wink and her father wave, Leah dropped her hand, smiled back at them briefly, and then continued walking, trying not to think about the intermittent back spasms she had been having.

She had beaten every one of her competitors at least once during her collegiate career, and she knew that she only needed a second-place finish to be guaranteed an Olympic spot. She had already won the two-hundred-yard butterfly, and she had a lock on at least one other relay race. If she won the current race, she'd be a shoo-in for a second team relay race, and then Anthony's three-gold-medal mantra might actually become a reality. Her nervousness had less to do with winning the race or three gold medals than with the mysterious back spasms she had been experiencing. She hadn't had a spasm in hours, but she remained concerned because the last time one had surfaced she had been exhausted, and now, after the semifinals, she was nearly dead on her feet.

She stared down at the slick ivory-colored tile, ignoring the possibility of a spasm and thought about how far she had come. There was hardly a trace of the reticent twelve-year-old who, after her mother had died of a massive stroke following a New Year's Eve party, had for years trailed her powerful corporate-lawyer father around in his downtown Denver 17th Street high-rise offices after school and accompanied him on business trips halfway around the world. There was little remaining evidence of the girl who had cried herself to sleep every night for years, begging God to return her mother to her side. Years of counseling had helped with bouts of anorexia, and then, at just the right time, Anthony had entered her life. Her metamorphosis now almost complete, she watched the water slip between her toes and tried to relax, telling herself that she had absolutely no reason to be so concerned over a simple muscle cramp.

Her arms dangling loosely at her sides, Leah shook her hands back and forth vigorously in an effort to release any remaining unfocused energy. Glancing up one final time at the partisan local crowd, she wondered how she would be received by the Australians at what Anthony was calling *her* Olympics. She was still pondering the question when the familiar baritone voice of the race starter announced, "Swimmers, please move to your starting blocks."

Immediately she climbed up onto her starting block above lane two, well ahead of the rest of the swimmers. Blocking out the crowd noise, she waited for further commands from the starter. When she heard the familiar call, "Judges and timers ready," her earlier unsteadiness disappeared and a surge of calmness swept through her body.

"Swimmers, take your mark."

Leah bent into her starting crouch, arms swept behind her, her toes gripping the edge of the starting block. The noise of the starter's gun and her smooth entry into the water were nearly simultaneous. By the time her first powerful half-dozen strokes cut into the water, she knew she was on a record pace. She made it a rule to never look for other racers until she had completed her first turn. Another half-dozen strokes and she was ready for the turn. She eyed the pool's bulkhead, made her turn, and was halfway into the second twenty-five yards of the race before she surveyed the lanes next to her and realized that she was half a body length ahead of everyone.

Her lead held coming out of the second turn and

through the entire third lap, but her lungs began to burn and her head started throbbing when she completed her final turn and broke for home, a full body length ahead of her competitors. The crowd was screaming, most of them on their feet and out of their seats as they sensed that Leah was about to shatter the NCAA individual medley record. Nathan Tanner and Anthony Rontella were shouting, arms extended in the air, as Leah devoured the last fifteen yards of the race.

As Leah tagged the bulkhead, the time clock on the wall above the judges froze, brilliant orange, its numbers recording a new NCAA record. Groggy and spent, Leah rested her head against the pool's gutter, gasping for air. Without warning, a spasm of pain filled the small of her back. Panting, she reached for her back as the painful knot exploded, doubling her over. She told herself, *relax,* but she couldn't. Suddenly a phlegm-rattling cough rose from the depths of her stomach and her eyes rolled back in her head. Rubber-legged, she lost her grip on the side of the pool and slipped beneath the water.

Anthony was over the first-row railing and racing for her by the time the two swimmers in the adjacent lanes realized that Leah was in trouble. Grabbing her by the arms, they struggled to keep her head above the water. A corkscrew of pain shot down her spine as a surge of fluid burst up from the pit of her stomach. Fuzzy-headed, she told herself that throwing up was something that some-times happened after an energy-expending race. A second muffled gurgle brought up not stomach contents but a gush of blood. The two swimmers at her side screamed and Anthony jumped into the pool.

By the time a hysterical Nathan Tanner reached poolside, her coach, Ellis Drake, had helped Anthony pull Leah from the water. Blood streamed from her mouth as she jerked in a series of uncontrollable convulsions. Two paramedics raced toward her, one carrying oxygen and a crash bag, the other pulling a collapsible stretcher. As Anthony and Nathan Tanner leaned over her convulsing body, Leah stared up into their faces with a terrified look that begged for an explanation.

"Paramedics are on the way," said Anthony, water dripping from his face onto Leah's.

"Hang on, baby," said Nathan Tanner, his ashen face drained of blood.

When Leah's eyes closed and the puzzled look on her face began to fade, Anthony stood up and screamed, "Hurry!" But by the time the paramedic with the oxygen knelt down to probe for an airway, Leah Tanner was already dead.

Chapter 2

Y ou still there, Hernández?" asked Jamie Lee Custus in her thick Texas hill-country drawl, shouting over a rush of phone-line static. Jamie Lee was seated in the kitchen of her rusted-out Winnebago in a leased one-acre sagebrush thicket outside Beaumont, Texas, nursing a cup of hot chocolate and rocking back and forth on the back legs of a press-backed wooden chair. She had never liked the name Jamie Lee—hated it, in fact. The name was too masculine and back-woodsy, too much like her father's name, Jimmy Lee. But as long as Jimmy Lee was alive there was no changing it. Change had never come easy for him, or her, and dropping the name that he had stuck her with would just be another progression in the alcoholic depression that was killing him.

"Yeah," came the muffled answer on the other end of the line.

"Can't you fucking Cubans fix your goddamn telephone lines?" asked Jamie Lee.

Manuel Hernández, who had just been jerked out of a deep, peaceful sleep, wasn't in the mood to defend his homeland. "Fuck you, Custus. In case you forgot, it's five A.M. here in Havana. What the hell's so important you need to roust me out of bed at this hour?"

"We've got a code-red on Cardashian. Seems as though the son of a bitch is acting flaky and on top of it, he's sick."

"You sure?" Hernández stood up from the edge of the bed, tugged at the frayed elastic waistband on his grimy boxer shorts, and glanced back at the outline of the woman's body beneath the dingy gray sheet.

"Word came down from the top. Sweets called from somewhere out in cell-phone space."

"Shit," said Hernández, still eyeing the woman. "What are we supposed to do?"

"Handle it."

"Meaning?"

The phone line crackled, a staccato lead-in to Jamie Lee's answer. "Come off it, Hernández; you know the score. Have your lecherous little Cuban ass in Denver by midnight. I'll be there ahead of you by five."

Hernández looked down at the dust-covered Day-Glo alarm clock on the nightstand, then again at the woman next to him before reaching inside his shorts and massaging his testicles. The problems he was going to encounter trying to get to Denver on such short notice would wreak hell with his day—a day he had promised to the woman. "Can't you handle it alone?"

"Listen to me, you little Caribbean rodent. I don't care

about the piece of commie ass you've probably got lined up for tonight, or whether you stand to lose a bundle on some back-alley cockfight. Be in Denver by midnight."

A lengthy buzz interrupted their conversation. Uncertain whether Custus could still hear him, Hernández shouted into the phone, "You talk big for a broken-down relic of a redneck, my friend. Especially since our problem seems to have surfaced on your end of this deal."

Jamie Lee took a long sip of hot chocolate before leaning her chair into the wall and then lifting her arthritic, next to useless left leg up onto the edge of the kitchen table. Balancing her stocky five-foot-nine-inch frame on her bad leg, she shook her unruly mop of red hair in disgust. "Save the finger pointing, Hernández. This thing's not over yet. A lot can still go wrong out there in the middle of the ocean among you commies."

Hernández smiled. "Yeah, like I might suddenly turn into a gimp."

Infuriated, Jamie Lee was out of her chair and on her feet in seconds, her large square face red with rage. Slipping the Bowie knife strapped to her belt from its leather sheath, she jammed it into the tabletop. "Can your comments, runt. Unless you'd like to end up losing a tongue."

"I'll chance it," said Hernández, smiling, enjoying the opportunity to yank Jamie Lee's chain.

Jamie Lee gritted her teeth, and looked down at the stacked three-inch orthopedic platform heel of her right boot. *When this job is over, I'm going to even the score,* she told herself, mouthing the words. "Meet me at the United passenger service counter, and don't be late." She glanced at her boot once again before slamming down the receiver.

Hernández was still grinning broadly when the sleepy-eyed girl with matted hair, sparkling white teeth, and a golden tan poked her head from beneath the filthy sheet.

"Quién era?" asked the girl, sitting up in bed, exposing her naked torso.

"A gringa, a very ugly and stupid woman, is who it was," said Hernández, slipping out of his shorts, pulling back the sheet, and easing into bed.

The girl giggled. "Stupid and ugly," she repeated in broken English as Hernández pulled her toward him.

Hernández nuzzled his face between the girl's large, perfectly rounded breasts, asking himself why he continued to work with Jamie Lee and why he had agreed to get involved in a scheme that could get him in trouble with the Cuban government and possibly cost him his life. As always, the answer came up the same: *money,* and his friendship with Neil Cardashian, an egocentric American loner who prided himself on operating from the position of a rogue. He had roomed with Cardashian decades before during college, just before Castro's revolution in the years when Cuban athletes like himself were still sent to study and hone their skills in the United States.

Fully aroused, Hernández positioned the girl on top of him. Instinctively, she reached out to brace herself on his shoulders. As she did, a question surfaced at the edge of his subconscious. *What idiotic thing could Cardashian have done that would risk his getting killed?* Hernández was about to run the possibilities through his mind when the rhythm of the girl's supple body started to work its magic.

10

"Stupid and ugly, stupid and ugly," she repeated in her thick Spanish accent, quivering as she moved her body in sync with his, until all thoughts of Neil Cardashian dissolved from Manuel Hernández's mind.

Chapter 3

Dr. Neil Cardashian had left the University of California and the hills of San Francisco for the Rockies two years earlier, with a $5 million federal research grant in hand to accept a position at the University of Colorado Health Sciences Center in Denver. He had been courted for months by the university's president, who offered him $2 million in state matching funds and the directorship of a new state-of-the-art molecular biology research institute to come to Denver. Here he could investigate his passion, the pathophysiology of human development and aging. On the day of Cardashian's arrival, the university president, a former U.S. senator and never one to shy away from a television camera, called a press conference to announce his enthusiastic support of Cardashian's mission, which he claimed would define the cradle-to-grave genetics of human aging "once and for all."

Six months later the president was gone, vacating his position for a European ambassadorship, leaving Cardashian and his research programs to drift on the winds of a promise of matching funds that never surfaced.

The fifty-seven-year-old, ruggedly athletic, and charming Cardashian, with his reputation as a research gun for hire, knew enough about the ups and downs of high-stakes academic research to not let the president's departure be a setback, and in nine months he was top copy once again after managing to ingratiate himself with several of Denver's moneyed socialites.

Armed with community support and backed by the strength of federal funding for his institute, Cardashian had only one remaining difficulty: scientific credibility. Ever since his arrival in Denver, a handful of colleagues had grumbled behind his back that too many of his research claims regarding the genetics of human development and aging were pie-in-the-sky exaggerations and experimentally unreproducible. Cardashian had initially been able to nullify their criticism by charming decision-making administrators on the Health Sciences Center campus and cranking out research papers in droves, but when the whispers challenging the veracity of his research wouldn't disappear, he was forced to appoint a reluctant campus darling, Dr. Theresa Gilliam, as his associate institute director and co-investigator, gambling that her participation would quiet the voices of academic discontent. Plausible and timely, the appointment was brilliantly insightful, save for one miscalculation. Cardashian badly

misjudged the tenacity, integrity, and gritty straightfor-
wardness of the sixty-year-old, wheelchair-bound Gilliam.

Eyeing each other guardedly, Cardashian and Gilliam
were just outside the doorway of Cardashian's eighth-
floor private office in the biomedical research building,
engrossed in their third acrimonious engagement of the
day. It was seven P.M. and the research laboratory behind
them, bustling with activity only thirty minutes earlier,
now sat silent and empty.

Tess Gilliam eyed Cardashian, who had been complaining of a stuffy nose and a fever all day, as if she expected
him to bolt. "I don't care what you say, Neil. Your latest
autoradiographs just don't wash, and there's something
strange about the mitochondria in the electron photomicrographs I took the other day. They're the size of
peanuts." Dr. Gilliam inched her wheelchair toward Cardashian, forcing him to take a half step backward into his
office.

"Maybe the P32 was bad. As for the EM photos, perhaps there's a problem with your scope's resolution."

"Come off it, Neil; you know better."

Cardashian took another step backward and swallowed
hard, knowing the P32-radioactive DNA label they used
for identifying telomerase didn't just go bad and that
Tess, an expert in electron microscopy, had prepared the
EM photos herself.

Grasping the arms of her wheelchair, Tess arched herself up straight, thinking for the first time in a long while
how confining the *damn contraption,* as she called it, actually was. If she could have, she would have leaped out
of the wheelchair, grabbed Cardashian by the shoulders,
and shaken him senseless. It was all she could do to keep

from screaming, *You're not only tinkering with the truth and risking our reputations, you're an idiot, Neil!* Restraining herself, she said instead, "Who ran the gels?"

"Veronica." Cardashian's raspy, nasal response was barely audible.

"Veronica doesn't make those kinds of mistakes; you know that, Neil. The granules in nearly every cell in the autoradiographs are bursting with P32. It's almost as if the telomerase product's pure."

Cardashian eyed the floor and ran his tongue back and forth across the inside of his lower lip without responding.

"I don't know what's going on here, Neil, but I intend to find out. When Henry Bales gets back from Durango I'm going to have him call a meeting of the research oversight committee. Given our research protocol, the results I'm seeing just aren't possible."

"You can't do that, Tess." Cardashian's voice was suddenly booming. "It'll kill our funding." Agitated, he moved toward the wheelchair. "Remember, your name's on this project too."

"All the more reason for Henry to have a look."

Cardashian knew that Henry Bales, the chair of pathology and also a molecular biologist, was a man he couldn't afford to antagonize. His face turning crimson, he reached down, grasped Tess's right hand firmly, and squeezed it. "I'm sure the P32 counts and EM discrepancies are just a mistake."

Looking him squarely in the eye, Tess pulled her hand away. "I hope so," she said, rubbing the back of her hand.

"Any more problems we need to address?" asked Cardashian, realizing that his clumsy attempt at persuasion had been a mistake.

"No."

"Well, then, I suggest we call it a night. I'm sure we'll be able to answer all of your questions tomorrow." Cardashian stepped back into his office, serving up a broad, this-conversation-is-over smile. It was the kind of insecure, ingratiating smile that Tess had seen from Cardashian scores of other times, a smile that he usually unleashed just before he lost his temper, and one that told Tess it was indeed time to leave.

"I hope so," repeated Tess, wheeling her chair out the doorway, turning to leave, and telling herself that her decision to collaborate with Neil Cardashian had been a stupid idea from the start. She had known he was overbearing and had a penchant for establishing scientific conclusions before they were readily apparent. But the lure to do cutting-edge work, her sense of loyalty to the institution, and the notion that she could keep Cardashian scientifically honest had placed her where she was.

Rubbing her hand again, she spun her wheelchair fully around and headed down the center aisle that led out of the laboratory. She hadn't thought about the college skiing accident that had put her in the wheelchair in years, but glancing back toward Cardashian's office one last time and seeing snow-capped Mt. Evans through his windows, the memory of her accident resurfaced in a rush. She remembered the cold, numbing desperation she had felt as she lay at the bottom of an Aspen ski run, unable to move her legs. She recalled the strange feeling of guilt that had surfaced when she realized that she had let her

University of Washington teammates down. Most of all she recalled wondering whether she was paralyzed and thinking that if she were, she'd just as soon lie there and die. And she might have if it hadn't been for a rehab team led by a world-class neurologist, a gaggle of compassionate physical therapists, and modern medicine. It was her spinal cord injury that had opened her eyes to the wonders of neuroscience and eventually charted her career in medicine.

After a moment, she left the lab, mulling over what to do next. First she'd call Henry Bales, who was as close to her as a son and unfortunately on vacation at his southern Colorado Flying Diamond Ranch outside Durango, to inform him that she planned to press for an investigation of Cardashian. Then she would call Dr. Sandra Artorio, a National Institutes of Health research scientist and good friend, who aside from Cardashian was one of only a handful of scientists who had an understanding of the full potential of the enzyme known as telomerase.

Chapter 4

The temperature was just a few notches above freezing and the hay meadows of Dr. Henry Bales's Flying Diamond Ranch were still partially covered with snow. The remnants of eight hundred tons of neatly stacked hay that had kissed the rafters of the ranch's mammoth hay sheds the previous fall sat forlornly in the stack yard. A week earlier Henry had instructed his foreman to increase the mineral supplement to the herd of three hundred Black Baldy cattle he ran on the Flying Diamond in hopes that the cattle could hang tough and remain healthy until the tender timothy grasses of spring poked up from beneath the soil.

The aroma of lodgepole pines hung in the late March air and although the rolling hills of chickweed and sage looked the same as they had for a hundred years, the ranching culture that Henry had grown up with was slowly fading. Sooner or later ranching as he knew it would disappear, going the way of nineteenth-century trail drives, cattle barons, and the once sprawling grasslands of the West. But until then, branding at the Flying Diamond took place the same week it had since Henry was five years old.

Henry, his foreman, Scotty MacCallum, a neighboring rancher's two pimple-faced teenaged boys, and CJ Floyd, one of Henry's closest friends, were busy branding a corralful of six-week-old calves. The calves had been separated from their mothers into a crowding pen, and the bellows of mother cows, bawls of the calves, and authoritative barks from Henry's seven-year-old Border collie, Cody, reverberated from the corral.

Rest broken by their early-morning start and saddlesore from moving a hundred head of cattle from a mucky, subirrigated outlying pasture the previous day, Henry and CJ stood next to the rusty old propane heater Henry's father had also used to fire branding irons. Rubbing their hands above the heater's warmth, they watched Cody work the first reticent calf toward a calving table where the calf would be laid on its side and branded.

It was half past six that evening before they finished branding, doctoring, and pairing all the calves back up with their anxious mothers. The sun had started its slow dance behind the mountains to the west, and a layer of wispy clouds served as the perfect diffusing filter for a brilliant sunset. Bone-weary and dehydrated, Henry nodded for CJ to follow him down the center alleyway that led from the corrals. In the distance, Scotty Mac-

Callum and his two young hands moved off on horse-back, driving the Flying Diamond's herd of Black Baldys back to their familiar pasture while Cody nipped at the legs of three lazy cows bringing up the drag.

CJ swung the alleyway gate closed and looked ahead to catch Henry gazing at the sunset. "Ever wonder why things seem to have to change so much in life?" said Henry, sounding miffed. Instead of answering, CJ stopped in his tracks and stared at his friend of more than twenty-five years. He hadn't seen Henry in such a philo-sophical mood since the last days of their navy tour in Vietnam.

Henry had been in college in 1969 when he decided his life needed a little more adventure, and a war was the perfect place to start. CJ had been a gang-banging black kid with nothing to look forward to but an uncertain life on the Denver streets. They had ended up serving in the navy together, assigned to the 42nd River Patrol group at Can Tho. CJ was transformed into a gunner's mate aboard one of the dozens of 125-foot swiftboats the navy used to patrol the twisted creeks, dense jungle, and humid swamps of the Mekong delta, Henry into a corps-man. Linking up as shipmates on the patrol boat the *Cape Star*, they had served together for a year.

Neither of them had ever been able to put their finger on just why they became friends. Perhaps it was their Colorado roots. It could have been their single-minded loner's view of the world. Whatever the reason, their friendship had endured through the war and the nearly three decades since. Over the years they had laughed and cried about their Vietnam experience, but nothing seemed to make either of them break into laughter more quickly than when Henry recounted the two things he had said every night for a year before he squeezed into his *Cape Star* bunk: *When I get home, I'm never leaving the Rockies again,* and, *This war gives me gas.*

While CJ stayed on for a second tour, returning stateside to become a bail bondsman with a Bronze Star, a bad attitude, and months of recurring night terrors and sweats, Henry came home and enrolled in medical school at the University of Colorado within the year. Following medical school he remained at the Health Sciences Center through a pathology residency and a molecular biology Ph.D. He currently served as chair of pathology and chief of diagnostic molecular biology and led a research team investigating the role that viruses play in the human cancer cascade. True to his Vietnam mantra, except for work-related research conferences he rarely set foot beyond the boundaries of the West.

Breaking his stare and finally responding to Henry's question, CJ said, "On occasion, but I try not to let it spoil my day."

Henry smiled at CJ's response as they began walking side by side up the quarter-mile gravel lane that led to Henry's rambling hillside home. "Have you ever second-guessed becoming a bail bondsman or thought about why at forty-seven you're still bounty-hunting bad guys on the side?"

"No more than I've ever second-guessed why my folks deserted me or why I was raised by an uncle who was a drunk instead of president of the United States. Something's eating at you, Henry. Spit it out."

Henry stopped, stroked his chin, looked at CJ pensively, and then continued walking. "I think I'm caught between the proverbial rock and a hard place."

"Woman troubles?" asked CJ, knowing Henry's MO for getting caught up in relationships with either dyed-in-the-wool cowgirls or career-crunching fast-track types unable to adjust to the dual aspects of Henry's life.

"No, but a woman's involved."

"Might as well get it off your chest," said CJ, shortening his stride as the lane leveled off near the house.

"You remember Tess Gilliam, don't you?"

"Sure. That tough-as-nails lady doctor in the wheelchair. The one who keeps your ego in check?"

"That's her," said Henry, surprised at the accuracy of CJ's description. "She called me the other night while you were in dreamland sawing logs to tell me she's got a problem back at work. She beat around the bush for a while until I finally pushed her into telling me what was wrong. It seems as though a colleague of ours back at the Health Sciences Center might be fudging scientific data."

"That's what's got you so worked up? A problem back at the shop? Shit, Henry, you're here at the ranch to get away from that. If it was me, I wouldn't give it a second thought."

Kneading his lower lip thoughtfully as he mounted the steps leading up to the porch that wrapped around three sides of the house, Henry said, "To tell you the truth, CJ, there's nothing I'd like to do more, but Tess is a co-investigator on the fudger's research project. If things turn sour, some major-league bad stuff just might rub off on her." Henry walked down the full length of the porch, bypassing several chairs before plopping down in a frayed wicker chair next to a support post. Dog-tired, CJ slumped in a chair next to him. They sat in silence for a while, staring out toward the fading sunset, until Henry spoke up. "I've been preparing myself to deal with what might happen to this ranch for a long, long time. Guess I'm just not as prepared to deal with people cheating at medicine."

CJ sat back in his chair, hat tipped forward, his hands clasped behind his head. "That scientific world of yours is way out of my league, Henry, but I can tell you this. When it comes to human nature, there's one sure constant: people cheat. Doesn't matter whether you're dealing with bond-skipping bottom feeders, doctors, preachers, or bums."

Henry sighed. "That's what's got me so spooked, CJ. I always thought I could tell pond scum from sweet water."

"Take my word for it, Henry. Sometimes you can't," said CJ, knowing that Tess Gilliam represented the sweet-water side of Henry's equation. He didn't know many people tough enough to come back from cracking their spine to earn an M.D. "I think Dr. Gilliam can take care of herself. And for what it's worth, here's some advice. Get rid of your rotten apple."

Henry thought for a moment as he stared out into the fading light. "Easier said than done. The person I'm referring to is pretty well connected, and to make matters worse, his research involves investigating the genetics of the very essence of life."

Catching a glimpse of the last rays of light bouncing off Cedar Creek, CJ pointed toward the approaching darkness. "I'll tell you what's the essence of life. It's coming home alive and in one fuckin' piece from Vietnam."

Henry got up and smiled without answering. They stood in silence, staring out into the enveloping night, until Henry finally broke their vigil and headed toward the front door. As he opened the door and reached inside to flip on a hallway light, he couldn't shake the thought that CJ was absolutely right. Stepping across the threshold, he turned back to CJ, shaking his head. "Looks like I've got a new kind of war on my hands, CJ. Hope I live through this one too."

Chapter 5

Vernon Lowe didn't like freelancing. It put too many miles on his car. More importantly, it had a habit of interfering with his weekly gospel choir practice. The only thing that kept him tied to the freelancing autopsy gravy train was the fact that he got paid $150 for each one.

A five-foot-seven, bug-eyed, fancy-dressing slip of a black man, Vernon had been chief morgue attendant at Denver General Hospital for more than twenty years. During that time, he had garnered such a reputation for skillfully prepping and eviscerating the dead that a half-dozen hospital pathology departments in the Denver metro area routinely called him whenever they found themselves shorthanded in the morgue.

Vernon had been called to Boulder Community Hospital on a freelance job early that morning. He disliked freelancing at Boulder Community because, as he told close friends like CJ Floyd, college towns gave him the willies—too many leftover hippies. Nonetheless, with money as the magnet, he found himself in the middle of the Boulder Community morgue the morning Leah Tanner's body arrived for autopsy.

If he'd had any inkling that the autopsy was a coroner's case, he would have passed on the job. Over the years, he had been involved in enough coroner's cases to know that they sometimes morphed into legal beasts full of hungry lawyers. Beasts that could put him on the witness stand two years down the road, defending why the Y-shaped incision he had made to open someone's body hadn't been perfectly symmetrical.

Vernon wolfed down the last of a stale hospital cafeteria doughnut and chased it with a rush of bitter coffee before walking across the morgue to the men's dressing room to gown. Belting out a chorus of "What a Friend We Have in Jesus" as he changed, he checked his watch and told himself that he'd be back on the Boulder Turnpike headed for Denver in less than two hours. When he stepped back out into the morgue humming "Rock of Ages," he found Dr. Lyndon Nelson, a Boulder County deputy coroner, thumbing through a wafer-thin medical chart and talking to another man.

"Vernon. What a relief," said Nelson, placing the chart on the lip of the gleaming silver autopsy table beside him. "I was afraid I might get some rookie assisting me. I sure don't need that on this post."

Vernon smiled at the backhanded compliment without answering, thinking that of all the Boulder pathologists he could have drawn, Nelson was the one he would have chosen. He wasn't sure who the man with Nelson was, or why he was there, and it must have shown on his face because Nelson immediately spoke up: "Vernon Lowe, I'd like you to meet Dr. David Patterson. He's the doctor for the CU swim team. Unfortunately, we're about to post one of his swimmers." Turning to Patterson, he added, "Vernon's the best in the business."

Patterson smiled and nodded at Vernon without shaking hands. "Glad to hear that." Looking back at Nelson, he added, "Like I said, I promise not to get in your way."

"What happened to your swimmer?" asked Vernon, retrieving the medical chart Nelson had set aside.

"We're not certain. We're speculating she had a seizure or a stroke."

Vernon looked at Nelson for his take on the cause of death.

Nelson shrugged. "Afraid I'm going to have to let the autopsy speak for itself."

Vernon wasn't surprised by Nelson's response. He knew Nelson as the kind of man who never liked to take a stand unless he was certain he could back it up. Scanning the cover of the medical chart, Vernon's eyes locked on the red name tab in the upper-left-hand corner that spelled out *Leah Tanner* before he quickly flipped through the contents. "Awfully young," he said, setting the chart aside.

"Twenty-two, and just hitting her prime," said Patterson. "She was in line for a couple of gold medals at this year's Olympics."

"Sad," said Vernon, a non–sports enthusiast who had forgotten that it was an Olympic year. Looking at Nelson, he said, "How'd the autopsy end up in your lap?"

Nelson frowned, as if to say, *You don't know?* Then, realizing that Vernon deserved some explanation of why they were about to autopsy a young woman in the prime of her life, he said, "I know you're not into sports, Vernon, but this thing's been on the news for the past day and a half. To tell you the truth, I'm surprised we're not down here sharing the morgue with the press."

"Guess I missed it," said Vernon. "We won't have any media people in here today, will we?"

"No," said Patterson. "The girl's father has made certain of that. In fact, that's why the autopsy was delayed until today."

Vernon didn't know what power Leah Tanner's father had over the press or how he had been able to delay an autopsy, a coroner's case at that, for two days, but he was relieved not to have to share the morgue with anyone other than the out-of-place-looking, square-faced Dr. Patterson.

"Might as well get started," said Dr. Nelson, nodding for Patterson to follow him to the dressing room to change. Vernon watched them disappear before he strolled over to the morgue's bank of refrigerated coolers, checked the computer-generated name tag that read *Leah Tanner* in a slot above cooler number one, swung the door open, and rolled the pale, lifeless body out on its bed of stainless steel to begin the autopsy.

Forty-five minutes later, Vernon laid aside the Striker saw he had just used to remove the bony skullcap from Leah Tanner's cranium in order to access the brain. "Ready for a neuro inspection over here," said Vernon, wiping a fine saw-generated mist of bone off his goggles before turning back to glance at Dr. Nelson, who was in the midst of examining Leah Tanner's lungs while Patterson peered over his shoulder.

"There's fluid in these puppies," said Nelson, squeezing both lungs and listening for crackles. "But she certainly didn't drown."

"We already know that," said Dr. Patterson, his abundant midsection tugging at the seams of the undersized green smock he had struggled into.

Continuing his examination of the lungs without responding, Nelson snipped off several small wedges of lung tissue and dropped them into a couple of jelly-sized jars of formalin for processing and later microscopic examination. He was about to head across the room to get a couple of fresh bottles of formalin before moving to the brain inspection when Vernon called out, "Hey, Doc, think you better step over here and have a look at this."

Aware that Vernon prided himself on never asking for help from an attending pathologist unless he really had a problem, Nelson glanced toward Vernon with surprise. "Stroke?" he said, suspecting that Leah Tanner's neurologic damage was so dramatic that Vernon could see it on his cursory examination of the brain. "I sort of figured all the real pathology here would end up being neurologic." Then, looking at Patterson, he said, "You could almost bet on it from the comments in the resuscitation notes."

Not wanting to burst Nelson's bubble, Vernon remained silent as he stared down at Leah Tanner's brain. Stepping aside, he let Dr. Nelson take his place at the head of the autopsy table, staring at the bewildered look arching across Nelson's face, a look that Patterson, who had followed him, quickly mimicked.

"Damn," said Nelson, sounding as though he needed to

convince himself that he wasn't looking at a mirage. Instead of seeing the gray-white, convoluted surface of a normal brain, he found himself looking at a mass of BB- to pea-sized nodules. Red, black, and sometimes purple knots ballooned up from the brain's prominent fissures, odd pebblelike excrescences resembling grotesque strands of pearls.

"What do you think?" asked Patterson, his eyes ballooning.

Nelson leaned down for a closer look at the unusual pathology. "I don't know," he said, running a gloved hand along a string of the nodules, trying to formulate a list of diagnostic possibilities in his head. The knots were too firm to be abscesses, and they seemed too confined to the brain's surface to represent any kind of lethal tumor. They certainly weren't blood clots, but hemorrhagic fungus balls remained a possibility. The fact that the strange nodules seemed to occupy not only the brain's fissures but also the minuscule space that had existed between Leah Tanner's brain and her skull had him wondering how they had been able to maintain any kind of blood supply without dissolving into massive pools of dead tissue. The nodules didn't appear to extend much beyond the brain's outer cortex, but there was no question they must have penetrated into the depths of the vital regulatory compartments of Leah's brain. The bizarre findings had him baffled. Snapping the fingers on his surgical gloves, Nelson looked at Patterson and frowned.

While Nelson and Patterson stared at one another, Vernon prepared to document the findings with a Polaroid camera he had retrieved from a nearby cabinet. Easing down into a semisquat, he framed the photograph, adjusting the image until the knobby surface of Leah Tanner's brain came into sharp focus. He snapped three quick photos, laid them aside to develop, and straightened back up, telling himself as he did that in twenty years of autopsy freelancing, he had never seen anything so strange.

Chapter 6

Bottom line is, Tess, I don't care what you and Henry Bales think. Neil Cardashian and his research simply are not, as you so offhandedly put it, expendable." Louise Adler, microvascular surgeon and dean of the University of Colorado's medical school, adjusted the slipknot in her expensive handcrafted silk scarf, as she always did when she was about to rebuff a subordinate. Then, glaring down at Tess Gilliam from her perch of authority against the front edge of her desk, she added, "I never expected you, of all people, to be capable of leading a witch hunt."

Recognizing the reason for Adler's agitation, Tess slammed the legal pad she was clutching facedown in her lap in frustration. She knew that Adler couldn't afford to have a single blemish on her record during her CU stewardship if she expected to work her way up the deanship food chain. They both knew that Colorado was just a way station on the wealthy Harvard-educated Adler's goal of administering some Ivy League school, perhaps even her alma mater. Nonetheless, Tess was determined to not let Adler's career plans interfere with the purpose of their meeting.

"You're not hearing me, Louise," said Tess, knowing how much Adler hated being called by her first name. "Neil's playing with fire." Negotiating her wheelchair closer to Adler, Tess dropped her legal pad on the desktop with a thump. "I've summarized things here." She tapped the tablet with her index finger for emphasis. "I'm not sure what Neil's up to, but I've spent the last week checking through six months of his daily research logs and reevaluating every experiment he carried out in that time. I've talked to his research assistants, postdoc fellows, residents, and secretary. I've even spoken to our scientific product reps. In short, I talked to everyone who might know anything about the unusual series of Neil's telomerase experiments I stumbled across two weeks ago—experiments that Neil seems to have purposely kept me in the dark about. And you know what, Louise? I think your golden boy is cooking his research books."

"You can prove this?"

Tess ran her hands up and down the arms of her wheelchair in frustration and glared up at Adler. "I'm not out to prove anything. I simply want you to make certain that any irregularities get looked at by the research ethics committee and dealt with. In other words, Louise, I'd like you to do your job."

Adler shot Tess an icy stare. Adjusting herself against

the desk's edge, she turned and looked down at the legal tablet. "Have you any idea what's at stake here?"

"Are you kidding, Louise? Have you forgotten that Neil's experimenting with telomerase? You and I both know the stakes."

Concerned that her authority was being tested, Adler pointed an index finger squarely in Tess's face. "You're right. I do. First off, there's the university's reputation to consider, and very likely yours and mine to boot. Second, there's five million dollars in federal research funding this medical school stands to lose, not to mention collaborative research projects and future funding. And finally, there's not only the embarrassment Neil would suffer given an unwarranted ethics committee investigation, there's also the lawsuit I'm sure he'd slap on us if you're wrong."

Surprised by the fact that Adler had all but ignored her mention of Cardashian's possibly inappropriate experimentation with the enzyme telomerase, Tess gritted her teeth and sat up in her wheelchair. Her eyes narrowed in a challenge to Adler. "Maybe I need to remind you of our potential liability if Neil's somehow managed to coax the telomerase genie out of its jar."

"Don't be coy with me, Tess. I've got an M.D. and a Ph.D. just like you, and mine came from Harvard. I know the telomerase story as well as you."

Tess swallowed hard and counted to ten before responding. "I'm aware of your credentials, Louise, but you haven't been in the operating room or your physiology research lab for nearly three years."

"Save your sarcasm, Tess. Everyone from the janitor who sweeps out Neil's lab to our freshman medical students knows that Neil's been trying to define how the telomerase enzyme controls human maturation and development."

"Suppose I told you Neil may have found what he's been looking for."

"Then I'd say Neil should dust off his tux, buy a plane ticket for Sweden, and begin polishing his Nobel acceptance speech. You're his co-investigator; you should be jumping for joy. Don't tell me there's a twinge of scientific jealousy operating here."

"Don't be stupid, Louise. I'm not jealous. I'm scared."

"Spare me the melodrama, Tess, and get to the point. So far all you've convinced me of is that Neil Cardashian has been doing his job."

Trying to maintain her composure, Tess leaned back in her wheelchair and brushed an errant lock of her stunning silver hair out of her face. "Are you familiar with the telomerase experimental model that Neil's been working with?"

"Certainly. In case you've forgotten, I hired the man. He's working with a protozoan, I believe."

"*Euploidies aediculatus,* to be exact. There's only one other lab in the country experimenting in the same arena," said Tess, surprised by the accuracy of Adler's response. "Sandi Artorio's at NIH. Here's our problem. From what I've seen, I think Neil's moved up from working with a one-celled protozoan to something more complex, and I'm almost positive he's working outside the bounds of our NIH-approved protocol. If he is, as his lead co-investigator, my butt's in the wringer, and yours will be right behind."

"Have you talked to Neil about your concerns?"

"Yes, but he brushed me off."

Adler's face turned ashen. She was well aware of the rigid oversight responsibilities the university had to the National Institutes of Health. "Damn it." Adler walked around her desk to an intercom and buzzed her secretary. The look on her face was bitter, her voice authoritative. "Get me Neil Cardashian on the line." Then, flipping on the speaker phone, she looked at Tess. "Maybe you should hear what Neil has to say."

Tess shrugged. "As long as you tell him I'm here."

The secretary was back on the line before Adler had a chance to respond. "I have Dr. Cardashian's research fellow on the line. He says Dr. Cardashian's not in. Thinks he's nursing a cold."

"Please tell him to have Dr. Cardashian give me a call as soon as he gets in. It's urgent."

"I certainly will."

Frowning at Tess, Adler switched off her speaker phone. "You heard the dirt. Neil's out." Then, almost accusingly, she added, "Why didn't you come to me about this sooner?"

"I came to you as soon as I had something I thought was concrete."

"Have you spoken to Henry Bales or any of his research ethics committee members about this?"

"I've only spoken to Henry."

Knowing that Henry Bales was the kind of man who would never compromise on an issue related to abuse of medical ethics, Adler shook her head in disgust. "This could get sticky."

"That it could," said Tess, sensing that their meeting was about to come to an end.

"Are you prepared for that?"

"The question is, Louise, are you?"

Adler stood up from her desk. A worried expression covered her face. The look told Tess that Adler was having difficulty answering the question.

"Call me after you've heard from Neil," said Tess, positioning her wheelchair to leave the room. "I don't think we can go any further with this today." She was almost to the doorway when she turned back to Adler and added, "And Louise, if the shit hits the fan, don't bury it. Remember, all I've got to lose is my reputation. You've got Harvard waiting in the wings."

Chapter 7

Neil Cardashian was sitting on the floor in his eighth-floor research laboratory, legs spread-eagled, his back propped against the side of his antique rolltop desk. Jamie Lee Custus and Manuel Hernández stood watching him from a few feet away. Cardashian's insides had been burning for hours, but surprisingly he wasn't sweating. The tips of his fingers were numb, and his mouth turned fuzzy as a parade of lights continued to flash on and off behind both eye sockets. Fighting back a runny nose, he snorted, reached up, listless and dizzy, and wiped a thick pool of mucus from his upper lip onto the monogrammed cuff of his tailored shirt.

Suddenly he heard voices, painful, piercing voices that seemed to be coming from the same spot as the flashing lights behind his eyes. As the voices reached their zenith, Cardashian urinated on himself seconds before defecating into his Armani pants. Custus and Hernández wrinkled their nostrils and backed away in unison as the offensive smell filtered up toward them. Groaning, Cardashian threw up on himself, convulsing until only a rubbery string of vomit hung from his lower lip.

Shaking her head in disgust, Jamie Lee flipped down the mouthpiece on the cell phone she was clutching and nonchalantly punched in eleven numbers. After six rings, there was an answer. Without announcing who she was, Jamie Lee whispered, "We're standing here watching Cardashian shit and piss himself to death. The smell is something awful. What do you want us to do?"

"Take his jewelry, watch, wallet, and clothes, and dump him," said the muffled, obviously disguised voice on the other end of the line, an undulating, robotic voice that sounded as if it were being filtered through a dictaphone losing battery power. "And clean him up, even the shit."

"Say what?"

"You heard me. Clean him up and be sure to wipe his ass. I don't want to risk anything coming back to bite us."

"In your dreams."

"Do it, or you won't see a dime."

"Come wipe his ass yourself, Sweets!"

"I can't do that. And just for the record, if you ever mention my name again during a cell-phone conversation, count on it, you'll end up like Cardashian."

Jamie Lee, unconcerned with the threat, said, "It's a code name, for Christ's sake." She looked at Hernández and shook her head. Hernández nodded understandingly before returning to picking his teeth with a paper clip he had picked up from Cardashian's desk. Adjusting the cell phone to her ear, Jamie Lee grumbled, "You've been watching too many Cold War movies, my friend."

After a half minute of silence, Sweets responded, "This whole thing's over your head, Custus. We're dealing with something here besides Bowie knives and switchblades. Just clean up the mess and cart him out of there the way we planned. And don't forget to leave behind a little present to point the finger at Gilliam."

"Everything else the same as we planned earlier?" asked Jamie Lee.

"Yes. Now, how about moving off the dime?"

Jamie Lee suddenly found herself listening to a dial tone and wondering whether the money she was getting for her current assignment had been an undersell. She disliked Sweets, a strange voice on the phone, a phantom that she had never met. She detested the lecherous Hernández just as much, and she didn't give a rat's ass about Cardashian. All of a sudden she felt as though she should have doubled her price.

Slipping the cell phone into her pocket, she ran her tongue across her teeth and scanned Cardashian's laboratory, watching the last rays of twilight arch their way through the windows. Deciding that what she needed at the moment was a fresh perspective on the outside world, Jamie Lee threaded her way between a scintillation counter and a DNA sequencer and squeezed past two banks of on-line printers until she was at the laboratory's outer wall of windows, looking directly at Mt. Evans in the distance. *Pretty*, she thought. *Pretty as a picture.* She didn't know how long she stared at the mountain, but when she began working her way back through the maze of lab equipment, the laboratory was capped in early-evening darkness.

She glanced down at Cardashian and turned up her nose at the rancid smell wafting from him. "Is he still breathing?"

"Barely," said Hernández, kicking Cardashian in the ribs just to make sure he was giving the right answer.

Cardashian let out a winded moan.

"Don't worry; it won't be much longer." Jamie Lee knelt down and passed her hand back and forth in front of Cardashian's face just as he began twitching and flailing in a series of arm tics and head jerks. When she jumped back cautiously, landing on her bad leg and losing her balance, Hernández began laughing. Embarrassed, she swung back her good foot, launching it squarely into Cardashian's groin. Cardashian let out a muffled cry and listed over on his side. When Hernández moved to prop Cardashian back up, Jamie Lee waved him off, her face brimming with satisfaction. "Sweets should have let you put a bullet in his head. It would have been a whole lot simpler." Hernández shrugged and moved away without responding.

Irritated by Hernández's silence, Jamie Lee gazed down at the logger's boot she had used to kick Cardashian, and then at the stacked three-inch orthopedic heel of her other boot. Polishing the toe of the orthopedic boot on the back of her jeans, she looked over at Hernández, smiled, and nudged Cardashian with her boot once again. When Cardashian didn't respond, she gave him another kick. Then, looking at Hernández and shaking her head, she said, "Son of a bitch Sweets wanted us to clean up Cardashian's shit before we dump him. Can you believe that? Clean up a dead man's shit. Ain't that a hell of a stretch?"

Chapter 8

The old Cuban adage *El tabaco nare; el azúcar se hare*—Tobacco is born; sugar is only made—touts the fact that although sugar may represent the heart of the Cuban economy, it is tobacco, and the mystique of the Cuban cigar, that is Cuba's true economic soul.

Cuba's Pinar del Río province, which accounts for eighty percent of Cuba's tobacco crop, is also home to some of Cuba's most mountainous terrain, including limestone bedrock dotted with caves, underground rivers that stretch for miles, dense pine forests, and a swampy coastline that buffers the province from the outside world. The tobacco leaves that are rolled into Cuba's famous Havana cigars come from the province's Vuelta Abago region, where tobacco farmers still spend much of their time as they have for nearly two hundred years, nurturing a crop that has a tenuous three-month growing season.

Atina Mesa Salas, a sleepy-eyed, sixty-six-year-old Pinar del Río City native, had been a *torcedora,* a tobacco roller, for nearly fifty years until retiring two years earlier. During her career she had seen bumper crops, the nationalization of the tobacco industry, and crop failures due to everything from droughts to monsoons. She had worked her way up from a post–high school two-year *torcedor* apprenticeship to a grade 7 star roller for the Cohiba Tobacco Company at its world-famous El Laquito factory, specializing in the handling of difficult cigars. Revered for her ability to roll mammoth *figurados,* Atina was one of the most respected tobacco rollers in the province.

Rolling cigars was one of Atina's two claims to fame. The second was equally compelling. In a country infatuated with home-grown sports heroes, her grandson, Ernesto, was the premier heavyweight on the Cuban boxing team.

Over the course of the last two years she had squirreled away enough money, bribed the proper officials, and managed to wriggle her way into a travel slot with the boxing entourage so she would be able to attend the Olympic games and watch Ernesto box. When asked how she had managed to set aside the necessary funds, her answer was always the same: *Like the water's edge, I have prepared for a lifetime to meet the shore.* This terse stock answer warned most people not to pursue the subject.

Dreaming of the Olympics, Atina sat cross-legged in a dimly lit room filled with rows of tables, rolling a cigar along with several other *torcedores.* A Monte Cristo cigar hung from the corner of her mouth, its tangy, aromatic smell punctuating the humid air. Although the Cohiba had surpassed the Monte Cristo as Cuba's premier cigar, Atina preferred the less trendy brand she had wrapped and smoked most of her life. Dressed in a red-and-white-striped, loose-fitting blouse, Levi's that had been smuggled in from the United States, and a four-strand liquid silver necklace that she had recently bought on the Cuban black market, Atina worked methodically without looking up.

Twenty minutes later, her wrapping complete, Atina arched her glasses off her nose, shoved them into her coarse-textured, closely cropped silver hair, and looked at the teenaged roller beside her. The girl had been helping her for months. In a legitimate cigar-making operation, the clumsy-fingered, mistake-prone girl would never have been assigned a seat next to Atina, but Atina had retained her for three special reasons: the girl was coachable, she was willing to run the risk associated with rolling counterfeit cigars, and she spoke nearly perfect English, a language Atina desperately needed to practice for her Australian Olympics trip and a language Atina had rarely used since the 1960s.

"Relax, girl, you're not rolling a log," said Atina, proud of her English. "Play gently with the leaf and it will pay you back."

The stringy-haired girl smiled sheepishly and stopped what she was doing.

"Handle the leaf as if it were the skin of an angel. Don't poke at it like it's the hide of a cow." Atina set her cigar aside in a charred clamshell and demonstrated her rolling technique. Taking the leaf from the girl, she quickly folded and rolled the leaf along its length. "Now you do the same," she said, looking expectantly at the girl.

The girl pulled a new leaf toward her and followed Atina's lead.

"Better; much better, my child."

The girl smiled, tossing her limp, oily hair, buoyed by the praise from a master *torcedora*. Continuing to work, she asked, "Will you go to watch Ernesto practice today?"

"I will, but it will be late. I prefer to go when my baby is spent. By then he's exhausted, ready to go home like a puppy in my arms." Atina thought about all the times the now solidly built, six-foot-four-inch, 235-pound grandson she had raised had fallen asleep in her arms as a sickly child, and how as an overly sensitive bullied youth he would pout for hours when she scolded him to stick up for himself and meet the demands of his schoolwork. Ernesto had sulked for weeks when he realized just after turning thirteen that he lacked the skills to make his school's soccer team. His introduction to boxing had come purely by chance when he stumbled across a cache of mildewed boxes belonging to his late grandfather, boxes chock-full of 1950s and '60s American boxing magazines. Eventually he became fascinated with the sport and mesmerized by the boxing style of Sugar Ray Robinson, who seemed to be featured in every magazine. Poring over the magazines until they were dog-eared pulps, learning English in the process, he ultimately mastered Sugar Ray's boxing style.

Atina had tried her best to stop him from becoming caught up in such a brutal sport. She had no desire to watch her grandson repeat the mistakes of his grandfather. But she was no match for a boy who had found his calling. By his twenty-third birthday, and in the midst of an Olympic year, Ernesto Salas's face had been featured on the cover of every major boxing magazine in the world, and his boxing skills were being touted as matching those of Muhammad Ali.

Hoping for her grandson's continued success, Atina began rolling a new *figurado* as she prayed that the recent joint pain in her fingers wouldn't reassert itself today and that the American-financed cigar-counterfeiting operation that she had reluctantly agreed to spearhead in order to finance her Olympics trip and retirement wouldn't be discovered.

Finished with a new cigar, the stringy-haired girl nudged the completed product over to Atina. "What do you think of this one?"

The new creation was an improvement on what the girl had been producing. But Atina's intuition and eye for the art told her that the girl had probably reached the limit of her skills. She smiled at the girl, thinking of Ernesto's initial failure at soccer. Then, fingering the poorly rolled cigar, she said, "You're improving," hoping as she did that the girl had other talents.

Beaming, the girl said, "Thank you," and pulled a new tobacco leaf from the stack at her side.

Atina retrieved her Monte Cristo and took a long, satisfying drag. As she did, a dull ache spread down her fingers and into the back of her hand. She flexed her fingers back and forth until the pain finally passed. Setting her cigar aside, she allowed her thoughts to drift back to the years before communism and the good times with her husband, Orente, as she considered the downside of the risky second career she had chosen, and whether her brother-in-law, Manuel Hernández, would be on time to pick her up and take her to Ernesto's sparring practice.

Chapter 9

It wasn't the impact of Leah's death, Nathan Tanner's incessant pacing, or even the look of doom on Anthony Rontella's face that had Ellis Drake wheezing in frustration and perspiring from every body pore. What had Drake truly upset was that for forty-five minutes they had all been cooped up in a stark white broom closet of a room in a university honors dormitory, forced to inhale stale air and listen to the numbing buzz of the room's single dying overhead fluorescent light while waiting for the University of Colorado athletic director.

The room and the buzz reminded Drake of the sparse Kansas farmhouse where he had grown up, a farmhouse he had learned to hate and that he had fortunately left behind long ago to become first an NCAA champion swimmer, then a small-time Nebraska college coach, and finally head swimming coach at the University of Colorado.

For a few seconds the buzzing stopped, and Drake's thoughts turned from his own troubled and abused childhood to Leah Tanner. In twenty-six years as a coach, he had seen his share of sprains, torn ligaments, and even a fracture or two, but Leah was his first fatality. Her death had him rattled, and for two days his stomach had felt like a sack of wet cement, precipitated by the fact that the day before her death she had come to him complaining of back pains and dizziness, which he had passed off as pre-competition jitters.

He wasn't quite sure why he, Tanner, and Rontella had been called to meet with the University of Colorado athletic director and the team doctor, David Patterson, for the third time since Leah's death, but he was certain that neither the AD nor Patterson was aware of Leah's earlier complaints. In the two days since Leah had died, he had recounted the circumstances surrounding her death to university officials, NCAA bureaucrats, doctors, reporters, and the hierarchy of security officers in charge of the tragic event. He was positive that Anthony Rontella and Nathan Tanner had done the same, so he couldn't help but wonder, *Why another meeting?*

Drake glanced through the room's tiny window and watched a family of squirrels dart across the freshly mown lawn outside. It was twilight, two hours past the time he normally left for home. Peeved at the wait and the lateness of the hour, he looked over at Nathan Tanner, who had stopped pacing and was now staring blankly at the opposite wall. Tanner's face was a mask of sorrow.

"The least they could do is show up on time," Tanner

grumbled, aiming his remark at the wall. For nearly two days his finely tuned life had spiraled out of control. He had bitten the inside of his cheek the previous night while tossing in his sleep, dreaming of Leah, awakening to a mouthful of blood.

He had spent the better part of Leah's teenage years building a successful corporate law practice, taking time out only to drive her to excel as a swimmer. Now, before she had a chance to enjoy the fruits of her labors, she was gone. Burdened with guilt, numb from his loss, and frustrated with waiting, he turned his gaze from the wall to Anthony Rontella. "Wait if you want to; I'm calling it a day."

Crossing the room to leave, he opened the door to find himself facing Lowell Harper, the crusty, short-tempered University of Colorado athletic director, and Tanner's friend of twenty years, Dr. David Patterson.

"Sorry to be late, got held up in traffic," said Harper. Then, dropping his arm sympathetically over Tanner's shoulders, Harper added, "It's been hectic, Nate. I've had the media, worried parents, the coroner's office, and even NCAA and university security nipping at me all day. How are you holding up?"

"Okay," said Tanner, stepping back into the room.

Harper removed his arm from Tanner's shoulders and acknowledged Anthony Rontella with a quick nod before walking over to Ellis Drake and giving him a firm shoulder pat. Clearing his throat, he said in a raspy, apologetic voice, "I hate to say so, Nate, but what we've got on our hands here is a first-rate media mess. That's why I wanted to have this meeting off the beaten path." Pausing, he looked Tanner directly in the eye. "I know this will sting, but I'll give it to you straight. We still don't know what happened. Can't get an honest answer out of the NCAA, the Olympics people, or the coroner. They all keep telling me that as soon as they have something firm they'll let me know." Looking at Patterson for support, he added, "Right, Doc?" sounding as if he'd been coached.

"Correct," said Patterson.

"I understand. I've been told the same thing. I'm pushing for an answer too," said Tanner, his tone of voice letting everyone know that he was busy directing his own investigation.

Anthony Rontella, who had been sitting alone just within earshot, moved toward the center of the room. "So why this meeting?" he said, directing the question to Harper.

Harper cleared his sinuses with a quick snort. "I just wanted us to all be on the same page."

"Meaning?" asked Tanner, a half frown crossing his face.

Anthony responded before Harper could. "Meaning he needs a little spin control for nervous parents and the press."

The retaliatory look Harper shot Anthony said, *Butt out!*

Tanner's eyes narrowed in frustration as he looked for help from Patterson. "Is that what this is all about, David? Damage control for the press?"

"Certainly not. We just don't want anyone jumping to conclusions before we have all the facts."

"Conclusions about what?" Tanner fought back the urge to grab his old friend by the official black-and-gold-striped University of Colorado tie he was wearing and give it a healthy tug.

"Conclusions suggesting that a controlled substance might have been involved in Leah's death," said Patterson.

Tanner's move toward Patterson was so quick that Anthony barely had time to slip between them.

"You saying my Leah was using drugs?" asked Tanner, spitting the words at Patterson and clenching his fists.

"I'm not saying anything of the sort. I'm just anticipating what might come next."

Pushing his solid two hundred pounds past the much smaller Rontella, Tanner inched his nose directly into his old friend's face. "You know what you can anticipate for me, David? You can anticipate your sorry bureaucratic ass out of my sight."

"Calm down, Nathan; it's only a statement, not a fact," said Patterson.

Tanner took a step back from Rontella, shook his head, and stared at Patterson. Four years earlier Patterson had helped convince him that for the good of God, country, the state of Colorado, and motherhood, Leah had to attend CU. Although not a coach, Patterson had perceived that Leah could be the cornerstone of a new University of Colorado swimming presence and that with Ellis Drake as her coach she could be part of a wave of athletes capable of leading the university into female sports dominance in the West. He had boasted about how clean the CU athletic program was, and now he was just short of accusing Leah of using drugs. "You're a shill, David. A fast-talking shill." Tanner took another step backward, hands in the air defensively, shaking his head in disgust as if Patterson were contaminated.

The room was suddenly quiet except for the heavy breathing of Tanner and Patterson, the buzzing sound of the room's dying fluorescent bulb, and Ellis Drake's wheezing.

Drake, who had watched the entire episode unfold without saying a word, felt a sudden and very healthy twinge of guilt, a twinge that stung even more because he had been as instrumental in recruiting Leah to CU as Patterson. Leah, in fact, had been his personal reclamation project, so he wasn't quite sure why Patterson was bearing the brunt of Tanner's frustration. He, not Patterson, had molded Leah into an Olympic-caliber swimming star.

His insides churning, he asked himself if perhaps he had misconstrued a substance-abuse or performance-enhancing problem as her pre-race jitters. He was the one responsible for knowing his athletes inside and out. Most of the time Leah was levelheaded, but it wasn't unusual for her to turn quixotic or even morose before a race. Maybe Leah's jitters had been more than a case of nerves. He could have missed the telltale signs of an athlete on drugs; he'd done so before.

He was still pondering the possibility when a smallish, balding man with a jet-black, pencil-thin mustache and a mop of unruly hair pushed the door open tentatively and stepped inside. Drake recognized the man as one of the NCAA team doctors who had swarmed to Leah's aid at poolside. The man smiled apprehensively as he walked across the room, nodding greetings to everyone but clearly moving toward Dr. Patterson. "They told me I might find you here," he said, stopping directly in front of

Patterson. "I'm not breaking up anything important, am I? Lawrence Carter, NCAA," he added, announcing his name as if he were a cop.

"No," said Patterson, puzzled by the man's appearance.

"Good. I just wanted to ask you to drop by my office when you're through."

Patterson looked surprised. "Why?"

"Just a few questions about Ms. Tanner's medical history, that's all. Won't take but a couple of minutes."

Stepping back, Carter found Nathan Tanner directly in his path. "Do you know what happened to my daughter?"

"No, we don't. Nothing's come back from the coroner's office yet."

"Then why the secret meeting between you and Dr. Patterson?" Tanner shot both men a distrustful look.

"I can assure you it's just doctor talk. I'd like to know a little more about your daughter's past medical history. It may help us understand what happened."

Tanner took a deep breath, exhaling so loudly that it startled everyone. "Then there's no reason you shouldn't share your discussion with me. I know more about her medical history than anyone."

"I guess not," said Carter. "Why don't you come along?"

"Are we done here?" asked Tanner, glancing at Harper, looking for an okay to leave.

Harper shrugged. "Guess so."

"Fine," said Tanner. Then, turning to Patterson and Carter, in a voice dripping with sarcasm, he said, "Glad you doctors decided to include me in your meeting."

Carter, looking as though he had been caught in a

whirlwind, looked at Harper and said, "Thanks." Without exchanging another word, Tanner and the two doctors quickly left the room.

Disappointed that he hadn't been included, Anthony Rontella swept his windbreaker off the chair next to him and slipped it on, ready to leave. "Think they'll find out what happened to Leah?" he asked, looking at Harper.

"Hard to tell. One thing for sure, it'll take a while to dig out the truth," said Harper, looking past Anthony toward Coach Drake. "Hey, Ellis, you wanna go grab a bite to eat?"

"No. I'm not in the mood. Why don't you go on with Anthony?"

Harper glanced back at Rontella, embarrassed at not having included him in the initial offer. "You up for some food, Anthony?"

"I guess so."

"Have anything special in mind?"

"Anything's fine by me."

"Good; how about Italian?"

"Okay," said Anthony, looking as if he'd just said yes to something he might end up regretting later.

"I'll talk to you tomorrow," Harper called out to Drake as he and Anthony left the room.

Once again Ellis Drake found himself staring at four stark-white walls and listening to the irritating buzz of the overhead fluorescent light. He knew he had done the right thing by passing on dinner. His stomach was too upset to tolerate a meal. But he wasn't sure whether he'd made a mistake by not going with Patterson, the NCAA doc, and Tanner.

If they were going to rehash Leah's medical history,

there was plenty he could have added. Like the fact that their discussions needed to move beyond Leah's history of anorexia and concentrate more on recent events. Someone needed to address the question of why a few months earlier Leah had had a flurry of near-Olympic-record fifty-five-second hundred-yard butterfly times, followed by a month when she could barely break a minute. Someone should have looked into why Leah and Anthony Rontella had been so defensive about her swimming dropoff and why they had insisted at so many recent team practices that Leah be the only one in the pool. He wasn't a doctor, but he had coached long enough to know that when it came to evaluating people with psychological baggage like Leah's, it was too easy to get bogged down in the past and miss seeing the present.

His already queasy stomach grumbled at the thought. As he moved to leave the room, the fluorescent tube overhead buzzed one last time and flickered out. Moving from the room's darkness into the well-lit hall, he couldn't help thinking that Leah's death was more than another random event, and far more complex than just another fluorescent tube finally dying.

Chapter 10

Until lighter, more energy-efficient upright freezers came along, the gunmetal-gray, thirty-cubic-foot Revco 1000 was the preferred workhorse of research laboratories around the world.

When Lieutenant Clifford Menton arrived at the Denver city dump thirty minutes into his day-watch homicide shift to find maggots as thick as cake icing covering the face of a dead man stuffed inside an open, half-buried Revco 1000, he suspected that the rest of his day was going to slide downhill. The jaybird-naked dead man smelled like a backed-up sewer. Pecan-sized blood clots filled both nostrils, and his hair was matted with blood. A tattoo of crossed rowing oars arched across his biceps.

Dodging a garbage bag full of dog feces and a decaying pile of sanitary napkins, Menton bent over the open Revco to get a better look at the victim. After surveying the body, he looked back up and said, "Never seen one of these babies in a place like this," to the young uniformed patrolman standing guard over the Revco.

"It's a research freezer."

"I know what it is, *son*." Menton spat his words out in admonition. "You may not believe it, but I'm not as dumb or as slow as I look. I've actually logged evidence into hummers like this."

The patrolman stared down toward the chalky fragments of plasterboard at his feet, frowned at the gypsum residue clinging to his soles, and swallowed hard. Menton, who had skirted the pesky plasterboard, smiled at the young officer's predicament as he pulled a pair of latex gloves out of his pocket, slipped them on, then reached over and pushed the fleshy parts of the dead man's nose from side to side. "It's not broken," he said, running his right hand around the curvature of the man's skull. "And his noggin's intact." Menton stepped back, nearly tripping over a two-by-four. "Shit, if I didn't know better, I'd swear somebody's trying to build a fucking house out here. Any ID on the victim?" he said, regaining his balance.

"None."

"Who found him?"

The young cop nodded toward two dump scarfers Menton had missed while zigzagging his way around the field of garbage and construction scraps to the freezer. The men were seated on rickety barstools fifteen yards away, partially hidden from Menton's view by an idle front-end loader and a mound of garbage.

Menton worked his way over toward the scarfers, avoiding a trail of rotting banana skins and a cache of Styrofoam fast-food containers that he suspected would grace the dump's soggy floor for the next hundred years. Stopping short of the two men, he nodded. "I understand you two found the dead man. What made you look inside the chest?"

The taller of the two men, a slim, square-faced black man with smooth, ageless skin, pulled a cigarette butt from the corner of his mouth and nodded at his friend. "You askin' him or me?"

"You're the one talking."

The man took a final drag on his cigarette before flicking the butt into a pool of maroon-colored slime at his feet.

"The property tag, my man. That's what hooked my attention. Made me wonder what might be inside."

The look on Menton's face turned pensive as he mulled over the scarfer's words, pondering a probable source for the dead man's coffin. Realizing that it was unlikely that whoever had stuffed the man inside the chest would have risked traipsing across a quarter-mile of dump with a naked body in tow just so they could stash the body in a half-buried freezer chest they stumbled across, Menton said, "Mind showing me the property tag?" suspecting that the chest and the dead man had departed from the same place at the same time. Then he eyed the taller scarfer suspiciously, wondering why he would have been scrutinizing one of his dump finds for indications of prior ownership.

Menton's doubtful look wasn't lost on the scarfer. "I know what you're thinkin'," he said, staring at Menton as if he could read his mind. Rising from his stool, he headed for the chest, nodding for Menton to follow. "You're askin' yourself why a dump scavenger diggin' through garbage would be lookin' for any kind of personal identification on one of his finds. Simple. Everybody and everything on this earth, including you, me, and my friend Earl back there, has a history. And the way I figure it, there's no harm in knowin' where somethin' you might take possession of has been."

Reaching the freezer, the scarfer dropped to his knees. Oblivious to the rancid waste he was kneeling in, he waved for Menton to follow suit as he ran his hand across a metal emblem hidden beneath the rounded flange that rimmed the top of the freezer.

Menton jacked up his trouser legs, pulled his sport coat up over his butt, and squatted for a better look. A buckled rectangular property tag was glued to the freezer's gray outer shell. Gripping the freezer lip to maintain his balance, Menton bent toward the tag until his forehead nearly touched the freezer. The property tag's seven-digit ID number was worn and difficult to read. But there was no mistaking the silver-and-black University of Colorado seal or the words *Medical School* embossed beneath the seal. Menton ran a gloved finger across the tag several times before standing up and letting out a satisfied grunt, thinking as he did that the philosophical scarfer had turned out to be one hell of a sage.

Everything and everybody's got a history, Menton thought as he slipped off his gloves, secure in the knowledge that the University of Colorado, like his own Denver Police Department, maintained the kind of weighty bureaucratic documentation that would no doubt tell him exactly where the dead man's coffin had come from.

Tossing his gloves into the muck at his feet, he smiled and watched the gloves disappear as if they had been sucked into quicksand, thinking that maybe his day wouldn't slide downhill after all.

Chapter 11

The time-consuming cab ride from Washington's Dulles Airport back to her research laboratory at the National Institutes of Health had Dr. Sandra Artorio frustrated. Eight hours earlier, at the annual meeting of the American Society for Genetic Research in Los Angeles, she had presented the world's first scientific abstract documenting the fact that a protein she had discovered in a common protozoan was an essential part of telomerase, the enzyme thought to play a seminal role in determining how long an organism might live.

The abstract was another first in a stellar career that had earned Sandi A., as she was known to her friends, a reputation as one of the world's premier molecular geneticists, and colleagues at NIH whispered that she was on track for a Nobel prize. Forty-five minutes after her presentation, she had rushed to catch a flight back to Dulles, and her plane had landed on time. What had her Venezuelan blood on a slow simmer was the fact that after arriving on schedule, she had spent the next hour and a half stuck in Beltway gridlock in the back seat of a cab reeking of incense, listening to her cab driver complain about the political corruptness of the last three presidents.

By the time she negotiated her luggage and jet-lagged body down the empty corridors of the NIH building that housed her second-floor research laboratory, it was seven P.M. and she was asking herself a lingering and all too frequent question: *Why in the world hadn't she gone straight home?*

She knew the answer. She was in a race, one that she was leading and intended to win. As the acknowledged front-runner in a research trial designed to unmask the so-called molecular stopwatch that controls life, she could ill afford significant downtime. Her meticulously conceived and relentless investigative efforts were the engine driving her, what she allowed her colleagues and the rest of the world to see. Cloaked behind an ebullient personality and exotic good looks was the real reason for her efforts: a need to prove to herself and the world that the first-generation daughter of clannish Venezuelan immigrants, someone who had never had a new dress until she was ten, a girl who had never had a real boyfriend or left her neighborhood until she went to college, could indeed turn the world of science on its ear.

Pausing at the doorway to her lab, she slipped her key out of her purse, fumbled with the temperamental lock, and asked herself a second question, one that had been nagging her recently: *Did she have the stamina to win her race?*

Years earlier, when she had become the first National Merit Scholar from her predominantly Latino school in the grimy steel-mill town of East Chicago, Indiana, the challenge had started. It had escalated throughout college at Indiana University, a Ph.D. in genetics at Dartmouth, and a three-year postdoctoral research fellowship at Johns Hopkins. Following her postdoc she had spent a three-year stint as an assistant professor and full-fledged academic at Ohio State, and she had hated it. She hadn't realized when she accepted the job that university life was as much bureaucracy as science. She had left Columbus after a failed relationship with a criminal defense lawyer, disenchanted and searching for a way to get back on the scientific fast track.

Her current position at NIH gave her the opportunity to rebound from her academic experience, reset her goals, and take aim at a new objective. In the decade since her arrival, she had risen to the challenge, but in the past four months, as she approached thirty-eight, in spite of all her scientific successes she was beginning to wonder if she was going to get her second wind.

Jiggling her key back and forth and overcoming the idiosyncratic lock, she swung back the door, flicked on the overhead lights, and let out an uncharacteristic sigh. A stack of autoradiographs of polyacrylamide gels, prepared by her new postdoc while she was gone, had been neatly stacked in a bin on a table by the door. She picked up the films, quickly scrutinized them, and set several aside as not up to par. Making a mental note that the postdoc could use some technical assistance, and probably some encouragement, she placed the rest of the gels back in the bin, put her suitcase down next to the door, kicked off her heels, and headed across the open laboratory toward her private office.

Before leaving Los Angeles, she had returned all of her phone calls, checked in with her still vigorous marathon-running father back in Indiana, and answered all her e-mail messages, so she was surprised to find a stack of new phone messages and an e-mail printout sitting in the middle of her desk. She suspected that most were research protocol questions from collaborators and colleagues. And if luck would have it, one might even be from her favorite Georgetown antiquarian bookstore informing her that the hard-to-find West Indian cookbook she had been trying to locate for months had been found and was ready to be picked up.

Flipping through the messages, she pulled out what she considered to be the most urgent one, an e-mail from Dr. Tess Gilliam in Denver. Longtime friends, she and Tess shared mutual interests, not only in science but in cooking, literature, and sports. They had become close friends when Tess had done a nine-month sabbatical in Sandi's laboratory five years earlier to hone her skills in molecular biology after spending most of her research career as a cell organelle electron microscopist. The admiration Sandi had for Tess Gilliam's research expertise and indomitable spirit couldn't be measured.

The message was typical Tess, offering a view of the world before getting down to business. *Sandi, you know how I hate e-mail, but since I couldn't catch you by phone at the ASGR meeting, I've been forced to lower myself to its de-*

humanizing level. I'm sure everyone at the meeting is singing your praises. Double theirs and add mine.

Now the reason for this note. I have a telomerase signal problem that's driving me crazy, and I need help. How often have you seen HeLa cell antisense clones bursting with telomerase signal, and if you have, is it associated with altered cell growth, mortality, or doubling? Bottom line: I've got cells out here that are gorged with the stuff and I'm worried that Neil Cardashian's working outside of our approved telomerase protocol. Tess.

Dropping exhausted into her chair, Sandi pulled an unopened roll of fruit-flavored candies from the top drawer of her desk, teasing off the top one as she thought about the sea of differences that existed between Tess Gilliam and Neil Cardashian. She had never understood why Cardashian and Tess had ended up working together, but she suspected that it had a lot to do with the forced relationships that are often fostered at universities, one of the reasons she had left academia. Tess, after all, was a doctor's doctor who believed, occasionally to a fault, that when it came to science, you dotted every I and crossed every T. Neil Cardashian, on the other hand, whom Sandi had known almost as long as she had known Tess, although undoubtedly brilliant was also flamboyant, manipulative, and, on the research side of things, downright sloppy.

During her years on the faculty at Ohio State, Sandi had served on a molecular biology and genetics study section, one of the hundreds of National Institutes of Health peer-review committees assigned to regularly meet and evaluate extramural research grant requests for funds. During the three-year committee assignment, she had gotten to know Cardashian, whom she found to be conniving, charming, cavalier, dashing, and abrasive, some-times all in the space of minutes. Near the end of the committee's first three-day meeting, Cardashian had taken to calling her Snake Eyes, in reference, he said, to her aqua-green eye color and slinky, near-six-foot height. It was a nickname some of her colleagues still snickered about, and one she had been unable to shake over the years. She had never liked Cardashian, and although they often sat on the same panels at scientific meetings because of their mutual interest in telomerase, she had also never trusted him.

During their last year of committee service, Cardashian had been committee chair, and she had had the unshak-able feeling that he was somehow manipulating research-grant priority scores, the grading system used to rank grant proposals for funding. She was never able to prove her suspicion, and years later, when she heard that Car-dashian had left the University of California for Colorado and that he and Tess were serving as co-investigators on the $5 million telomerase research project, she wondered whether Cardashian had mended his ways. The e-mail from Tess dashed her optimism.

Knowing that Cardashian was neither the mad-scientist type nor stupid, she suspected that if he were doing something inappropriate without informing Tess, it was either to stroke his ego or to gain a research or funding advantage. He'd never take the chance of scuttling his re-search career unless the potential rewards outweighed the risk.

Weary of speculating about the scientific integrity of a man who had once told her point-blank at a cocktail party that he'd lay odds that she was too driven to be very good in bed, Sandi flipped to Tess's phone number in her Rolodex and dialed it, hoping that since it was just five P.M. in Denver, she'd still catch Tess at work.

"Gilliam's lab," answered Tess.

"Tess, it's Sandi. Got your message. Sounds like you've got a Cardashian problem out there in the mile-high city."

"Great to hear from you, Sandi, and thanks for getting back to me so fast. I saw your telomerase abstract in the ASGR proceedings booklet. I know it turned some heads." Tess punched on her speaker phone and rolled her wheelchair over to a nearby microscope.

"They had me bobbing and weaving like a heavyweight during the discussion session afterward."

"Sounds to me like you're still standing."

"More like floating, but not from the Q and A. To tell you the truth, I'm plain jet-lagged out."

"I won't keep you long. Promise. Hold on a second." Tess moved her wheelchair up to a dual-headed microscope that flanked a metal tray filled with microscopic slides. She took the top slide out of its slot, readied it for low-power magnification, and focused the microscope. "Okay," she said, talking into a speaker next to the scope. "I needed to grab a slide and take a look at it while we're talking. I don't want to pass along any bogus information." Adjusting herself in her seat, she refocused on the slide. "I'm sitting here looking at an in situ prep I received from one of Neil's lab techs a couple of days ago. I don't know why his tech decided to run it past me. Normally Neil screens all his own preps. Could be it's because Neil hasn't been at work the past two days—probably somewhere in the mountains blowing out the pipes on his

73

Ferrari. Anyway, his tech needed the slide screened, so I agreed to give him a hand. What I saw knocked me for a loop. The cells in the prep are bursting with what are undoubtedly P32-labeled telomerase granules. Here's my question: Have you ever been able to get that much telomerase activity on something as crude as an in situ prep?"

Sandi thought for a moment. "No, not using any of our in situ models."

"Do you think Neil could be using a radioactive label that he hasn't told me about? One that would light up like the northern lights?"

"It's possible, but why would he use anything besides standard labels like P32 or S35?"

Tess eased up the condenser on her microscope and flipped to a high-power magnification. "There're a couple of strange things about these cells, Sandi. They're gigantic, and I swear they look like they have desmosomal attachments between them."

"You're kidding."

"I wish," said Tess, focusing up and down on the slide, scrutinizing the fingerlike cell-to-cell attachments she was describing. "I need your help."

"Send me the slides, matching tissue that's not labeled with isotope, and any frozen homogenized tissue extracts you've got."

"I was hoping that would be your answer. I'll have them sent to you by tomorrow morning."

"Do you think Neil's really working outside your research protocol?"

"I'm afraid so." Tess sat back from her microscope.

"And from the look of these slides, I think Neil's way past the fringe."

"I'll buy the fact that Neil's out there sometimes, but do you think he'd chance being fired?"

"I'm not sure. I'll tell you what, though, these in situ preps of his have me scared. I confronted him about some other research discrepancies a couple of nights ago, and I haven't seen him since. I've talked to the chair of our research ethics committee, Henry Bales, about the issue, and I've shared my concerns with our dean. I can't push this much further without an expert's take on the slides. That's why you're up to bat."

"Happy to help. I just hope you're wrong about Cardashian. I've never liked him, but I'd hate to think he'd risk putting you or his career at risk."

"He's a strange bird, Sandi. As odd and egotistical a bird as I've ever run across. I can't honestly say what I think he'd do."

Sandi thought about her previous encounters with Cardashian. Inching a new candy out of her roll, she wondered whether Cardashian was brazen and unethical enough to do what she knew Tess suspected. Deciding reluctantly that he was, she slipped the candy into her mouth. It was a tart lemon-flavored one, the only flavor she had never grown to like.

Chapter 12

The Hotel Nacional, constructed in 1930, remains Cuba's most elegant and scandal-ridden hotel. Despite the fact that during the 1950s the hotel was stripped of much of its original Italianate charm when it was converted into a gambling complex managed by American gangsters, the enchanting Caribbean grande dame has nonetheless survived mobsters, gamblers, decadence, and communism, and done so in style.

Bleary-eyed, his ears still ringing from his all-day flight from Denver through Toronto to Havana, Anthony Rontella sat, cognac in hand, in the Nacional's bar just down the hallway from Havana's finest nightclub, the Cabaret Parisién. He was nervously waiting for his contact to appear and looking for all the world like a thirty-something, upscale, fast-track international businessman instead of an underpaid, fearful athletic trainer who, in his haste to amass a quick fortune, may have bitten off more than he could chew. Sporting closely cropped hair and a light tan tropical suit, Anthony hoped that no one in the bar would mistake him for anything but the American businessman he was purporting to be.

Anthony ran his eyes down the backside of his dark-haired, statuesque waitress, unable to stop his gawking until a man at the next table grumbled something in Spanish and shot him a cold stare. Ignoring the look, Anthony sat back in his chair, rolled the remaining splash of cognac around in his snifter, and surveyed the room.

Subdued lighting and pastel-colored walls had never been his cup of tea. He preferred the more flashy surroundings of Las Vegas, his hometown, the place where, after a successful high-profile undergraduate athletic career at Philadelphia's Temple University, he had tried to parlay his athletic notoriety and hometown connections into a singing career that had failed. Nonetheless, he had to admit that the room had a kind of understated elegance, and it was a perfect place for carrying out his end of the deal that he hoped would change his life.

Taking a final sip of cognac, he placed his empty snifter back down on the table and glanced around for his waitress, who had disappeared. He realized he needed another drink to steady his nerves. He hadn't planned to make an unscheduled trip from the comforts of Boulder to Cuba, but Leah's death and orders from Sweets had left him little choice. It concerned him that he was taking orders from someone he had never seen, someone who was no more than a disguised voice on the phone. All their communications had been by telephone, wire, or messenger. Sweets always contacted him, never the reverse, and Sweets seemed to revel in not simply barking orders, but in playing a role.

He did know that there was a link between Sweets and Neil Cardashian, the man who had given him $50,000 of the $100,000 he stood to make. He also knew that the Cuban connection was designed to sidestep rules of legitimate scientific investigation required in the United States. Given the circumstances, it was either pay a visit to Cuba to make certain that their agenda was going well or risk incurring the wrath of Sweets.

In the year that he had been shuttling back and forth to Havana doing Sweets's and Cardashian's bidding, he had also been busy developing a Cuban-based project of his own. One that he expected to ultimately net him far more than $100,000 and a project nearly as daring as Cardashian and Sweets's. After both deals were done, he planned to return to the Rockies and fade into the sunset, damn Sweets, Cuba, and his paltry $40,000 a year athletic trainer salary.

He felt bad about what had happened to Leah, but she had known the risks going in. She had been an easy recruit. The insecure ones always were. He had used his clean-cut looks, his fraternity-of-athletics spiel, and everything he had ever learned during his youth on the streets of Vegas about the psychology of gaming to string her along. All he could hope for now was that Leah's father wouldn't pursue her death too vigorously.

He was still pondering the problem of Nathan Tanner being a loose cannon when a stoop-shouldered waiter with bloodshot eyes edged up to his table. *"Otro, señor?"* said the waiter, staring down at Anthony's empty glass.

Anthony frowned, looking around the room for the tight-bodied waitress who had snatched his attention earlier. Unable to find her, he said, "Why not?"

As the waiter sauntered away, Anthony looked up and spotted his contact walking through the door. He watched Manuel Hernández thread his way across the crowded room, thinking Hernández was the kind of man it would be foolish to turn your back on. Just before Hernández reached the table, Anthony stood up to greet him.

"Señor Rontella," said Hernández, his Cuban accent barely noticeable. He extended his hand loosely toward Anthony's. "My apologies for being late."

Anthony pumped Hernández's hand once and quickly let go. He knew more about Hernández than Hernández thought, including the reason for Hernández's command of English: years of prep schools in the United States, and four years of college at the University of Pennsylvania. "No problem; I've been enjoying a few libations and gawking during the wait." He nodded toward his empty snifter, then at the curvaceous waitress, who had reappeared at the table next to them.

"I see," said Hernández, glancing at the waitress. "I admire your taste."

Anthony sat back down, motioning for Hernández to join him. Hernández seated himself and then reached inside the pocket of his baggy, badly sweat-stained tropical sport coat and pulled out a couple of cigars. Handing one to Anthony, he glanced behind him and waved the waitress over. Holding up two fingers, he said, *"Para los dos."*

As the waitress scurried away, Hernández held up his cigar. "As I've told you before, *el tabaco nace*. Tobacco is our soul." He snipped off the end of the Cohiba with a polished-nickel cigar cutter he had slipped from his pocket and smiled. "And, my friend, tobacco after all is at least partly why you are here," he said, handing the cutter to Anthony.

"To tobacco," said Anthony, lifting his empty cognac glass from the table in a mock toast, wondering how much Hernández knew about his second non-Sweets-related reason for being in Cuba. Uncertain of the answer and worried by the question, he snipped the end off his cigar and lit up. Enjoying a long, ceremonious drag, he blew a stream of smoke into the air and shot a look of thanks toward Hernández.

As the smoke swirled toward the ceiling, evaporating in the overhead lights, Hernández relaxed back in his seat, and Anthony caught a glimpse of the pearl-handled .357 Magnum that Hernández always kept tucked in his inside coat pocket. The butt end of the .357 was flanked by one remaining Cohiba. The gun only reaffirmed the fact that he was involved in a double-edged scheme that could turn dead-end ugly.

The evening breeze blowing off the Cuyaquateje River did little to modulate the stifling 95 degree heat inside the Quonset hut that sat just beyond the city limits of Pinar del Río. The antiquated swamp cooler used to cool the training facility chugged in agony, its pre–World War II motor grinding and scraping. Three modern boxing rings dominated the stifling metal building. Each ring featured sparring matches between members of Cuba's Olympic boxing team. A handful of unenthusiastic spectators milled around the two peripheral rings watching four middleweights flail away at one another.

A crowd of close to two hundred lined the perimeter of the center ring. A few, like Atina Salas, were lucky enough to have seats in a rickety stand of bleachers on the north side of the ring. All eyes were on the ring's contestants: a stumpy, mahogany-skinned, thick-muscled boxer in dark blue trunks with a youthful baggy bulldog of a face and a taller, lighter-skinned, athletically built boxer in scarlet trunks. The taller man's left knee bore the unmistakable linear scar of surgery.

The shorter boxer flicked three quick, powerful left jabs at the taller man, who skillfully deflected the three blows with his forearm. The high-pitched squealing-tire sound of leather grazing the taller man's skin seemed to encourage the shorter boxer. Sensing an opening, he launched a bold right cross toward his opponent's jaw. Arching his neck, the taller man dodged the blow, responding with a right-jab bullet to the temple of the slightly off-balance shorter man. The shorter man staggered backward before collapsing into a heap on the canvas, triggering a series of catcalls, cheers, and whistles, and chants from the crowd of "Ernesto, Ernesto, Ernesto!"

Amid the noise, several trainers jumped into the ring to check on the unconscious boxer. It took the better part of two minutes to get the boxer to sit up. In that time, another man slipped through the ring ropes. Silver boxing robe in hand, he stepped across the ring and draped the robe over the shoulders of the perspiring Ernesto Salas.

Adjusting the robe with a shrug, Ernesto looked out into the boisterous crowd. Spotting his grandmother

Atina, he smiled and waved his gloved right hand in triumph at her. Atina blew him a kiss before she rose from her seat and, with both arms extended in the air, led the crowd in a new wave of "Ernesto, Ernesto, Ernesto!"

As Ernesto made his way out of the ring, he leaned over toward the man who had brought him his robe. *"La segunda entrada y ya estoy agotado, Rulon,"* he complained in a pronounced nasal tone. *"Agotado como un perro cansado. Algo no está bien, mi amigo. Nececito un doctor."* Ignoring Ernesto's complaint, Rulon Mantero reached up and patted the boxer on the shoulder reassuringly. As they left the ring and headed down the steps toward Atina, Rulon thought about the five thousand American dollars he had squirreled away beneath his house in a tobacco box dug into the sandy soil. And that triggered thoughts of the promise he had made to the American Rontella, who had given him the money to, as he had put it, "tend to Ernesto." His hands suddenly began to tremble. With his stomach gurgling and his mind racing, Ernesto's complaint began to swirl around inside his head. *Two rounds and I'm winded, Rulon. Winded like a dog. Something's not right, my friend. I need to see a doctor.* The words kept repeating themselves until he passed his life-long friend into the comforting arms of his grandmother and, more suspicious than ever of Rontella's so-called protein nutrient package for Ernesto, quickly disappeared into the still raucous cheers of the crowd.

Chapter 13

Lieutenant Menton's take on the long arm of bureaucracy had been right on the mark. The Revco freezer property tag had been the key to identifying his dump victim as University of Colorado physician and research scientist Neil Cardashian. He hadn't even had to waste time researching the unusual tattoo on Cardashian's right biceps to make him. Cardashian's half-dozen unpaid speeding tickets and an arrest record from the Colorado State Patrol documenting that six months earlier Cardashian had been clocked in his Ferrari doing ninety-two in a fifty-five-mile-an-hour zone on a mountain road outside Vail enabled Menton to quickly match the speeder's fingerprints with those of his dead man. Menton still had one small problem, however. The Denver coroner's office hadn't pinpointed the cause of death.

After spending the better part of the morning interviewing several University of Colorado Health Sciences Center faculty members, two surly inventory-control staff people, and a recalcitrant dean who seemed more worried about her reputation than Cardashian's death, Menton had finally verified that the Revco 1000 from the dump was the property of Dr. Tess Gilliam's research laboratory.

Menton grabbed a hot dog, a bag of the stalest chips he had tasted in years, and a Coke from a street vendor in front of University Hospital before heading across the street to the UCHSC biomedical research building to talk to Dr. Gilliam. As he crossed Ninth Avenue in the shade of the bridge of offices and research labs that connected the hospital to the medical school, Menton glanced back at the conga line of health care workers now queued up at the hot dog vendor and wondered why people who were paid to know better were lined up to wait for the same cholesterol and sodium meal he was wolfing down.

By the time he reached the research building's entrance, his hot dog was history. Tossing his chips into a trash can and wrinkling his face in disgust, he caught the elevator to the eighth floor. He was still nursing his Coke when he walked unannounced into Tess Gilliam's laboratory. Engrossed in reviewing slides at her microscope, Tess didn't realize Menton was there until he said, "I'm looking for Dr. Theresa Gilliam," in a booming voice that made her jerk her head up from the scope.

"You found her," said Tess, rotating her wheelchair to face Menton.

Surprised that the woman who, he had been telling himself, by all accounts had the most to gain from Cardashian's death was wheelchair-bound, Menton moved across the lab to greet Tess.

"Lieutenant Menton, I'm guessing," said Tess, forcing a tentative smile. "When the dean's office called and told me about Neil's death, they said you'd be dropping by. I'm still a little numb from the news." Tess reached out and shook Menton's hand. "From the look on your face, I'd guess Dr. Adler forgot to tell you about my chariot," she said, tapping both arms of her wheelchair lightly.

"As a matter of fact, Dr. Adler didn't mention that you were disabled."

"I'm not. Just need a wheelchair to navigate."

"My error."

"Everybody's entitled to one," said Tess.

"Before I make any more, I've got a few questions I'd like to ask you, if you don't mind."

"No need for such a low-key approach, Lieutenant. I've got enough street smarts to know that since Neil was found in my freezer, I'm someone you have to talk to. I've had three calls already this morning from colleagues asking me about Neil. One person even said that word on campus is that I'm a suspect. Hard to figure out how I could've stuffed Neil in a freezer operating from this contraption, though, isn't it?" said Tess with a wink.

"It would be a problem. That is, if you were a suspect, and if I knew for certain that Dr. Cardashian was murdered," said Menton, stepping over to a laboratory stool, out of the path of the wheelchair. "Mind if I have a seat?" he said, pulling the stool out from beneath the countertop.

"Please."

Menton plopped his once lithe but ever softening body

onto the metal stool. "You don't sound too surprised to hear about your colleague. Mind telling me why?"

"You'd have to have known Neil, Lieutenant. He was the kind of person who raced through life without a seat belt. He didn't like rules, and he didn't care a gnat's eye about taking chances. I think flying by the seat of his pants stemmed from his college days as an athlete."

"I see," said Menton, leaning forward on the stool. "Your dean tells me that you and Cardashian were co-investigators on a five-million-dollar project. There wasn't any bad blood between the two of you, was there?"

Tess frowned at the mention of Adler. "I was about to file a charge of unethical conduct against Dr. Cardashian. Other than that, we got along fine," said Tess sarcastically, certain that Adler had probably already filled Menton in on the friction between her and Cardashian.

"Was Cardashian aware of the impending charges?"

"Of course."

"What was he doing that was unethical?"

"Let's just say I thought Neil was pushing the envelope of the research guidelines governing our project."

Menton adjusted his weight on the increasingly uncomfortable stool, deciding as he did not to press the issue. He had other ways of learning more about the grievance, and from people he suspected might be more objective. "Considering what you've just told me and the fact that Cardashian was found in one of your freezers, you may want to get some legal counsel before answering any more of my questions, Dr. Gilliam."

"Thanks for the advice, Lieutenant, but since I didn't kill Neil, I'll take my chances."

"Have it your way," said Menton, wondering if Tess

Gilliam were truly as feisty and stubborn as she appeared at first blush. "What's the story on the freezer?" he said, changing his tack, deciding that linking Tess to Cardashian's coffin might just change her self-assured tune.

"There's no story. That Revco you found Neil's body in has been gathering dust in one of my equipment storage rooms for years. I'd be happy to show you the room if you'd like."

"Why don't you?"

Heading her wheelchair in the direction of the storage room, Tess said, "Let's go."

Menton followed, staring at the array of high-tech gizmos, computers, and exotic-looking glassware lining the countertops as Tess led him down an aisle to the storage room. Halfway down the aisle he stopped to gaze at a strange gurgling apparatus that reminded him of a Kentucky hill-country backyard still. "What are you making in here, doctor?"

"Plasmids," said Tess, reaching into a lab coat pocket, extracting a set of keys, and unlocking the storage room's door. "They're self-replicating pieces of DNA," she added, flipping on the lights as she moved into the room. Menton nodded as if he understood, following her into the room.

Except for a narrow aisle down the room's center and a washer-and-dryer-sized space near the back, the storage room was jam-packed with the same kind of high-tech paraphernalia that filled the larger laboratory outside. A few pieces of equipment were draped in plastic, but most sat unprotected and forlorn-looking, gathering dust. Menton eyed the mass of equipment. "Looks like you're well prepared for breakdowns," he said as Tess spun her wheelchair around to face him.

"Afraid not, Lieutenant. What you're looking at in the current vernacular of science is a roomful of '55 Buicks and even a few Model-T Fords. Most of the equipment in here is obsolete."

Menton whistled in amazement, stepping around Tess as he moved down the room's center aisle. Glancing at a freestanding centrifuge, something he recognized, he patted it and smiled. "Big money tied up in this stuff, I bet."

"Hundreds of thousands, at least."

Menton ran his finger across a dusty plastic slipcover that draped a boxy-looking apparatus, leaving behind a snail track in the dust. "That much, huh? Why don't you sell it?"

"Can't. It belongs to the state. It can only be transferred to another lab here on campus or traded to another state institution. Since most of it's obsolete, it ends up staying right here and gathering dust."

Noting that he didn't see any Revco freezers, Menton moved toward the room's open space in the back. "Seems like a waste," he said, pointing to a dishwasher-sized piece of equipment just to his left. "What's that?"

"A DNA synthesizer."

"And this?" Menton tapped an object draped in plastic at his side. Tess backed away from the synthesizer and watched as Menton extracted two limp latex gloves from his jacket pocket.

"Looks like a wheelchair to me," she said, frowning.

Menton removed the slipcover and spun the wheelchair

around, scrutinizing it before his eyes locked on the chair's seat. "One of yours?"

Tess moved forward for a better look. "Yes," she said, reaching out for the wheelchair.

"Don't touch," warned Menton, his tone of voice suddenly authoritative. "Do you know how long this chair's been in here?"

"Years, probably."

Menton ran a gloved finger across the chair's metal frame and down both arms, never diverting his eyes from a series of ink-blot-like splotches on the chair's leather seat. Spinning the chair toward Tess, he asked, "Were you ever injured while using this chair?"

"No."

"Are you sure?"

"Yes."

Menton stepped back and stroked his chin. Then, looking at Tess, he said, "Take a better look at the seat, Dr. Gilliam, and tell me what you think the stains on the leather seat might be. Remember, don't touch."

Tess leaned forward toward the wheelchair, staring down at the half-dollar-sized stains on the seat. At first the stains reminded her of grease spots, but on closer inspection she realized what they were. "You're thinking it's blood?" she said, looking at Menton.

"Afraid so, and it doesn't look that old."

Tess swallowed hard, her eyes still glued to the seat of a wheelchair she hadn't thought about in years. She had no idea how the blood had gotten on the seat, but she could see that although dried, it was fresh enough. Suddenly the ghost of every experiment she and Cardashian had ever run began to swirl around inside her head. She was certain that Cardashian's death had something to do with him treading on the integrity of science, and she had the feeling that the microscope slides she had FedExed to Sandra Artorio had been the catalyst. Finally looking back up from the wheelchair at Menton, she said, "Should I call my lawyer, Lieutenant?" forcing a smile that never came.

Menton's answer surprised her. "It might be smart. We could be here for a while. Why don't we go back out to your office?"

As she gripped the wheel of her wheelchair to turn and leave, an eerie feeling that she hadn't experienced in years surfaced at the edge of her subconscious. It wasn't until she was back outside in her laboratory, trying her best to recall her lawyer, Julie Madrid's, phone number, that she realized that the feeling was the same terrible helplessness she had felt decades before as she lay immobile at the bottom of a ski run.

Chapter 14

Balancing three piping-hot catfish luncheon specials in the crook of her right arm, Thelma Carsen clamped her free hand over the badly chipped mouthpiece of the telephone on the back wall of Mae's Louisiana Kitchen. "CJ, telephone," she screamed, her voice raising every eyebrow in the room. Readjusting her meals, she dropped the receiver, letting it plummet to within inches of the floor to unravel on its greasy cord.

CJ was seated at a table just beyond the restaurant's narrow, tunnel-like entry, waiting for Thelma to deliver his meal of deep-fried catfish, okra, coleslaw, New Iberia Louisiana dipping hot sauce, and corn bread. Mavis Sundee, the feminine soft spot in CJ's otherwise hard-edged life and the restaurant's owner, sat across the table from him.

"Who'd be calling you here on that phone?" asked Mavis, cocking an eyebrow to let CJ know that the phone call was cutting into her time.

"Beats me," said CJ, just as Thelma delivered his lunch. He looked down at the steaming plate of catfish, then over at Mavis. "Sure all you're having is a Diet Coke? Seems a little on the obsessive side of healthy for the owner of a soul food restaurant."

Ignoring the comment, Mavis popped the top on her Coke and smiled. "Go ahead and take your call. I won't let your food run away."

"I won't be long." CJ slid out from behind the table and trailed Thelma back down the length of the long, narrow restaurant that had always reminded him of a New Orleans shotgun house. Nodding greetings to people at tables along the way, he kept asking himself, *Who, besides some Five Points lowlife looking to get bonded out of jail, would be calling him on the restaurant's public telephone?*

Five Points, the core of Denver's black community since early in the twentieth century, had been home to CJ for most of his life, and although he now lived in a converted second-floor apartment in the rambling Victorian Painted Lady that housed his bail-bonding business on Denver's notorious block-long Bail Bondsman's Row, Five Points was still home turf.

CJ looked back toward Mavis as he bent down to retrieve the dangling phone, recalling the promise he had made to her the previous summer—a promise she had extracted after he had gotten himself entangled in a bounty-hunting case that had cost the bail bondsman next door to him his life and nearly gotten CJ killed. It was an irrevocable promise to never get involved in another bounty-hunting job again.

CJ slipped the receiver up to his ear, hoping his commitment wasn't about to be tested. "Floyd here."

"CJ, it's Julie. I've had a heck of a time tracking you down. I'm over at the CU Health Sciences Center playing referee between Henry Bales and a Denver police lieutenant named Menton. Henry's about to get himself thrown in jail for impeding a murder investigation if he doesn't cool his jets. Thank God I got you. This was a last-chance call."

Petite, green-eyed, curvaceous, and with a toughness belying her looks, Julie Madrid had spent seven years as CJ's secretary while attending law school at night. Eight months earlier she had graduated, passed the bar, and tearfully left CJ's employ to hang out her shingle in the first-floor office of the Victorian building next door to CJ's. CJ liked to joke that Julie couldn't bear to be too far away from his contagious bad attitude and brotherly love, and there was more than a little truth to the statement. He had once beaten Julie's physically abusive ex-husband nearly senseless when, after repeated warnings, the man had continued to threaten Julie. Since that encounter, Julie and her ex had never crossed paths again, and CJ and Julie had cemented what had turned into a siblinglike ten-year friendship.

CJ leaned against the wall and transferred the phone to his right ear, trying to hear over the din of the noonday lunch crowd. "Where's Henry now?" he said, unable to shake the words *murder investigation* from his thoughts.

"About twenty feet away in Tess Gilliam's lab, arguing with the cop and acting way past stupid. I stepped into Tess's private office to call you. CJ, you need to get over here right now. I've never seen Henry like this. He's acting . . . ah, damn near as knee-jerk as you."

"Isn't Dr. Gilliam's lab just down the hall from Henry's?" said CJ, trying to recall the layout of a place he'd seen only twice at best.

"Yes."

"I'm on my way." In half a dozen long strides, he was back at the table with Mavis, shaking his head, wondering what the hell had gotten into Henry. "That was Julie on the phone. She's got an emergency over at CU."

"Medical?"

"No."

"No bond skippers, I hope."

"No. But it's serious. Henry Bales is in a verbal face-off with some cop."

Mavis sat back in her chair, shaking her head. "Henry? No way!"

"Afraid so," said CJ, giving Mavis a look that she hadn't seen in years, a frozen-faced, no-comment, secretive kind of stare that she had had to fight through for months following his return from Vietnam. A stare she called CJ's foggy look. Visibly shaken and trying to hide it, Mavis looked across the table at CJ's lunch. "Go on. I'll make you something special at my place this evening," she said.

"Deal," said CJ, recognizing that Mavis was upset. Feeling guilty for leaving so abruptly, he stooped down and planted a gentle kiss on her lips. "Was I looking foggy?"

"Yes. Promise me you won't get your and Henry's behinds in a sling."

"I won't. Promise. See you around seven."

"Seven," said Mavis, smiling at CJ as he turned to leave.

CJ knew the smile was meant to let him know she was okay. But the puzzled look that he saw replace it as he left the restaurant told him Mavis was worried that he just might go back on his word.

By the time CJ reached his showroom-spotless drop-top '57 Chevy Bel Air a block down the street from Mae's, his heart was thumping. Henry's out-of-character behavior had him scared. In the nearly thirty years that they had known one another, he had seen Henry lose his composure only once, during a *Cape Star* search-and-rescue mission in Vietnam after a sniper-downed chopper pilot Henry had pushed IV fluids into for thirty minutes and tried to resuscitate finally lost his battle to maintain blood pressure and died.

Teary-eyed, with his voice wavering and his hands shaking, Henry had unsheathed the pilot's sidearm and pocketed it. On their way back through a quarter-mile of dense jungle to the *Cape Star*, Henry had stopped, slipped the gun out of his pocket, and fired blindly at the treeline just ahead until he was out of ammunition. Then, in a voice just above a whisper, he had turned to CJ and handed him the gun, saying, "Know what, CJ? If I had seen that fucking sniper, I would have killed him. Piss on the Geneva Convention's goddamned noncombatant rules." CJ later learned that Henry and the dead pilot had been high school rodeo team roping partners back in Durango, Colorado.

CJ swallowed hard as he slipped behind the wheel of the Bel Air and pulled out into traffic, knowing that everyone, even someone as even-tempered as Henry Bales, had a button that could be pushed.

Chapter 15

The congestion around the Health Sciences Center forced CJ to park nearly four blocks away from the basic science research building. He jogged across campus, cowboy boots clunking, Stetson in hand, past a string of baby-faced twenty-somethings whom he pegged as medical students, sensing that he was out of place. The suspicious look he got from a woman in a white lab coat pacing the entryway of the research building as he stood waiting for the elevator, thumbs jammed inside the pockets of his riverboat gambler's vest, reinforced the feeling.

He spent the quick ride to the eighth floor reading the half-dozen notices taped to the elevator's walls asking for volunteers to participate in research trials investigating everything from diabetes to Alzheimer's disease. One of the notices promised to pay enrollees a hundred dollars for their participation. Surprised by the blatant solicitations, CJ wondered how often people actually signed on to become human guinea pigs.

On the eighth floor, it took him a few seconds to get his bearings before heading south down the hallway past Henry Bales's laboratory. On the way he kept telling himself that since he hadn't seen any police cars outside the building, at least the cop Henry was arguing with hadn't called for backup.

The teal-and-white sign next to the last doorway before the fire exit read, *Tess Gilliam, M.D., Ph.D., Division of Molecular Genetics.* A decal of a downhill skier flanked the degrees. Prepared for the worst, CJ walked through the door and past the hum of two gigantic upright minus-70 freezers in the entryway. A young Asian woman stood at a sink just inside the laboratory. Engrossed in what she was doing, the woman didn't look up until CJ cleared his throat and said, "I'm looking for Dr. Gilliam."

Startled, the woman glanced up, her eyes locked on CJ's Stetson. "Are you Mr. Floyd?"

"Yes."

"Everyone's in Dr. Gilliam's office. They're expecting you. Down the middle aisle and to your left. It's the first doorway back by the windows."

"Thanks." As CJ headed for the office, he could feel the woman's eyes still glued to him. Ignoring the urge to look back, he walked briskly past a dizzying array of scientific instruments to the door to Tess's office and tapped lightly.

"Come in."

Recognizing that the voice was certainly not Henry's, CJ stepped into the office to find Tess Gilliam seated in her wheelchair behind her desk and a subdued-looking Henry Bales in a chair next to her. Julie Madrid and a man with the essence of cop stamped on his face sat in chairs on either side of the desk.

"Everything okay?" asked CJ, looking first at Julie and then at Henry.

Henry raised a handcuffed wrist from the arm of his chair in response.

CJ slapped his forehead with his palm and shook his head. "Shit." Then, turning to Menton, he added, "Is he under arrest?"

"No. Just enjoying a time-out. I'm Lieutenant Clifford Menton, and you are?"

"CJ Floyd."

Menton eyed CJ, trying to place him before turning to Julie. "I didn't realize you had sent for reinforcements, counselor."

"Just looking out for my client's best interest."

"How do you expect Mr. Floyd to help?"

"Is moral support a good enough answer?" Julie looked at Henry for a response, but he only continued to look embarrassed, eyes locked on the floor.

"It's *an* answer." Menton glanced back at CJ, and a sudden hint of recognition crossed his face. "Floyd. You're a bail bondsman, right? I knew I'd place the face."

"Yeah," said CJ, uneasy that a cop he didn't recognize had pegged him so quickly.

"I've seen you around. What's your connection here? Besides moral support, I mean."

Before CJ could answer, a tall, blue-eyed, underfed-looking man sporting a fresh buzz cut opened the door. CJ figured the younger man, who remained standing in the doorway, arms clasped behind his back, for Menton's partner.

Menton gave the man a nod. "The room I want swept is outside the office and to your left. It's a storage room in the back." Sensing the man needed to be shown the room, Menton added, "I'll show you." Moving to head out the door, he looked back around the room. "Hold your places, everyone; I'll be right back."

During Menton's absence Julie offered two snippets of advice she'd been hoping to slip in. "Tess, don't volunteer any more information about your relationship with Neil, and CJ, make sure Henry stays seated in that chair."

Menton was back in less than a minute, rubbing his hands together expectantly. "Now that halftime's over, ladies and gentlemen, let's get back to the game. That is, if you have no objections, counselor," he added, looking at Julie.

"I don't have any," said Julie.

"Fine." Menton reseated himself, scooting his chair closer to Henry. Then, looking at Tess, he said, "Can you tell me why anyone might want to kill Dr. Cardashian?"

"Not really," said Tess, noting that CJ had positioned himself directly behind Henry's chair. Uncertain just how much of her suspicion concerning Cardashian's research she should share with Menton, she said, "Neil was a little on the eccentric side and he could be overbearing, but those aren't reasons to kill someone."

Menton smiled. "Maybe not in your world, Dr. Gilliam.

"What about you, Dr. Bales?" said Menton, eyeing CJ as if daring him to move as he reached over and unshackled Henry. "Know of anybody who might have disliked Dr. Cardashian enough to have killed him?"

Henry rubbed his wrists, looked up placidly at Tess, and shrugged. "No one specifically."

"I see." Menton slipped his handcuffs into the pocket of his sport coat, noting that neither of the answers he'd gotten had been an outright *no*. "Any bad karma between you and Dr. Cardashian?" asked Menton, looking back at Tess.

"Only the professional disagreement I told you about."

"What about other people he worked with? Did anyone dislike him enough to want to kill him?"

"Like you said earlier, Lieutenant, we don't function like that in our world."

Menton smiled, glanced at everyone once again, and sat back in his chair, aware that not only was Tess Gilliam feisty, she also had a lot of loyal friends. "Did Dr. Cardashian have financial or ah . . . relationship problems?" he said, directing the question to Tess.

"Neil wasn't married, and as far as I know he played the field. As for money, I have no idea about his finances."

"He drove a Ferrari," Menton said pointedly.

"And I drive a Chevy truck," said Henry.

Julie shot Henry a look that said, *Shut up*, followed by a glance toward CJ that told him she expected him to keep Henry in line.

Ignoring Henry's comment, Menton continued questioning Tess. "Any professional jealousy between you and Cardashian?"

"That's a ridiculous question," protested Julie, rising from her chair.

Tess pushed her wheelchair back from her desk and

motioned for Julie to sit down. "But one that's easy enough to answer. No, there wasn't."

Unfazed by Tess's adamant response, Menton said, "I understand from your dean, Dr. Adler, that you and Dr. Cardashian were working on a five-million-dollar National Institutes of Health research project. Mind telling me a little bit about it?"

"What would you like to hear?" asked Tess, suspecting that Adler had probably also run down her life story for Menton.

"The project's purpose, for starters?"

"Neil and I were trying to identify what role an enzyme that synthesizes the ends of chromosomes plays in the longevity of cells."

"Were you having any success?"

"Some," said Tess, looking at Julie to see if she had given the right answer and receiving a supportive nod.

"Would it be possible for me to get a summary of the project? One that a layman could understand?"

Tess reached across the arm of her wheelchair, pulled out the side file drawer of her desk, thumbed through a row of Pendaflex files, and extracted a red-tabbed folder that read, *Telomerase Abstracts.* Slipping a sheet of paper from inside the file, she handed it to Menton. "Here's a synopsis."

"Used to handing these out, I take it?"

"As a matter of fact, yes. But usually I'm passing them out to colleagues or the press. This is my first request from the police."

Menton scanned the title at the top of the page, "The Role of Telomerase Reactivation in Immortalized Cell

Lines." "Were you part of the project too, Dr. Bales?" he said, glancing over at Henry.

"No," said Henry, just as Menton's buzz-cut partner stuck his head back inside the doorway.

"Can you spare a sec? I need to see you in the back room," said the man.

Menton left without saying a word. He returned before Julie had a chance to offer any advice. "Dr. Gilliam, did Dr. Cardashian have a habit of changing clothes in that back storage room of yours?"

Looking stunned, Tess turned to Julie for direction.

"You can answer," said Julie.

"No."

"Strange," said Menton, stroking his chin. "We just found several articles of clothing and a lab coat with Cardashian's name embroidered on it stuffed behind some equipment." Menton looked at Julie and shook his head. "Afraid I've got to play strictly by the rules now, counselor. I'll be asking for a search warrant."

"On what grounds?" asked Julie.

"On the grounds that Dr. Cardashian may have been murdered right here." Menton tapped the desktop with his index finger for emphasis.

"That's insane," said Julie.

"Afraid not, Ms. Madrid. I'm going to have to ask Dr. Gilliam to come downtown with me so she can answer a few more questions."

Henry was halfway out of his chair before CJ grabbed him by both shoulders and shoved him back down in his seat.

"Smart move on your part," said Menton, eyeing CJ. "I'd hate to have to bring the cuffs back out."

"Do we have to go now, Lieutenant?" asked Tess, grasping the seriousness of the situation.

"In a few minutes. I'm going to want to hear a lot more about your and Dr. Cardashian's research."

"Looks like I'll be stepping outside my world after all, doesn't it, Lieutenant?" said Tess, trying her best to sound unintimidated. Then, turning to Henry, she said, "While I'm giving the lieutenant my story and the scoop on the telomerase, why don't you do the same for CJ?" Tess winked at CJ, knowing that her request would keep Henry from coming with her and Julie and possibly doing something that might get him arrested.

"Guess it was important for Mr. Floyd to come over here after all," said Menton, aware of Tess's maneuvering.

"It's always important to have friends, Lieutenant, and it never hurts to have a little knowledgeable backup when you're entering a world you don't fully understand."

Smiling at Tess's logic, CJ gave Menton a look that said, *Touché.* As he did, he could almost see the wheels turning in Menton's head as he tried to determine what a world-class research scientist like Tess Gilliam and a bail bondsman would have in common. He could have told Menton that Henry Bales was the connection, but realizing that the way things were headed he might need a little advantage of his own, he smiled and thought, *Why spoil the fun?*

Chapter 16

CJ and Henry sat alone in Henry's office, taking turns staring out the window at the cloudless sky. A few minutes earlier Henry had told CJ exactly how the police had found Cardashian's body and admitted that it had been Tess's concern over Cardashian's research conduct that had upset him while they were at the ranch. CJ knew Henry was capable of staring out the window poker-faced for hours, his methodical mind grinding away at the morning's events.

CJ decided to break the silence. "How about telling me about what happened between you and that cop Menton that made him slap handcuffs on you? Then you can bring me up to speed on that enzyme Cardashian and Tess were studying. First the handcuffs."

"I don't know. Menton just seemed to jump-start something inside me that I hadn't felt since Vietnam."

"Bad attitude on his part?"

"No." Henry paused and stared back out the window. "I just didn't like the way he kept picking away at Tess."

CJ knew the influence Tess had had on Henry. Not only had she mentored Henry for most of his professional career, she had also helped him put his all but fractured life back together after a heartbreaking failed marriage. Like Tess, CJ could have predicted the marriage's outcome, knowing that his introspective, intellectual research scientist friend was also too much pure cowboy for the daughter of an Eastern transplant blueblood. The marriage crumbled in less than two years, as much from the inertia of two polar opposites unwilling to look for a middle ground as from anything else.

Afterward it had been Tess who had rescued Henry from a blue funk, insisting that he take a three-month leave of absence from the university and spend it reenergizing himself at his Durango ranch.

Watching Henry sit motionless and stare out the window, CJ finally said, "Maybe Menton has something against women doctors."

"Nah," said Henry, his southwest Colorado drawl surfacing as it always did when he was upset. "He just seemed to be pushing too hard for another notch in his case-solved gun. When he asked Tess whether she was temporarily or permanently wheelchair-bound, I just lost it."

CJ shook his head, surprised at Henry's inability to read Menton. "He's a homicide cop, Henry, looking for a button to push. All he wanted to do was gauge Tess's reaction."

"Well, he got one from me instead," said Henry, getting up from his chair. "Will they put her in jail?"

CJ couldn't help but smile at Henry's lack of under-standing of the criminal justice system. "A prominent doctor with her lawyer at her side, no murder weapon, and no probable cause. No way. Menton just wants to put the fear of God in Tess to tilt the scales his way. It's like drill sergeants at boot camp. Cops like to show everyone who's in command. Tess'll be just fine. With Julie run-ning interference, she'll be back in a couple of hours. Now, how about filling me in on that mysterious enzyme of Cardashian's?"

"I'll hold you to your prediction," said Henry, check-ing his watch. Then, striding quickly across the room as if he needed to rev himself up in order to talk about Car-dashian, he added, "The enzyme's called telomerase. Some researchers claim it's the scientific mother lode. Maybe, maybe not. One thing for certain, though: Car-dashian was searching for something that would make the whole world sit up and take notice."

"Clue me in."

"In a nutshell, that telomerase project of his is geared at identifying the genetic stopwatch that tells us how long we'll live."

"Damn! And I always thought you scientists were more interested in finding ways to create life."

"Not really. We've been looking for the molecular stop-watch that controls life's calendar for a long, long time."

"Sounds a little Twilight Zoney to me."

"It's not. When you get right down to it, it's no differ-ent than building a house or for that matter, tearing one down. You can start with a foundation or a wrecking ball either way."

CJ pulled a cheroot out of his vest pocket and lit up. "Where does the telomerase stuff fit in?"

Suppressing the urge to give CJ another lecture about his smoking, Henry said, "Our normal cells have a limited number of times they can divide. Once they reach the end of that number, they can't divide anymore. No division, no new cells, and bingo, like the buzzer at the end of a basketball game, the old clock ticks out. It's a ruthless system, one that's based on the fact that DNA strands at the end of our chromosomes called telomeres get eaten away as we age. Have I lost you yet?"

"No," said CJ, not fully appreciating Henry's high-tech jargon but clearly understanding that Cardashian had been screwing around with something that controlled the very essence of life. "Maybe we shouldn't be mucking around with this shit."

"Maybe. But the snowball's rolling and it's gaining speed. Cardashian wasn't the only one investigating telomerase. Most of the people working in the field think that those telomeres I just mentioned are the keys that turn the telomerase switch."

CJ took a drag on his cheroot. "What's the scientific party line, and Henry, try giving it to me in something close to plain English."

"Easy enough. Telomeres are sort of like the plastic tips at the ends of shoestrings. We continually eat away at them throughout life. When the plastic tips become too short, cell generation can't continue without snipping off a piece of what's behind the tip, the shoestring itself. To keep the string from unraveling, something has to keep the cells intact. Telomerase seems to be the glue."

"Is this stuff ready for the drugstore yet? Sounds like just what I need to get myself rejuvenated."

"The best thing you can do about rejuvenation is toss those cheroots. As for telomerase, the stuff's a long way from pharmacy shelves because nobody's been able to identify its catalytic protein."

"You're spewing jargon again, Henry."

"Sorry. The bottom line's this. No one's been able to put their finger on the fuel that makes the telomerase engine run. From what Tess tells me, only one scientist in the U.S., Dr. Sandra Artorio at the National Institutes of Health, has even come close."

"So here's the long and short of it," said CJ. "Stop me if I'm wrong. Cardashian and Tess are busy looking for some kind of immortality clock. They're close to finding it when, just short of Tess turning Cardashian in for cheating in class, Cardashian ends up dead. Next thing we know, our friend Menton shows up and fingers Tess as the prime murder suspect. Am I close?"

"Right on the money."

"Glad Julie's with Dr. Gilliam," said CJ, frowning at the scenario he'd just run down.

"I thought you said Tess would be back in a couple of hours."

"That was before I knew about your damn telomerase house of cards. Menton will push Tess pretty hard, knowing that she and Cardashian were working on some kind of mumbo-jumbo fountain of youth. With Cardashian out of the way Tess gets all the credit. Speaks to motive for a cop. Let's just hope Tess doesn't get too talkative."

"She doesn't have to. That summary she gave Menton

spells out the whole telomerase story. Tess could be in real trouble, CJ. She may need your kind of help."

"I don't know, Henry. This sounds way out of my league."

Henry's eyes turned glassy as he paused to gather his thoughts. "Any chance you remember what I said to you after Tommy Haskins died on that search-and-rescue mission back in Vietnam?"

"Yes," said CJ, looking at Henry apprehensively, recalling Henry's jungle threat to kill whoever had shot his friend. "Yes."

"I'd feel the same way if Tess somehow got hurt. I'll pay you myself."

CJ stepped over and draped his arm across Henry's shoulders. "Money's not the issue here, Henry. When it comes to murder, Menton was right. It's a different world altogether, and Tess could end up getting hurt."

Henry slipped out of CJ's grasp and gave him a look that only two people who had shared the same war could appreciate. "You wouldn't send me in country alone, would you?"

Sensing that he was about to board a roller coaster, CJ shook his head and stubbed out his cheroot on the heel of his boot. Then, remembering his no-bounty-hunting-or-problem-cases promise to Mavis, he crossed his fingers. "Give me everything you can on Cardashian and his research, including a list of his and Tess's enemies and friends, and whatever you can dig up for me on exactly how he died."

Recalling Mavis's admonition once again, CJ second-guessed himself, but the smile on Henry's face told him he was doing the right thing.

Chapter 17

The abandoned ramshackle tobacco barn sat in the middle of a defoliated, sickly-looking grove of palm trees three miles off the road leading to Guanahacabibes Peninsula, the crooked spit of land that is Cuba's westernmost point.

Anthony Rontella had spent the last two and a half bone-jarring hours enduring a ride from the Hotel Nacional and through the hills of the Pinar del Río province in an open-topped World War II–vintage jeep. Not once during the trip had Manuel Hernández, who was driving, stopped singing the virtues of the Castro revolution, sounding as if he needed more convincing about the righteousness of the cause than Anthony.

Turning onto the narrow cowpath of a road leading to the barn, Hernández made a final comment: "When in

Cuba, one must always remember this. There are only three natural states for a Cuban dissident: in exile, in prison, or dead." The comment struck Anthony as almost remorseful, and it made him wonder just what a ruthless freelancing entrepreneur like Hernández really thought of the Castro regime.

Hernández seemed to enjoy Anthony's befuddlement. He pulled the jeep to a stop in front of the barn, leaving the vehicle's barely functional low beams directed on the barn's front door. "Some of us are special, amigo. Blessed like María la Gorda, untouched by the dust of revolution."

According to legend, Venezuelan-born María la Gorda was captured by pirates and abandoned near the Guanahacabibes Peninsula following a shipwreck. Destitute, María turned to selling fresh water and her large, voluptuous body to passing sailors, eventually enjoying a long and comfortable life in Cuba. "I know the story," said Anthony, recognizing that Hernández, like Mary the Fat, was a man who was quite capable of weathering whatever storm he might find himself in.

"Then you have looked into my mind," said Hernández. Grinning broadly, he stepped out of the vehicle, peered expectantly into the semidarkness, then reached back and flashed the jeep's headlights on and off twice before sounding the horn and stepping away from the jeep. Within seconds the barn door swung open. Hernández slipped back into the jeep and eyed Anthony pensively. "Should we ever find it necessary to pull up to an abandoned structure such as this at night again, you would do well to follow my lead and get out of the vehicle. There are people I pay whose very lives depend on my monthly gratuity, and then there are those who would rather be heroes of the revolution. It is the heroes one must never lose sight of. People have been known to become the victims in situations like this. I am certain you wouldn't want to go up in mortar fire and flames."

A bolt of fear shot through Anthony as he squinted toward the barn, realizing for the first time what his gambling nature had gotten him into. He had placed himself in a situation in which Sweets, Hernández, or someone waiting inside the barn could have easily killed him. And he ran the risk that his secondary scam, the one that Sweets knew nothing of, could play out so that he ended up rotting away in some Cuban jail. Second-guessing himself as the vehicle bumped forward and then pulled into the barn, Anthony let out a sigh of relief as Atina Salas quickly pulled the barn door shut.

The dimly lit barn was empty except for a recently constructed thirty-foot-long, fifteen-foot-high enclosure near the back that was partially hidden from view behind stacks of ninety-weight oil drums. Anthony had the urge to rush beyond the drums and check on his side bet but suppressed the urge and stepped from the jeep grinning from ear to ear, greeting his star counterfeit Cuban cigar roller with a brief hug.

"*Buenas noches,*" said Atina before turning to Hernández and complaining, "You're late."

"It's my fault," said Anthony, hoping to defuse what he knew from past experience could turn into a lengthy argument if he didn't head it off.

Atina shot Manuel a disdainful look. "Did you do everything to make sure you weren't followed?"

"I ran enough hillside reverses to make us dizzy."

Atina looked at Anthony for confirmation. Anthony nodded, hoping to bridge the gulf of distrust.

"You waited at the peninsula turnoff for fifteen minutes for the bicycle rider to come by before you proceeded?"

Manuel cocked a defiant eyebrow and cracked his knuckles. "I told you already. We did everything as planned."

Atina looked at Anthony for a second verification. "Is it as he says?"

"Yes," said Anthony. He wasn't sure of the reason for the friction between Manuel and Atina, but he wasn't going to let it interfere with the cigar-counterfeiting sidebar he had been setting up for over a year. Now that he and Atina had successfully field-tested their product, he couldn't afford to let petty animosities scuttle a project that he had pumped so much money into. "Let's see the production," he said in a voice meant to let Atina and Manuel know that they should save their jousting for later.

Atina rolled her eyes at Manuel and then turned to Anthony with a smile. "I'll show you what we have on hand. You'll be impressed."

"I'll stay here," said Manuel, thankful that he wouldn't have to endure another of Atina's lectures on entrepreneurship and pleased that it would offer him a chance to call his contact, Rulon Mantero, to find out how Ernesto Salas was doing.

"Suit yourself," said Anthony, trailing Atina across the dirt floor, dodging chicken droppings along the way.

Atina stepped up to the oil-drum facade, swung two hinged cantilevered drums aside, and stepped through a partially open sliding metal door into a well-lit, recently drywalled room filled with dozens of tables stacked high with Honduran-grown African cedar cigar boxes. Most of the boxes were covered with ornate, exquisitely detailed, professionally produced—but counterfeit—labels. They included most of Cuba's elite cigar manufacturers: Cohiba, Davidoff, Monte Cristo, Sancho Panza. Hundreds of unlabeled boxes rested next to their labeled counterparts, and bundles of forged cigar labels, all wrapped in tissue paper and held together by featherweight rubber bands, sat next to them.

Lighting up a Cohiba, Atina smiled and waved her arm at her stash. "Impressive enough?" she said, taking a long drag on her cigar and beaming at Anthony.

"I'd say."

"I thought it would be," said Atina, surveying the fruits of six months of intensive labor that had been completed while she also had to hide her efforts from grandson Ernesto. Wanting to make certain that Anthony understood the pressure she had been working under, she added, "Depending on size, an expert *torcedor* can produce one hundred to one hundred fifty cigars per day. A well-coordinated team close to five hundred. As you can see, I have had a team producing around the clock. I'll ship five thousand boxes to your contact in Montreal, who will then move them on to your person in Boston within a week or two."

"What's the total?" asked Anthony, wanting the bottom line, knowing that Atina couldn't make a move without him.

"One hundred and twenty-five thousand cigars."

Anthony crunched the numbers in his head. Five thousand boxes at an average of $80 per box meant that he stood to gross $400,000 on the shipment, close to half that after expenses. Satisfied that his gamble was about to pay off, he walked to one of the tables and scrutinized an open box of cigars. "You're certain that the bulk of the tobacco leaves that the cigars are rolled from are genuine?"

"The leaves, the binder, even the *capa*," shot back Atina.

Extracting a Cohiba, he inspected it and then rolled it back and forth beneath his nose, pleased that on a cursory inspection he couldn't tell the cigar's *capa*, or outer wrapping, from the genuine article. It appeared that, as she had promised, Atina had pilfered a hefty batch of the real thing somewhere along the line.

Anthony rolled the cigar around in his hand, sniffed it again, and gently pressed it between his fingers before extracting a lighter from his pants pocket and lighting up. After savoring several long drags, he kissed his fingertips and smiled at Atina. "How have you done it?"

Atina smiled and took a puff on her own cigar. "Like the water's edge, I have prepared for a lifetime to meet the shore."

"It's a secret, then?"

"More a secret weapon than a secret. I prefer to credit my successes to my knowledge of the *cabildos*."

Unaware that *cabildos* were seventeenth-century Cuban communal slaves responsible for preserving the dances, music, and religious traditions of their African homeland, Anthony frowned and took another drag on his cigar. "Call it what you will. We all have secrets," said Anthony. "Speaking of secrets, how's Cuba's number-one counterpuncher?"

"Fine, although I think he has the stomach flu."

"Nothing serious, I hope."

"Mostly diarrhea and upset stomach, but he hasn't felt at all like sparring."

The muscles in Anthony's stomach coalesced into a knot. "That's too bad," he said, trying his best to sound less interested in Ernesto's health than in his and Atina's cigar-counterfeiting venture. "I'm surprised Manuel didn't tell me about Ernesto being ill."

"He doesn't know about it. No one does except me, his coaches, and of course Rulon Mantero, that hanger-on friend of Ernesto's who seems to like you so much."

Atina's mention of Rulon Mantero, the critical bagman Anthony had been using as a go-between for Ernesto, triggered a new knot in Anthony's stomach. "I should probably drop in on Ernesto while I'm here."

"Suit yourself. But don't blame me if you catch the flu."

"I'll risk it. By the way, has Rulon been by to see Ernesto since he's been sick?"

"Every day. Why?"

"Just wondering," said Anthony, slapping at a pesky mosquito on his arm. "I might need to use him on my end of this tobacco deal in Boston."

"You'll be wasting your time and money. He's worthless."

Aware that a chain was only as strong as its weakest link, and hoping that he hadn't squandered the $5,000 he had given Rulon to nursemaid Ernesto, Anthony said, "I'll talk to him anyway."

"Suit yourself," said Atina, surveying the barn with a

sudden sense of urgency. "Are you finished with every-thing you need to see here? We should be moving out."

"Yes," said Anthony, preoccupied with Ernesto's health as well as his own should he have to tell Sweets that he had bungled his assignment because he was setting up a cigar-smuggling scam. Swallowing hard, he sighed and swatted two additional mosquitoes that had landed on his arm just below his right shirt sleeve.

"Then I'll close everything up."

"Fine," said Anthony, glancing at the flattened mos-quitoes, flicking them away and leaving a streak of blood just beneath the tattoo of crossed oars on his arm.

Chapter 18

Sandra Artorio hadn't left her research laboratory since mid-morning, when Tess Gilliam had called to tell her that Neil Cardashian had been found dead in a minus-70 Revco freezer and to ask whether she had received the fresh frozen cell blocks, slides, and unstained microscopic tissue sections she had overnighted.

After listening to Tess detail what she said Denver police were now calling a murder investigation and summarize her afternoon grilling by a police lieutenant named Menton, Sandi decided to drop what she was working on and help Tess determine whether the answer to why Cardashian might have been murdered was locked somewhere in the cell blocks and tissue sections Tess had sent.

An overnight rainstorm and the accompanying humidity had turned Sandi's jet-black curly hair uncharacteristically limp. Running a hand through her hair and frowning at its texture, she realized that she hadn't taken a break in hours. Getting up, she pushed the slides her technician had just immuno-stained away from her microscope and thought about Tess's dilemma.

For the first time in a long while, she found herself questioning whether the scientific fast-track life that she was so wedded to might have a downside that she had never considered, and for some unexplained reason, she also found herself wondering whether she should be frightened. Especially since she and Cardashian had both been in hot pursuit of the same thing: identification of the key protein in the telomerase enzyme. Each of them hoped to determine how the enzyme could miraculously rebuild the ends of chromosomes after each cell division and whether its catalytic protein could indeed function as the principal switching mechanism in control of the human aging process.

They had been looking for the protein in two unique and divergent organisms; while she had been concentrating on isolating the protein from *Saccharomyces cerevisiae*, common brewer's yeast, Cardashian had been investigating a ciliated protozoan, *Euploidies aediculatus*. She glanced around her empty lab, reassuring herself that it was just science and there was no reason to be afraid.

In one sense she had been ahead of Cardashian. Just six weeks earlier she had identified what she was convinced was the possible DNA sequence for the catalytic protein, the critical starter component of the telomerase enzyme. She hadn't told anyone about her discovery, since she hadn't verified her findings by duplicating the experiment. Even with replication, she was at least six months away from a true end point. Now, considering what had happened to Cardashian, she was happy that she had kept her findings to herself.

She felt a strange sense of isolation as she pulled her chair back up to her microscope and slipped the first of the immunofluorescent-stained slides onto the scope's stage for review, focusing on the faint orange glow of what she recognized as fluorescent-labeled telomeres at the tips of chromosomes. The stain was almost assuredly staining chromosomes from the protozoan that Cardashian had been working with. But the staining was oddly intermittent and uneven, which made her wonder whether in her haste to help Tess she had run the in situ hybridization experiments too rapidly and made a procedural error. Especially since the matching sequence of radioactive-labeled slides that Tess had also sent, the ones that Tess claimed had made her suspicious of Cardashian's research in the first place, had stained evenly and uniformly dense.

Perplexed, she got up from her seat, walked to her office, and pulled out the top drawer of the lateral file behind her desk. She thumbed through a series of folders, stopping at the only one with a handwritten tab, and pulled out a two-year-old editorial from the journal *Cell Biology*. Neil Cardashian's editorial titled "A Probable Catalytic Subunit of Telomerase: A Proposal for Identification of Reverse Transcriptase Motifs" was simply a thoughtful opinion rather than a typical peer-reviewed scientific article. An opinion that had caused quite a stir when it was first published, generating in its wake several letters to the editor criticizing Cardashian's premise that RNA motifs rather than DNA motifs were the key to identifying the catalytic protein in telomerase. A premise that was in direct conflict with the scientific dogma of the time.

Cardashian's concept, which she remembered discussing with Tess Gilliam at length, had quickly disappeared into scientific oblivion as unfounded, but rather than dismiss it, Sandi had pegged a large portion of her own research on Cardashian's premise. It hadn't been until she began to experiment with *Saccharomyces* that she realized that Cardashian's theory was very likely on target.

As she reread the article's first page, her hands turned sweaty. *Human telomeres look nearly identical to the telomeres of other eukaryotes, since they all contain a spectrum of tandem DNA repeats. Humans thus share the (TTAGGG)n telomeric sequence with the full array of the rest of the world's other vertebrates, and a few very distant relatives in other kingdoms. Human chromosomes end in several kilobases of telomeric repeat DNA so that the G-rich strand extends out to the three prime ends of the chromosome. The catalytic protein necessary for telomeric extension almost assuredly resides, however, not in the DNA, but in the RNA subunit template.*

As Sandi read the last sentence of the paragraph a second time, and then a third, her hands began shaking as she began to understand why the fluorescent-labeled slides she had prepared from Tess's cell block had shown such weak and intermittent staining for telomerase, while the complementary Neil Cardashian–prepared radioactive-labeled P32 slides were bursting with what both she and Tess had very obviously been misinterpreting as telomerase enzyme.

Laying the paper aside, she rushed back out to her microscope and slipped one of Cardashian's radioactive-labeled slides onto the microscope stage for examination. This time, instead of concentrating on the forest of black-granular-staining radioactive P32 in the field, she focused her attention on the amorphous, indistinct cell outlines that enveloped the radioactive label. Focusing up and down on the slide, she realized that the radioactive label couldn't possibly be staining telomerase. If so, the staining would have to have been identical to the intermittent, patchy staining pattern she had seen in the slides she had prepared. *No*, she told herself, her hands now trembling. The Cardashian-labeled slides were almost assuredly staining not telomerase but the enzyme's catalytic component, the all too elusive protein that she had been trying to isolate and sequence for close to four years—the protein thought to be responsible for stopping human cells from ever growing old.

If that had been the only remarkable feature about the slides, her hands would have stopped shaking and the queasiness in the pit of her stomach would have subsided, but something else was evident. Something that struck her as decidedly strange, almost sinister. She returned to examining the Cardashian-labeled slides, trying to rationalize a conclusion she now couldn't avoid. She knew she was looking at the radioactive-labeled catalytic protein of telomerase, but the staining pattern was hundreds of times more dense than could have ever been generated via the normal RNA switching mechanisms within the cell. What she was viewing had to be something that had been introduced into the cell, not a product the cell had generated itself. It appeared that Cardashian had not only been correct in his assessment of how the telomerase catalytic protein was generated; he had also obviously isolated it in large enough quantities to be able to introduce into cultured cells.

Adjusting the fine focus on her microscope, Sandi struggled to make out the boundaries of the cells she was examining. After several minutes of scrutiny she locked in a field of prickly cell-to-cell attachments that made her silently scream. No longer awash in the rush of scientific discovery, she now found herself terrified. The cell-to-cell attachments she was looking at were desmosomes, attachments that could never be found in a simple one-celled protozoan. Suddenly she found herself facing the harsh reality of why Neil Cardashian might have been killed. The cells that he had been experimenting with, cells so rich in the catalytic protein of telomerase that they were bursting with it, were epithelial in origin and almost certainly human.

Sandi leaned back from her microscope and took a long, deep breath, knowing that with the head start Cardashian had, there was no telling what direction his clandestine research had taken. Not quite certain of what to do next, she reached for the phone to call Tess Gilliam, deciding halfway through punching in the numbers that she would catch the next nonstop flight to Denver.

Chapter 19

Unlike most Cubans, who must queue up for medical care at one of the country's numerous polyclinics, Ernesto Salas had the luxury of being attended to at home by Dr. Rafael Gómez, the Cuban boxing team doctor. Gómez's claims to fame included the fact that he had graduated from Stanford's medical school before Castro's revolution and had treated the premier for a middle-ear infection during a recent trip to the U.N. Ernesto hadn't been able to keep anything solid down for two days. He had lost six pounds, and his hand tremors and intermittent bouts of dizziness had Dr. Gómez baffled.

Equally puzzled, Atina Salas paced the living room floor of her apartment waiting for Dr. Gómez to finish his early-morning evaluation of Ernesto. She was fortunate to live in a recently constructed Pinar del Río rural apartment block built by one of Cuba's microbrigades, volunteer workers charged by the government with developing prefabricated rural housing. The apartment's workmanship was shoddy, but the brightness of her new home had replaced the dankness of a two-room hut she had lived in for years, so for Atina, quality was of little concern.

The morning was warm and breezy, and the intoxicating smell of fig and pine from the nearby jajuey trees and pine forest wafted through the open kitchen window. Until forty-eight hours earlier, all the things that Atina had worked so hard to develop had been falling into place. Her cigar-counterfeiting scheme was about to see the light of day. Ernesto was on the brink of becoming an Olympic champion, and it seemed a certainty that soon she would travel outside Cuba for the first time in twenty years. She never would have envisioned that Ernesto's health could turn out to be a barrier to her dreams, especially since she couldn't recall Ernesto having had more than a minor cold and one or two toothaches in his entire life.

She had packed Anthony Rontella back to the United States, puzzled by the fact that he seemed more concerned about Ernesto's health than their cigar-exporting arrangement, but in the eighteen months she had known him, she hadn't been able to quite figure out Rontella. Other than pegging him as an obvious gambler, she attributed his concern for Ernesto to the fact that Rontella needed to stay on her good side if he expected their business venture to succeed.

She couldn't help but notice that Ernesto's illness also had her lecherous brother-in-law Manuel Hernández and Ernesto's worthless friend Rulon Mantero out of sorts. In addition to Rulon pestering her about Ernesto's health twice a day, she had caught Ernesto in shouting matches with Rulon more than once, which made her suspect that they probably had a substantial amount of gambling money to lose if Ernesto didn't get better.

Dr. Gómez emerged from Ernesto's room and stepped into Atina's sparsely furnished kitchen, clunking his way across the room in a pair of expensive cowboy boots he had purchased on his last trip to the United States. His face was flushed and consumed by the same look of dismay Atina had seen for the past two days. "Is he any better today, Doctor?" Her eyes pleaded for the answer to be yes.

Gómez shook his head. "No. I'm afraid he's the same. In fact, I think his tremors are more pronounced. I'll check on him this evening. If he's any worse, he'll have to be hospitalized."

"Debe ser una maldición," said Atina, abandoning her pledge to converse in English whenever she had the chance.

Gómez rolled his eyes. "No. It's no curse. I thought he had an infection at first, but now I'm beginning to believe his problem is neurological."

Atina's knowledge of English didn't extend to medical terms. "Meaning?"

"Meaning he could have a brain injury from a blow to the head."

Atina squeezed her eyes closed, shaking her head in protest. "You're wrong, Doctor. My Ernesto delivers the blows. He doesn't absorb them. His problem is here," she said, patting her stomach.

Offended that Atina would discount his diagnosis,

Gómez stiffened. He slipped his stethoscope from around his neck, slammed it into a battered valise sitting on the kitchen table, and snapped the valise shut. "I'll be by to check on Ernesto this evening. If he's no better, he'll be hospitalized for tests. I've wasted more time than I should have letting him try to recuperate at home."

Atina realized that Gómez's concern was as much for his own welfare as for Ernesto's. There were those in the government who would frown upon the loss of a certain gold medal winner from the ranks of Cuba's boxing team. There would have to be a scapegoat.

"Buenos días, Doña Salas," said Gómez, gripping his valise with an air of self-assurance as he headed for the door in a poorly disguised huff.

"Buenos días," said Atina to Gómez's backside as she watched her front door open and then slam shut, barely missing the back end of the doctor's valise. Distraught, confused, and scared, Atina sat down on the rickety kitchen stool and reflected on her problems. Several minutes later, when she moved to get off the stool and head back into the bedroom to check on Ernesto, her front screen door creaked open and she found herself staring at Manuel Hernández and Rulon Mantero.

"We're here to check on Ernesto," said Manuel, backed up by a solicitous grin from Rulon.

"Come in," said Atina, considering how she might whisk them both out of her apartment as quickly as possible. But the look on Manuel's face and insistent frown on Rulon's forehead told her that she was going to have unwanted guests for a while.

*   *   *

Jamie Lee Custus was standing in front of the badly chipped bathroom mirror in her motel room, completely naked, massaging her reconstructed foot and ankle when the second phone call in ten minutes interrupted her daily rehab ritual. "Yeah," said Jamie Lee. Setting aside the hot towel she had soaked to wrap her leg in, she sat down astride the nearby toilet. On orders from Sweets, she had parked herself in a Denver motel room in the 9500 block of East Colfax Avenue. After two days of waiting for a new directive from Sweets, with nothing to do but lie naked in bed admiring herself in the room's mirrored ceiling and watch a big-screen TV that featured three channels of twenty-four-hour porn, her patience was wearing thin.

"Now that the dust has settled, I've got a new assignment for you," said Sweets in a mechanical voice that sounded as if it were being filtered through some kind of computerized synthesizer.

"What is it?" asked Jamie Lee, leaning back against the toilet tank, her voice noncommittal.

"I want you to keep tabs on the doctor who was working with Cardashian. Her name's Tess Gilliam. It shouldn't be hard; she's confined to a wheelchair."

Jamie Lee glanced down at her bad leg, wondering if Sweets thought she was stupid. After following Cardashian for months, she knew full well who the Gilliam woman was. She also knew that she needed to negotiate a better deal than the one she had been getting to shadow Cardashian. She knew Manuel Hernández had been paid more than she had to stick to Cardashian on two trips Cardashian had taken to Cuba. What she couldn't figure out was exactly what Cardashian had been doing in Cuba.

Her guess was that they were smuggling prescription drugs back and forth between the United States and Cuba on the very active Cuban pharmaceutical black market. She had a feeling that Hernández knew a lot more about what Sweets was really up to than he ever let on. "Why am I following her, and what's in it for me?" she said finally.

"The money's the same as with Cardashian, and you'll be following her because that's the job."

"Not enough," said Jamie Lee, listening intently to Sweets's strangely disguised voice, trying to place where she had heard similar sounds besides a carnival funhouse before.

"Three thousand a month, then."

"Why am I following the Gilliam woman?" asked Jamie Lee, sticking to her guns.

"Because she's sticking her nose where it doesn't belong," said Sweets, sounding exasperated.

"Not with me."

"Don't try my patience, Custus. I can always use Hernández if I have to."

Realizing that she had pushed the line as far as she could and thinking about how comforting $3,000 a month could be, Jamie Lee swallowed her pride. "There's no chance I'll have to off the lady in the wheelchair, is there?"

"I can't say. Why the sudden worry? I never pegged you for being squeamish."

"I'm not. I just don't like the idea of taking out someone who's handicapped."

Sweets laughed. "Don't worry. If I'm forced to, I'll handle the problem myself."

Jamie Lee could swear she heard the hint of an accent in Sweets's voice, an accent she couldn't place but one that always seemed to surface when their conversations turned to killing. "Suit yourself. Just make sure I get my money."

"You'll get it, don't worry. In the meantime, you'll be receiving a profile on Gilliam, complete with photographs, her personal habits, where she lives, even what she likes to eat. Stay on top of her."

"I know what she looks like. There's no need for photos."

"The information's not just on Gilliam. There's also information you'll need on another doctor, Henry Bales."

"Bales, yeah; I've seen the name in the building directory where Gilliam works."

"He and Gilliam are close, and he could be a stumbling block for us down the road."

"How's that?"

"That's not your problem. Just keep tabs on the both of them and do what you're told."

Jamie Lee gritted her teeth, gathered up the phone cord, and balled it up into a knot. Sweets's comment had struck a nerve—the same nerve that a logging foreman had tweaked when he had sent Jamie Lee and her crew into a section of Oregon forest to cut timber that he knew had been tree-spiked by environmentalists. The recoil from her saw hitting a spike had killed another logger and nearly cost Jamie Lee her leg. After a two-month hospital stay and six months of rehab, she had tracked the foreman down in the Washington backwoods. Surprising him as he urinated, she had snapped his neck as if it were a twig. The man's body and the felled tree she placed across it weren't found until months after Jamie Lee had moved to Texas. "Wire my money today," she said, releasing her grip on the cord.

"You don't like taking orders, do you, Custus? Strange for somebody who comes from a background that requires a team. I'll have your money on its way to you as soon as we're off the phone. Same account?"

"Yes," said Jamie Lee, surprised by Sweets's analogy.

"You'll hear from me soon."

Jamie Lee cradled the phone without responding. Months of playing lackey to a muffled voice on the phone had taken its toll. She told herself it was time to put a real face and name on the mysterious Sweets. She stood up from her toilet seat and admired, save for her leg, a solidly built, athletic body in the mirror on the back of the door, telling herself that if pressed, Sweets could easily suffer the same fate as the logging foreman. Then, wrapping a towel around her waist, she limped out of the bathroom, thinking that once she tagged Sweets with a real name, she'd never have to undersell herself again.

Rulon Mantero had sleep apnea so severe that his foundation-rattling snoring and fits of breathlessness were enough to scare anyone unfamiliar with his condition into believing that he might be having a heart attack. A man of predictable routine, Rulon slept with both the windows in his tiny one-room tar-papered shack fully open in order to take advantage of the tropical breezes he required to partially soothe the apnea beast he had to wrestle with every night.

He had looked in on Ernesto at six, eaten dinner at seven, checked on the money he had buried beneath his house, and set out the next day's special ration for Ernesto that Anthony Rontella kept him supplied with, before going to bed. He worried that Rontella's so-called power ration could have been making Ernesto sick, and before leaving Ernesto's bedside he had passed his concerns on to Manuel, who was also there. As usual, Manuel had disagreed to the point of screaming at him, and sent him on his way.

Given the loudness of his snoring, Rulon wouldn't have known that Manuel was outside his bedroom window if Manuel hadn't begun rattling the badly warped sash back and forth in its frame and screaming at the top of his lungs, "Rulon, are you there? It's Manuel."

"*Sí*," said Rulon, finally hearing the racket. Groggy with sleep, he sat up in bed, wondering why Manuel would be calling out to him in English.

"Are you awake?"

"*Sí*."

"I need to talk to you about Ernesto. It's important. Step over here to the window."

As Rulon moved over to the window, the fast-moving head of a baseball bat caught him squarely between the eyes, and a sudden flash of light sent him reeling backward. "*Qué chingados?*" he mumbled before passing out on the floor. Struggling to regain consciousness, he never saw the tennis-ball-sized incendiary device that Manuel tossed into the room, and he barely felt the flames scorching the delicate airways of his lungs. In the fifty seconds it took for Rulon to die and the less than five minutes it took for the fire to consume his isolated shack in the Pinar del Río flats, Manuel was already a mile away.

Stopping on a hillside to look back and admire the

glow from the fire, Manuel told himself that he should've rooted around in Rulon's crawl space for what he suspected remained of the $5,000 he knew Anthony Rontella had given Rulon on a visit to Cuba seven months earlier. He also questioned whether he should've searched the house for the remaining stash of power ration he knew Rulon had. But since there was no way of telling how much money he would've actually found, and the shack and everything in it were certainly history by now, he reasoned that the risk of being connected to an arson-murder far outweighed any additional monetary reward.

He watched the fire until it died down to just a faint glow in the woods before turning to begin the two-mile trek to his car. All in all, he would later report to Sweets, things had worked out well.

Chapter 20

Henry Bales had less than an hour to get to Denver International Airport, pick up Sandra Artorio, and make it back to the University of Colorado Health Sciences Center before a one P.M. surgical pathology seminar that he had to squeeze in before meeting with CJ and Tess at two. As he sped down Peña Boulevard, the access road to DIA, in his big-block Chevy pickup, he couldn't help but think that the medical puzzle he found himself involved in was getting stranger by the hour.

There was still no official word on how Neil Cardashian had died, although Tess seemed convinced that Cardashian had been murdered because he was involved in unethically tipping the scales of science. Henry was less certain but he was convinced that even though police hadn't been able to match the blood they had found on the seat of Tess's spare wheelchair to Cardashian's, Tess hadn't seen the last of Lieutenant Menton. The only solace in his own dead-end investigation of Cardashian's death was that he had CJ around to counterbalance Menton. Tess's last words to him before he had rushed out of her office for DIA were, "Sandi will meet you at the United pickup. She'll be easy to spot. She'll be wearing a burgundy suit and carrying a *Washington Post*. I told her that in case you miss one another, she should look for a shiny black Chevy pickup with the Marlboro man in a tie behind the wheel."

Henry had laughed at Tess's attempted levity, aware that deep down she was devastated by the whispered comments of longtime colleagues who were saying privately that she had killed Neil Cardashian. Even with her career in jeopardy it had taken some serious arm-twisting for Henry to get Tess to agree to let him dig through Cardashian's research records and even more of a push to convince her to let CJ rummage through Cardashian's private office.

In his search of the surprisingly skimpy research files, Henry hadn't found anything that pointed directly to why Cardashian might have been murdered. He suspected that one reason for the sketchiness of the records was that Lieutenant Menton had pulled anything of importance. Now he and Tess were counting on Sandra Artorio to fill in the blanks, hoping that she would be able to tie Cardashian's death to the mysterious telomerase-impregnated cells that Tess said Sandi had identified in one of Cardashian's cell blocks.

He had had an easier time convincing Tess that she needed CJ's help than he had convincing her she needed his. Her reluctance to accept his help had stung a bit. "You're a doctor, for Christ's sake, Henry. Not a private investigator or a cop," had been the way she had phrased it. "This Cardashian thing isn't just about research ethics anymore. Neil's dead, and I'm not certain where this whole mess is headed. I'll agree to CJ's help because he knows what he's doing. You'll just be in the way."

If it hadn't been for CJ's insistence that Tess's response was closer to that of an overly protective mother than a vote of no confidence, Henry wasn't sure how he would have handled the situation. He had no way of knowing that when Tess sat down to write CJ a check for a $3,000 advance for what she was calling his investigative assistance, she told CJ she expected two things: "Clear my name and reputation so that I can get back to my work, and promise me that no matter what, you won't let Henry get hurt." CJ had agreed to the terms with the realization that Henry probably didn't know how much Tess really cared about him and the knowledge that contrary to what Tess might think, Henry Bales was perfectly capable of taking care of himself.

Henry checked his watch as he slowed down and eased onto the access ramp leading to passenger pickup. There was a post-noon-hour lull in the normally congested area, and he spotted Sandra Artorio standing at the far end of the pickup zone almost immediately. Dressed in a figure-flattering dark burgundy business suit and standing next to a designer carry-on with a folded newspaper under her arm, she looked very different from what he had expected.

He found himself almost gawking at an exotically beautiful woman who looked more like she belonged on the pages of a New York fashion magazine than in the drafty halls of a research building at NIH. He pulled up to the curb just in front of her, suddenly feeling self-conscious about arriving in a pickup. Telling himself that it was too late to change chariots at this stage in life, Henry stepped out of the truck. He waved one hand above his head as he skirted the truck's front bumper, and said, "Dr. Artorio?"

"Yes," said Sandi, greeting Henry with a firm hand-shake.

"Henry Bales."

"Thanks for picking me up. Tess said you were a prince, and please call me Sandi."

"Okay," said Henry, grabbing Sandi's carry-on and slinging it over the bed rail, hoping he didn't look too much like some cowboy slinging hay. "Hope you don't mind riding in a truck. I grew up on a ranch, and I've never been able to get them out of my system."

"Not at all. I grew up riding in them too," said Sandi, thinking of the junk-heap pickups her father used to drive.

Stepping back from the bed rail, Henry opened the truck's door and extended his arm so that she could use it as leverage to get into the cab. Ignoring the gesture, Sandi smiled and slipped into the cab unassisted.

Impressed by Sandi's truck savvy, Henry had negoti-ated his way into departure traffic and calculated how fast he could get to the university when Sandi asked, "How's Tess holding up?"

"She's putting up a good front. But I think she's a lit-tle scared. The cops grilled her pretty good the other day, and she's still a suspect in what, at least for now, they're calling a murder case."

"I'm glad to hear she's hanging tough," said Sandi. Then with the hint of a frown, she added, "You sound as if you're not convinced that Neil was murdered."

"You have to remember, I'm a pathologist, and for some reason the autopsy findings aren't in yet. Guess I'm waiting for the bottom line."

"I see," said Sandi, admiring Henry's mid-March rancher's tan. "When do you expect the autopsy results?"

"This afternoon."

"And if it turns out Cardashian wasn't murdered?"

"I'll be real worried."

"Why's that?"

The look on Henry's face turned serious. "I'll let Tess explain the whole thing to you when we get back to the university. I don't want to leave anything out in the translation."

"Am I missing some deep, dark secret here?"

"Not really. It's just that Tess's directing the orchestra, and I'm letting her conduct."

Henry accelerated into the lengthy curve of highway that linked DIA's Peña Boulevard to I-70 and checked his watch, knowing that he'd have to speed up if he planned to make his seminar on time. Nudging the accelerator, he gave Sandi a guilty look. "Late-afternoon seminar," he said, shooting around a Volkswagen bus.

"I understand tight schedules. Besides, I like the wind in my face."

Henry smiled and watched Sandi slip casually back in her seat, legs extended, ankles crossed, and get comfortable in a way that he knew only came when someone was truly used to riding in the front seat of a pickup.

141

Chapter 21

Tess kept telling herself that no matter what kind of spin she put on it, she and CJ were breaking the law. Twenty minutes earlier they had slipped past the yellow police barricade tape sealing off Neil Cardashian's laboratory and office and begun rummaging through the contents. She didn't know how she had talked herself into doing something so stupid, but here she was, playing lookout, sitting nervously in her wheelchair while CJ burglarized her dead colleague's office.

"Everything okay?" asked CJ, calling out to Tess from inside the office.

"Yes. And please hurry up. I feel like a criminal."

"I'm moving as fast as I can," said CJ, committing his second illegal entry of Cardashian premises in as many days. The previous evening he had searched Cardashian's posh $400,000 lower downtown Denver condominium. He had thought that gaining entry to the condo would be a problem until his inventive ex-marine secretary, Flora Jean Benson, suggested that they could get in by posing as U.S. marshals investigating Cardashian's murder.

Armed with two shiny and very real U.S. marshals' badges that CJ had garnered in his twenty-five years of bounty hunting, bail bonding, and collecting all manner of American memorabilia, they had strolled into Cardashian's building shoulder to shoulder and flashed their badges to an unsuspecting building receptionist. They were escorted down the condo's central hallway to a bank of walnut-lined elevators, where the snooty director of residence whisked them to Neil Cardashian's fifth-floor condominium and let them in with less fanfare than if they had been tenants who had lost their keys. Flora Jean, who had a penchant for acting and an uncanny ability to mimic half a dozen well-known voices, had the balding director believing that she could have been Marshal Matt Dillon's long-lost black sister by the time she finished smiling at him and telling him what a wonder he was in a syrupy sensuous tone that left the director blushing.

They searched the condo for close to half an hour without finding anything of interest but several narcissistic-looking photos of Cardashian standing next to either a racing scull or a Ferrari, flexing his biceps and showing off the tattoo of crossed oars on his arm. There was nothing to suggest why Cardashian might have been murdered. In fact, CJ was so surprised by the neatness of the place that he was hard-pressed to believe that Cardashian had actually lived there. He left the building with no new insights into why Cardashian had been found dead in a dump in a research freezer and the distinct feeling that someone had been there ahead of them and swept the place. Whoever it had been, it was someone a whole lot neater than the Denver cops. He and Flora Jean had left the building as boldly as they had entered it, with Flora Jean gliding past the director of residence and flashing him a till-we-meet-again kind of look.

Cardashian's research office was the antithesis of his condominium. It was piled high with junk and stacks of papers, computer printouts, recombinant DNA gels, and photographs of his research work littered the room. A messy computer workstation draped with a hodgepodge of papers, half a dozen bulging cardboard files, and a table with a microscope hugged the back wall of the room. A couple of residue-caked coffee mugs sat on top of a wooden file cabinet next to a rolltop desk, and a cigar box that CJ immediately recognized as Cuban had been wedged between the two mugs.

Flipping open the top of the box, CJ eyed the cigars inside and thought about what he'd do if he had the money to afford Cubans instead of inexpensive cheroots. Turning back to the work at hand, he pulled out the top drawer of the file cabinet and found himself looking into an empty drawer. Moving quickly through the rest of the drawers, he found them all empty. Telling himself that somebody from Lieutenant Menton's crew, or the neat-nik who had beaten him to Cardashian's condo, had cleaned out the files, he turned back toward the room's doorway, where Tess Gilliam sat nervously waiting. "Cardashian's file cabinets are empty," he reported. "Not even a scrap of paper left behind."

A surprised look on her face, Tess rolled her wheelchair

into the room. "That's where he kept everything important, and he always kept a bottle of expensive cognac in
the bottom drawer for celebrating those special times
when a difficult research problem fell into place."

"Well, there's no cognac there now. What about the
stuff on his desk? There're a bunch of photographs on
top that look like pictures of fuzz balls."

"I know," said Tess, smiling at CJ's interpretation of
Nobel prize–caliber research and picking up the photos.
"They're bright-field photomicrographs of genetic alter-
ations on chromosomes and telomerase clones." Tess
turned her wheelchair to move back out of the room.

"Seeing as how I don't know a clone from a phone, I
need your help in here, Dr. Gilliam. How about turning
that wheelchair back around?"

"Sorry. I'm just not up to speed on breaking and entering," said Tess, angling her chair back toward CJ.

"I'll give you a lesson," said CJ. "First off, you'll need
gloves. I don't care about the cops finding my fingerprints in here; I'm not a suspect, but I sure don't want
them finding yours after they've probably already swept
the place."

"Neil always kept a box of gloves by his microscope.
He never handled slides without them; claimed his hands
were always too sweaty." Tess nodded toward the microscope table and an unopened box of latex gloves. CJ
opened the box, slipped on a pair of gloves, and handed
a pair to Tess.

"I'll sift through the papers on the desk and pull anything I think's important," she said, reluctantly slipping
on the gloves.

For the next half hour, CJ meticulously picked through

the pregnant cardboard boxes, a host of manila folders filled with research data, and even a dozen or so empty microscope slide boxes while Tess rummaged through the materials on Cardashian's desk, including a mass of telomerase transfection data, scores of telomerase repeat amplification gels, bright-field photomicrographs, and several handwritten research notes. By the time they finished, CJ had collated a stack of papers two inches thick and Tess had three manila folders bulging with research documents, photographs, and telomerase data that she had never seen before. Slipping a couple of large rubber bands around the folders, Tess said, "Why do you think the police left all this behind?"

"Two reasons," said CJ, tapping his stack of papers into place on the desktop. "They sealed the office off, not expecting that any of you God-fearing honest professorial types would venture back in for a look. More importantly, without autopsy findings to back them up, they don't officially have a murder case on their hands, just a dead man in a freezer at the dump. But you can bet that if they ever get to slap a murder tag on this, they'll be back."

"You're starting to sound like Henry. Don't you think Neil was murdered?"

"The only thing I'm certain of is that he's dead. Judging from the way his condo was sanitized and how that file drawer over there was picked clean, I'd put murder near the top of my list."

"His condo? You searched Neil's home?"

"In a manner of speaking," said CJ, deciding that the less Tess knew about some of his activities, the better. Tapping the face of his watch and frowning, he added,

"Time to get our butts in gear before someone comes in and catches us with our pants down."

"Fine by me."

As they moved to leave the room, the Cuban cigar box caught CJ's eye again. Unable to resist taking one for the road, he picked the box up from the file cabinet. "I take it Cardashian was as partial to expensive cigars as he was to cognac."

The look on Tess's face took CJ by surprise. "I don't think those were Neil's. He didn't smoke. In fact, he made a point of browbeating anyone who did. He liked to quote the fact that tobacco was responsible for more illness and death in the U.S. in a year than AIDS is expected to cause in a century."

Tess's declaration had CJ trying to understand what a box of expensive and very illegal Cuban cigars would be doing in the office of an antismoking zealot. Opening the lid, he rolled off the top layer of cigars, laying them aside on the file cabinet. Then, rolling the rest of the cigars up into a pyramid in his palm, he looked down into the box, glanced at Tess, and with a look of discovery plastered on his face said, "Well, I'll be."

"Is there something unusual in the box?"

"I'd say." CJ took the remaining cigars out of the box, set them aside, and removed the thin sheet of salmon-colored tissue paper that the cigars had been resting on. Laying the paper aside, he scooped a handful of gun-metal-gray, pearl-sized objects out of the bottom of the box and walked over to Tess. Aside from the fact that the oblong nuggets were shrink-wrapped in some sort of plastic, they reminded him of the bath-oil beads that Mavis liked to buy at a little shop on the Plaza in Santa

Fe. "Look like anything you can put a name to?" said CJ, holding the objects out in his hand for Tess to examine.

Tess ran her hand across the glistening nodules, picked one out, and rolled it between her thumb and forefinger. "I'd say they're suppositories of some sort."

CJ's eyes widened. "As in Preparation H? You wouldn't happen to be intimate enough with the details of Cardashian's . . . ah, health, to know why he might have needed these babies, would you?"

"No."

CJ rolled the gels around in his hand before stepping back to the cigar box and dropping them back inside. Tess slipped the gel she had examined into the pocket of her blouse.

"There're scores of these babies in the box," said CJ, running a hand across the top layer of the gels. "No one has hemorrhoids that bad."

"I'd tend to think not," said Tess, looking puzzled.

"Think we should take the box with us?" CJ leveled off his cache before placing the cigars back in place on top of the gels and closing the lid.

"It's your call," said Tess, staring at CJ, watching him intently as he slipped the cigar box under his arm. "Are we done in here?" she said nervously, glancing at her watch. "We're due to meet Henry and Dr. Artorio in my office in ten minutes."

"Done as a Christmas goose," said CJ.

"Then let's get out of here."

"Lead the way."

As he closed the door to the lab and made certain that the crime-scene tape across the door was back perfectly in place, CJ adjusted the cigar box under his arm and recalled a saying that his alcoholic uncle, the man who had raised him and taught him everything he knew about the bail-bonding business, liked to invoke when strange objects turned up in common places: *Out of sight out of mind, in plain view never mind*. Readjusting the cigar box, he headed down the hall behind Tess, thinking that as far as the unusual gels were concerned, his uncle had been right on the money.

CJ and Tess were well inside Tess's laboratory before Jamie Lee Custus moved out of the stairwell from behind the tempered-glass-windowed fire door that she had conveniently hidden behind while CJ and Tess rummaged through Neil Cardashian's office. She didn't know exactly what they had taken from the office, but she was certain that Sweets would be interested in the fact that their stash included a couple of bulging file folders and a box of cigars.

Chapter 22

Western State College is a picturesque liberal arts school tucked neatly into the town of Gunnison, Colorado. The town and college are encircled to the north by a crescent of mountainous national forest peppered with once bustling mining camps turned to ghost towns. Although Gunnison endures some of the coldest winter temperatures in the United States, Anthony Rontella had arrived at his graduate school alma mater the previous evening to a mid-March warm spell, ready to trigger the third phase of his gamble to set himself up financially for life. The campus, where he had earned a graduate physical therapy degree and a reputation as a former athlete with decidedly more nerve than brains or brawn, was quiet and forlorn in the midst of the school's annual spring break. Anthony was on campus to meet

151

with an athletic trainer he had been grooming for the past year.

He had six West Coast trainers online, ready to start his program in a week, and he knew that if he could score three additional trainers in his own Rocky Mountain backyard, he'd have the fifty athletes he needed to document what Cardashian had always claimed would put them on easy street for life.

Seated in a drafty coffee shop on the edge of campus, Anthony was halfway into his spiel to his mark. It was a polished, practiced pitch that he had been delivering to his select group of small-time athletic trainers for close to a year.

Leah's death had been a minor setback. Especially since it had taken him almost a year to fully explore Cardashian's premise with Leah serving as his lab rat. He had never understood why Leah had been willing to risk everything, even her life, in order to be champion for a day. Perhaps she thought that a gold medal would allow her to close the book on her anorexic lifestyle once and for all. He hadn't felt sorry for her, telling himself that she knew the score when she started, but for some reason he had the eerie feeling that before it was all over he'd have to answer for Leah's death.

Taking a sip of coffee and preparing for a new sales assault on his mark, Anthony recalled something Cardashian had told him about athletes. *Some athletes will do anything for an edge. Maim—even kill for a leg up in the race. Risk their lives for a little extra stamina during the closing seconds of a game. Make no mistake about it, they're the egotistical, surprisingly fragile, overcharged cellular factories we need. If you don't believe me, watch them in the heat of competition and you'll recognize the time bomb that defeat represents as it plays over and over in their heads.*

What convinced Anthony more than anything that Cardashian was right was the fact that Cardashian always ended their philosophical conversations with the words, *I know—I've been there myself.*

Now all he had to do was convince the man sitting across the table from him, a man to whom he had earlier given $10,000, to pluck a couple of experimental sheep from his athletic flock.

"I've already gotten all the people I need on the West Coast to buy in," said Anthony, pressing his mark for an answer, sliding a handwritten list of the West Coast trainers he had online across the table. "You know what that means." Anthony looked the droopy-eyed trainer straight in the eye. "You could be left out."

"I thought you said you didn't expect more than one kid in a hundred to belly up to the bar on this deal," said the trainer, scanning the list skeptically and handing it back to Anthony.

"You're right. And the magic number I need from you is two."

"I could get fired for this. Maybe even go to jail."

"No risk, no reward."

Looking nervous, the trainer stroked his chin and took a sip of the watered-down lemonade he had been nursing. "How am I supposed to get my kids to buy into this?"

Anthony swallowed hard and thought about the year and a half of legwork he had done and the risk he ran in crossing Sweets before answering. "Easy. Just remember that the kids who sign on will be the ones who are willing to break the rules for an edge." Smiling, he reached into his pocket, pulled out a wad of bills, and slid them toward the trainer.

"When do I get my other five grand?" said the trainer, slipping the money into his pocket.

"When you get me two kids who can stick the program out for a couple of months."

"I'll have two for you by the end of the week. Can't promise any more than that."

"No problem. I'll have everything you'll need to you by then."

The trainer took a final sip of lemonade, rolling what remained of ice cubes and a lemon slice around in his glass. "And nobody gets hurt?" he said in a voice filled with guilt.

"I guarantee it," said Anthony, wrapping his hands around his coffee mug, staring the trainer squarely in the eye, hoping the expression on his face didn't betray the fact that he was lying, and commending himself on the sale.

Chapter 23

"You're right. They do look like bath-oil beads." Sandi held a handful of the clear pearl-sized gels CJ had given her up to the light as they stood at one end of a long countertop in Tess's research laboratory while Tess hovered over a dissecting microscope a few feet away, examining a couple of the gels she had cut in half.

After greeting Sandi with a bear hug a few minutes earlier, introducing her to CJ, apologizing for Henry's absence, rehashing the details of her near incarceration, and bringing Sandi up to speed on what had happened to Neil Cardashian, Tess had produced the cigar box full of mysterious beads, saying, "We found these in Neil's lab. Somehow, I think they're tied to his telomerase research."

Surprised by Tess's statement, Sandi reexamined the

waxy beads. "From the looks of the in situ hybridization studies I ran back at NIH, you might be right. One thing for sure, Neil was well beyond working with one-celled animals. I'm guessing he'd already cloned the human telomerase transcript subunit, and I'd bet he was down the road to transfecting human epithelial cells."

"Further," said Tess, looking up from her scope.

Sandi laid her handful of gels on the countertop and looked at Tess quizzically. "You're saying Neil had moved beyond that?"

"I think so. Knowing his penchant for moving his research along no matter what the cost, I'd say he was already testing his hypothesis that accentuated telomerase expression increases the life span of human cells. Can you think of a better way to test your theory that cells can be kept in a perpetual youthful state than to cook yourself up a batch of telomerase cocktails in the form of suppository gels and start passing them out to people to see if you're right?"

Sandi shook her head in disbelief. "I hope you're kidding."

Tess picked up a couple of gels from the countertop. "I've got a real bad feeling about these little babies. One that tells me that when all's said and done, we're going to find out that these gels are laced with Neil Cardashian genetically engineered telomerase subunit constructs."

Unable to remain silent any longer, CJ said, "That fountain-of-youth stuff you've been talking about?"

Tess moved her wheelchair back from her microscope and waved for Sandi to take a look before answering. Then, looking at CJ, she said, "We'll find out as soon as

Sandi helps me run a TRAP assay on your little cigar box nuggets."

"Suppose they are, the telomerase subunits, I mean. What then? The only thing we'll know for certain is that Neil laced a couple of hundred bath-oil beads with telomerase," said Sandi.

Tess shot her a look of surprise. "I hope it's not bothering you that Neil was a few steps ahead of you in that scientific race that's always playing in your head. Just for the record, Sandi, this isn't a race. We need to find out what the nuggets inside our Pandora's box really represent before someone besides Neil becomes a casualty."

"I'll do what I can to help," said Sandi, feeling the sting of Tess's reprimand.

Realizing that he was missing something in the translation, CJ turned to Tess with a question of his own. "I thought this magic telomerase potion of Cardashian's was supposed to be some kind of fountain of youth. Now you're saying more people could end up dead. How about straightening me out on the facts?"

"Sorry," said Tess. "I didn't mean to leave you in the dark. The upside of the telomerase equation, the one that scientists love to talk about, is that given the right circumstances, a jolt of telomerase might give our bodies' cells a shot at immortalizing themselves. What gets lost in the hoopla is the equation's downside, the side that says that too much telomerase in the old human cellular engine might prove detrimental, even fatal. You see, the same telomerase switching mechanism that scientists love to tout as the great immortalizer also has the potential to tell cells to multiply forever."

"And?" said CJ, waiting for the punch line.

"And if that occurs, instead of having a stash of immortalized cells lying around waiting to give your body an extra kick, you have an avalanche of cells rolling downhill out of control in the form of a little disease known as cancer. Since we don't know how many waves of the magic telomerase wand it takes to get which response— forever youthful cells or cancer—theoretically it's just as easy to produce cancer in someone as it is to put a new spring in their step."

"Damn." CJ eyed the cigar box with newfound respect. "Is there any chance Cardashian could have figured out the telomerase dosage he needed in order to bypass the cancer risk?"

"I doubt it," said Sandi, answering in a rush. "Neil may have had a head start on the rest of us, but not enough of one to determine how to titrate a human dosage for telomerase that would give him the reproducible results he'd need. No, if Neil was passing out telomerase lollipops, he couldn't have been too far into the game, and that means that the downside risks that Tess is talking about are all too real."

CJ stroked his chin thoughtfully. "I hate to mention this, considering the fact that you both think this is all about science, but I'd bet Cardashian was looking at it from another angle, money. Big money. The kind that would force him to have to link up with someone else. Can you think of anyone around here who might have been willing to back Cardashian's approach to science?"

"I can't think of anyone offhand."

"Then Cardashian must have been using someone outside your research pipelines to move his project along. Somebody more interested in money than morals." CJ leaned against the countertop, contemplating how to continue to mount his investigation.

He was about to tell Tess that she could very likely spend her money more wisely when he remembered his pledge to Henry to marshal an investigation that would leave Tess's reputation laundry-day clean. Suspecting that any such investigation was likely to move him beyond the ivory towers of the Health Sciences Center, and into the realm of the second-rate hoodlums and bottom feeders he rubbed shoulders with every day, CJ said, "Did Cardashian have any enemies I should know about?"

"Not that I'm aware of."

"Friends, then."

"Neil didn't trust banks, businesses, or bureaucracies. And he certainly didn't trust anyone well enough to call them a friend. He did have a few car enthusiast contacts I heard him mention, but I can't recall their names. I think they all belonged to a Ferrari club."

Wondering how Tess could have worked with Cardashian for as long as she had without knowing more about him, CJ said, "Besides Ferraris, did Cardashian have any other serious passions?"

Tess's quick response surprised CJ. "Sports. Neil was an all-out football nut. He never let an experiment interfere with CU football or a Denver Broncos game. And I think he had season tickets to the Rockies and the Nuggets."

The hint of a smile formed on CJ's face. After coming up empty in his search of Cardashian's apartment and having nothing to show for his search of Cardashian's laboratory except a cigar box full of mysterious beads, he finally had what he liked to call a personality lead. He wasn't certain about what research scientists did when they slipped out of bed each morning to start their day, but he was used to tracking the daily activities of second-tier criminals—activities that often centered around gambling and the world of sports. CJ completed his smile, thinking as he did that it just might turn out that Cardashian wasn't that far removed from his bottom feeders after all. "Anything else about Cardashian's love of sports that I should know about?"

"There is one thing. Neil had season tickets to the CU football games that he shared with another faculty member. I know because the man called the lab a couple of times last fall to ask what time Neil would be leaving to pick him up for the game in Boulder. He missed Neil both times, and I took the messages."

"Another doctor on staff here?" asked CJ.

"No. But he is a doctor. His name's David Patterson, and I think he's the physician for one of the CU athletic teams. Gymnastics or swimming, I believe. I can get his name and phone number for you out of the university directory if you'd like."

"I'd like," said CJ, recognizing that although a tenuous connection between a research scientist at the Health Sciences Center in Denver and a doctor for one of the athletic teams on the main campus in Boulder might not be much of a lead in a murder, it was at least a place to start.

Reflecting on the possibility that his lead might go nowhere, CJ glanced up and found himself looking directly at Sandi. He suspected that her job of assaying the little pearls in the cigar box to determine whether they contained telomerase would be a lot tougher than running down Dr. Patterson. He watched as Sandi flipped back the top on the cigar box to examine the contents once again. It wasn't until that moment that he realized how striking she was, a fact that he knew hadn't been lost on the yet to arrive Henry Bales.

Chapter 24

The whole thing was infernal, as far as a God-fearing man like Vernon Lowe was concerned. In thirty years of splitting his time between autopsying the dead at Denver General Hospital, freelancing, and embalming bodies at Hubble's Mortuary in Denver's Five Points community, where he was legendary as a makeup artist and natural-look wizard when it came to laying Denver's black folks to rest, Vernon had never assisted on two coroner's cases in which the brain pathology of two dead people had been so nearly identical.

But there he stood, weighing Neil Cardashian's brain, trying to determine a reason for the similarity in pathology between Cardashian's brain and Leah Tanner's, the swimmer he had helped autopsy a couple of days earlier.

Bewildered, he ran his hand across the brain's irregular, knobby surface and sighed.

What made things even more problematic was the fact that Dr. Henry Bales, whom he had assisted on hundreds of autopsies over the years, and his friend, CJ Floyd, had both asked him to call them with the results of Neil Cardashian's autopsy as soon as there was a provisional diagnosis. Calling Bales about the autopsy findings was medically kosher. It was CJ's request that had Vernon edgy. The request had convinced him that both deaths, not just Cardashian's, had to be connected to the darkest side of the law.

Deciding for the moment that he wouldn't mention the link between the two autopsies to anyone besides CJ and Henry, Vernon continued weighing Neil Cardashian's organs while the frail-looking deputy coroner he was assisting, a perpetually depressed-looking woman who always wore too much perfume and called him Vern, a nickname he detested, continued inspecting Cardashian's large bowel while dictating her autopsy findings into a microphone inches from her nose.

"Vern, I swear this GI tract looks like it's peppered stem to stern with miliary TB," said the deputy coroner, looking up from the bowel and waving Vernon over. "Have a look."

Ignoring the name contraction, Vernon recorded the weight of Cardashian's brain, dictated it into his own dictaphone, and stepped over to take a look at the bowel, well aware that miliary tuberculosis, a form of TB that could swallow organs whole, morphing them into an unrecognizable mass of golfball-sized nodules, would be rare in two people as healthy as Cardashian and his swimmer. When he slipped up beside the coroner and realized that the four-foot length of intestine in front of him was peppered with the same strange-looking nodules as the brain, he said, "Brain's covered with the same kind of bumps."

"Snip a couple of brain samples off for me; I'll come have a look in a sec," said the coroner, degloving the section of bowel and turning it inside out for a better look. "Strange; real unusual for TB." She ran her hand over the lumpy bowel, kneading the lumps in its wall, trying to zero in on a diagnosis.

"No need to spend all day deliberating over that bowel, Doc. That's why the good Lord sent us microscopes."

The coroner smiled at Vernon's assessment and turned the bowel right side out. "Rectum's pretty callused over," she said, examining the terminal end of the bowel. "Looks like somebody took a scrub brush to it." She ran her hand across the rough whiteness of the rectal tissue, dictating into her mike: "The rectal mucosa demonstrates marked thickening. The texture is leathery and focally nodular. Ulcerations are numerous." Then, retrieving a pair of bloody scissors, she snipped off several pieces of bowel and plopped them into a string of specimen jars filled with formalin. "Like you said, Vern, guess I won't get a real answer until I sit down at the scope," she said, spinning the tissue around in one of the jars. "Guess we could be dealing with metastatic tumor, but if we are, I sure haven't seen anything that looks like a primary source, and most of all, I haven't seen one thing to suggest the man was murdered." She capped the jar and nudged it aside. Vernon capped the remaining jars and affixed preprinted labels with the words *Large Bowel and*

Rectum on their sides before glancing back across the room toward where he had been working.

While the coroner continued to dictate her findings, Vernon walked back over to where Cardashian's brain sat flattened into a dome-shaped mass. Retrieving a scalpel from an adjacent tray of instruments, he slipped one hand under the knobby-looking organ, snipped off several grotesque nodules from the surface, and dropped them into two jars of formalin. This time he labeled only one jar. The other he planned to deliver to Henry Bales, who had asked him to pass along anything unusual about Cardashian's autopsy.

He walked over to a small wooden bench in a darkened corner of the morgue, where he slipped the jar into a gym bag beneath the bench, zipped the bag closed, and strolled back to his workstation, bombarded all the while by the dull, monotonous drone of the deputy coroner. As he completed his preparation of the brain, he couldn't help but wonder what it was that connected the swimmer and Cardashian. Aware of Henry Bales's reputation as not just a research scientist but one hell of a diagnostician, he suspected that the answer would come down to something more complex than what the irritating deputy coroner could glean from a simple autopsy. He was hoping that whatever the link turned out to be, it wouldn't cause him to get caught up in something that was ungodly, but he was convinced that the connection had something to do with breaking the law.

Except for her noticeable limp and the fact that the left inside pocket of her jacket was weighted down with a Bowie knife, Jamie Lee Custus looked pretty much like the other half-dozen people working their way through the serving line of University Hospital's Wall Street Deli in search of a late-afternoon snack.

"Slim pickin's this time of day," the man in bib overalls just ahead of Jamie Lee mumbled. Slipping a slice of pecan pie off one of the dessert shelves and eyeing it dejectedly, as if it were too small to handle his appetite, he placed the pie on his tray and kept moving with a disappointed grunt. After a couple of steps he looked back at Jamie Lee, scanning her from head to toe. "Notice you got yourself a limp," he said, moving ahead to get a cup of coffee. "Got me a bad knee myself. Not why I'm here, though," he added, eyeing his crotch. "They're checking to see why I can't pee. Think maybe I've got something the matter with my prostate."

The man filled his cup to the brim with scalding hot coffee before turning back to catch Jamie Lee slipping the last slice of pecan pie off the shelf.

"Good choice. I've had it before. Tastes damn near homemade."

Agitated that someone would pay her special attention to the point of even commenting on her limp, Jamie Lee forced a smile and told herself to be more circumspect about her movements around the Health Sciences Center. When the man in overalls finally inched forward, Jamie Lee hastily grabbed a coffee mug, drew off a stream of decaf, and eyed a cloud of steam rising toward her. Watching the steam dissipate, she found herself second-guessing her decision to take the extra money Sweets had offered her to handle Tess Gilliam. "Keep an eye on her. Kill her if you have to, but don't let her derail my plans," had been Sweets's exacting new directive.

167

Jamie Lee didn't like the idea of having to kill a woman confined to a wheelchair. For some reason, she had the strange feeling that deep down she and Tess Gilliam were somehow connected. But business was business, she told herself, and sometimes that was just the way things sifted out. Looking back up from her coffee, she watched the man in overalls nudge his food tray down the service railing, wondering why someone who was having problems urinating would be buying a sixteen-ounce mug of steaming hot coffee. Casting her eyes floorward so as not to make any further eye contact with the man, she watched him pay for his fare with a rumpled $5 bill and waddle away.

The cashier at the end of the service line rang up her purchase with an artificial smile, and Jamie Lee quickly headed for an isolated table in the far corner of the room to enjoy her coffee and pie in solitude and decide how to best reconnoiter the hospital grounds unnoticed while she got a better feel for the lay of the land and the woman she would be stalking. She was closing in on the table when the man in overalls spotted her.

"You can share a table with me," he called out across the room, waving for Jamie Lee to join him.

Ignoring the man, Jamie Lee sat down, eyes on the table, and dug into her pie, hoping as she ran a plan for dealing with Tess Gilliam and her friends through her head that the man in overalls had gotten the message.

Manuel Hernández disliked partnerships, except for those involving women. So when Sweets called him in Havana and ordered him back to the United States, interrupting the lap dance that he was getting from a heavy-chested, doe-eyed girl who couldn't have been more than sixteen, Manuel cursed Sweets and the Sweets family lineage so savagely that the girl, whom he had paid $20 for her services, jumped up and darted for safety into a corner of his bedroom.

Waving unsuccessfully for the girl to come back, he growled into the phone at Sweets, "Can't I just handle the goddamn things down here?" Then, springing from his chair, he cornered the girl, and with one hand clasped over the receiver and the other down the front of the girl's pants, he whispered, "Twenty more dollars to finish."

"No," said Sweets. "I need someone to put a clamp on Custus in case she screws up handling Gilliam."

Manuel thought back to how swiftly he had solved the problem with Rulon Mantero. Thinking about Rulon's house bursting into flames seemed to enhance his erection. "Can't I just handle it like I did with Rulon?" he said, wondering how someone as thick-skulled as Rulon could have figured out that he was slipping Ernesto Salas a daily ration of something more than protein powder and vitamin C.

"No! We're operating in the U.S., not your Cuban backwoods."

Enticing the girl back to her original position with a $20 bill he had slipped out of the pocket of his sweatpants, Manuel nodded for her to restart her gyrations. Then, recalling how uneventful Rulon's death had been and how swiftly the wire transfer of $5,000 into his bank account had taken place, he let out a pleasure-filled gasp and said, "It'll cost you an additional five thousand. And for the record, I'm not playing Tonto to some dumbass, half-crippled ex-logger. If things turn bad, I'll pop her too."

"That's your decision," said Sweets.

"Next thing. If I leave Ernesto, what happens to the daily ration I've been slipping him?"

"Don't worry about Ernesto. His chances of being around for the Olympics are no better than fifty-fifty."

"You mean that shit your boy Anthony's been backing down here is that potent?"

"Yes."

"Ernesto's grandmother's not stupid. She'll ask questions."

Sweets let out a high-pitched laugh, one that sounded almost giddy filtered through whatever it was altering Sweets's voice. "Who cares? There's no one there to give her any answers."

"There's me," said Hernández, testing the waters to see whether Sweets might be amenable to blackmail.

Sweets thought about all the time and money invested in Cardashian's scheme and laughed. "I'd have to kill you, my friend, if that ever happened—and in the blink of an eye. I can't have you tinkering with my investment. The product I'll be offering for sale won't be just another one of your Caribbean trinkets. Count on it, there'll be plenty of demand for it, and all around the globe."

Hernández thought for a moment before adjusting the girl on his lap. He'd often wondered what made nut cases like Sweets tick. Now he pretty much knew. "Wire my five thousand."

"As soon as we're off the phone."

"Any chance that while you're at it, you can line up

some action for me in Denver?" asked Hernández, smiling at the girl, knowing that she barely understood English.

"I'm not your pimp, Hernández."

Hernández let out a booming laugh. "When I get there, keep Custus out of my hair."

"She's got orders to do her thing. You've got yours."

"Gotcha," said Hernández, grinning as he watched the girl's breasts bounce up and down.

"And Hernández, remember this. You'll want to come back home with all your organs intact. Cross me, and the organ you value the most may not make the trip back with you."

Hernández swallowed hard as the phone line went dead and his erection suddenly went limp. Ignoring Sweets's threat, he pulled the girl toward him, grasping her in a bear hug and nuzzling her breasts, concerned only with his immediate gratification and the future pleasures that $5,000 could bring.

Chapter 25

It was nearly eleven P.M. by the time Sandi finished setting up for her fourth attempt to assay samples from the cigar-box gels CJ had found in Cardashian's office. The telomerase repeat amplification procedure she needed to run to determine whether the gels were laced with catalytic starter protein would have taken the better part of a week, so she had hastily set up an in situ hybridization assay to test for telomerase itself. It was a less accurate but faster test designed to determine whether a microscopic artifact she had found in most of the gels was the result of a contaminant that she suspected was the source of the telomerase. But after three experimental runs she hadn't come up with anything to support her premise, and she was beginning to wonder whether the idea that the gels contained telomerase catalytic converter might be preposterous.

Tess and Henry had stayed around to help, but half an hour earlier Tess had called it a night, leaving Henry and Sandi alone in the lab snatching teenaged prom-night glances at one another while Sandi continued to try to coax results from her hybridization assays. The lab was strangely quiet except for the sound of an automated stirrer.

CJ left around seven to have dinner with Mavis. Before leaving he assured Tess and an overprotective-sounding Henry that he was set to run down the link between Cardashian and Dr. David Patterson first thing the next morning. It had taken only one phone call to the University of Colorado athletic department for CJ to learn that Patterson was the physician for the women's swim team. He left the lab joking that since they were now dealing with swimmers, perhaps Cardashian's death was linked to *jungle water*. The phrase was an inside joke between CJ and Henry, a reference to their days patrolling the Mekong River estuaries of Vietnam. Over the decades it had remained a code term that always seemed to surface when one or both of them was about to stick a hand into the hot flame of trouble.

Henry, who hadn't budged from Sandi's side since CJ's departure, was scrounging around in a storage cabinet near the back of the lab looking for a chemical accelerator that Sandi had asked for. Searching the cabinet and trying to ignore his fascination with Sandi, he had a sudden chilling thought about Cardashian's research: Should scientists really be tinkering with something that controls how long we live? Pondering the question, he found the chemical he was looking for when Vernon Lowe strolled into the lab, dressed in one of his trademark iridescent lime-green suits, carrying a greasy Burger King bag, and smiling.

Casting Vernon a wary glance, Sandi said, "Can I help you?"

"Vernon," said Henry, giving Sandi a look of reassurance and rushing up to shake hands before Vernon could respond. "Keeping late hours, aren't you?"

"Not that late, Doc. Just finished choir practice at my church a little bit ago. Your answering service told me I could find you here. I would've called, except what I've got to tell you needs a little face-to-face explaining."

Henry knew Vernon wouldn't have come all the way from a Five Points choir practice back to the university at nearly midnight unless he had a nugget to share about Cardashian's death. "Got a bottom line on what killed Cardashian?"

"Yeah," said Vernon, glancing at the greasy bag in his hand and then snatching an embarrassed glance at Sandi, wanting to say, *Wow.*

Smiling at Vernon's expression, Henry said, "Dr. Sandi Artorio, meet Vernon Lowe, best pathology assistant in the business."

Beaming at the compliment, Vernon shook Sandi's hand, surprised at how firm a handshake he got in return.

"My pleasure," said Sandi, wondering what kind of information Vernon could have on Cardashian that required a personal visit. "So what's the provisional diagnosis on Cardashian?"

Vernon set his Burger King bag down and extracted the formalin jar with Cardashian's brain tissue. "That's a piece of Cardashian's brain bobbing around inside. You can bet the answer to what killed him's in the tissue. The deputy coroner's betting on miliary TB or cancer. Neither one makes real sense to me, especially in a man without a history of either disease."

"Who did the post?" asked Henry, picking up the jar.

"Dr. Dawson."

Henry rotated the jar, eyeing the tissue. "No sign of anything that might suggest how he was murdered, was there?"

"Nothing. Except for a few bruises on his legs and back that probably got there when somebody shoved him into a freezer, according to a cop named Menton who hung around the morgue asking questions for half an hour before we started the post. By the way, he called back for a provisional diagnosis right after we finished. I didn't hear what Dr. Dawson told him."

Henry greeted the news about Menton by gritting his teeth. "Anything else?"

"Besides the fact that he wasn't bludgeoned to death, shot, or stabbed and his brain looked like the surface of the moon, his bowel was loaded with the same stuff in the jar, and his rectum was callused over like somebody took a scrub brush to it."

Henry rolled the tissue around in the jar once again, looked at Sandi knowingly, and nudged the jar down the countertop to her. "Have a look and tell me what you think."

"Besides the bowel and brain, did any other organs take a hit?" said Sandi, picking up the jar and looking at Vernon.

"No."

"Thinking what I'm thinking?" she said, glancing back at Henry and placing the jar back down.

"Sure am," said Henry.

"That bad?" said Vernon, suddenly looking nervous. "Remember, I'm the one who posted the guy. We're not dealing with some kind of Ebola virus here, are we?"

"No, we're not. The story you're telling doesn't support an infectious disease. A little too hit-and-miss. I'd agree with the coroner's second assumption, that we're dealing with some form of rapidly progressive cancer. And if I'm right, then as strange as it may sound, Cardashian was probably playing guinea pig to his own idea and killed himself."

"How'd he do that?" asked Vernon, his eyes ballooning.

"It's a long story, Vernon. For right now, let's just say he pushed the wrong button on a stopwatch."

Vernon looked mystified. "Must be one hell of a button, and if so, Cardashian wasn't the only one monkeying around with it. The other day I helped autopsy a woman up in Boulder who I bet my life had the same thing going on with her as Cardashian. Could've switched their organs with one another and never known the difference."

A look of astonishment arched across Henry's face, followed by Sandi's pleading, "No."

Sandi picked the specimen bottle up again and rotated it carefully in her palm, looking as if she were handling a plutonium trigger. "Are you sure the woman and Cardashian showed the exact same pathology?"

"As sure as I'm a God-fearing man. They were identical all right, right down to their callused rectums and the size and the shape of the knots on their brains."

Except for the rhythmic cadence of three people breathing and the swish of an automated stirrer, the room turned silent. Clunking Vernon's specimen jar back down on the countertop and casting Henry a look that said, *I can't believe what I'm hearing*, Sandi broke the silence. "I can run a quick assay for telomerase on one of Cardashian's brain tissue samples while you do a frozen tissue section to see if it's cancer. Any assay on real tissue is bound to be more telling than what we stumble across in sections from a bunch of bath-oil beads."

"Might as well," said Henry, then, turning to Vernon, he added, "How'd the woman from Boulder die?"

"Her paperwork said she either stroked out or died from a seizure at a swimming meet. Strange, considering what we found at autopsy. But it was one of my freelance jobs, I was running late on getting back to Denver for choir practice, and to tell you the truth, except for the brain knots and the unusual-looking bowel, I didn't pay it much attention."

"A swimmer!" said Henry.

"Supposedly top notch, named Leah Tanner."

Darting across the lab to a wall phone, leaving Vernon and Sandi mystified, Henry punched in CJ's number so quickly he thought he might have misdialed. "It's Henry," he said when CJ answered. "What are you doing?"

CJ rolled over in bed, relaxed his postcoital embrace with Mavis, and looked at her apologetically, silently mouthing, "Henry." "Relaxing with Mavis," said CJ, trying to mask his irritation.

"Oh. Sorry to break in, but this couldn't wait."

"Hope it's good."

Still tucked in the crook of CJ's arm, Mavis eased up in bed. Aware that CJ had been helping Henry with a problem involving Tess Gilliam and a possible murder, Mavis felt a nervous twinge pulse through her body, a familiar feeling that always surfaced when CJ became involved in a murder case.

"Shoot," said CJ, giving Mavis a quick kiss on the forehead.

"You know that doctor you're supposed to be checking on in Boulder?"

"Yeah. Patterson."

"Got anything on him yet?"

CJ slipped his arm from around Mavis, sat up in bed, and looked over at the alarm clock on his nightstand, which read 12:05 A.M. "I know as far as you type-A doctors are concerned, Henry, it's a brand-new day. But believe it or not, I don't start my day until eight."

"Sorry, CJ, but this is important."

CJ looked at Mavis and shook his head. "Damn it, Henry. You're breaking the rules. Yeah, I checked on him. I've got a meeting scheduled with him in the morning."

"Shit," said Henry, giving Sandi and Vernon an apologetic look for using profanity.

"What's got you so bent out of shape?" CJ hadn't heard Henry utter a profane word more than a handful of times in all the years he'd known him.

"Remember that telomerase story Tess told you the other day? The one about tipping the scales of science out of whack? Well, I think Cardashian may have tossed the scales. Vernon Lowe just dropped by Tess's lab with a little present in a bottle, a bunch of knots he took off Neil

Cardashian's brain. Along with his delivery he happened to mention that he helped autopsy a CU swimmer the other day whose autopsy findings were identical to Cardashian's. A girl named Leah Tanner."

"Damn."

"I'm thinking that both the Tanner girl and Cardashian caught the downside of the telomerase equation, and that they both very likely died from cancer."

"With no symptoms?" asked CJ.

"You're sounding like a doc, CJ. Yes, without symptoms. With the brain pathology Vernon claims they showed, I'm betting they both had rapidly progressive seizures that hit them like a ton of bricks. No time for symptoms. Scary, isn't it?"

"Yeah," said CJ, pausing to look at Mavis. "So you think Cardashian moved from testing out his everlasting-life premise in the laboratory to the real world?"

"Sure do. I'd wager he was testing it out on the swimmer, and on himself. Why a swimmer, I don't know."

"Using the bath-oil beads?"

"Makes sense. From the rectal disease Vernon said he found, I'd say Tess was right. Our bath-oil beads are probably some kind of telomerase-laced suppository."

CJ looped the phone cord over Mavis's head and sat up on the edge of the bed. "Think Cardashian had any other product out there in the pipeline besides what we found in the cigar box?"

"I wouldn't bet against it, and I'm betting that we're going to end up with a whole slew of dead folks on our hands if we don't move fast."

"Think Patterson's the key?"

"That's what I'm hoping you'll find out," said Henry.

"I'll do my best."

"Good. Just remember, CJ, this may be a whole lot bigger than just one off-center scientist running amuck."

"You're starting to sound like Mavis," said CJ, watching Mavis sit up uneasily in bed and frown.

"Just keep your antennae up, CJ. This thing has a *jungle water* smell."

Reading the code and trying to mask his concern, CJ said, "I'll check with you after I talk with Patterson, and just to keep him honest, I'll have Flora Jean call his office in the morning to let him know my agenda will include the Tanner girl as well as Cardashian."

"Think you'll be done by noon?"

"Yeah. And Henry, keep your eyes peeled to the rearview mirror yourself."

"Always do. I'll talk to you later," said Henry, cradling the phone and realizing that Sandi and Vernon were now standing next to him, drinking in every word.

CJ hung up the phone to find Mavis staring at him, a look of exasperation plastered on her face. "I know that if you're warning Henry to keep his head down, yours must be at flat-out ground zero."

"Nah, nothing that big."

Mavis ran her hand down the inside of CJ's thigh. "You're lying. What's so important about this appointment at eight?"

"I've got to meet some doctor."

Mavis frowned and started to remove her hand. "About what?"

CJ capped her hand with his own and slipped it back into place. "About living long and prospering."

Mavis wanted to ask more questions, questions that

would put her mind at ease, but the titillating warmth she felt as CJ began nibbling at her breast cut the Q and A session short. Consumed by a sudden rush of pleasure as CJ ran his fingers lightly up and down the inside of her thigh, Mavis relaxed and melted into his arms, thinking as she did about nothing but living long and prospering.

Chapter 26

Heavy early snows had prevented the maintenance crews from raking the leaves that still carpeted most of Fairlawn Cemetery. The unseasonably warm and misty late-morning air was rich with the scent of decaying leaves and the smell of freshly turned dirt around Leah Tanner's grave.

As Nate Tanner and Anthony Rontella crunched their way through leaves and away from Leah's grave site, all Tanner could think about was the fact that he should have kept closer tabs on Leah's health. For days he had been asking himself the same gut-wrenching question until now it seemed to be the only thought in his head: How could someone who seemed as healthy as Leah have had cancer at only twenty-two? Sidestepping a divot full of murky-looking water, he looked over at Anthony and said, "It doesn't make sense. Leah was as healthy as a horse. I don't remember her even having as much as the sniffles in the past five years."

"It's definitely strange." Anthony eyed the ground, maintaining a stoic look, camouflaging the fact that he knew the truth.

"How could cancer appear so fast?" Tanner's eyes pleaded for an answer.

"I have no idea. Maybe it was something genetic."

Tanner stopped in his tracks. "I won't buy that. I couldn't have passed along something that killed my only child." Glancing back over his shoulder at Leah's grave, he added, "You'll never make me believe that."

"Sorry," said Anthony.

"The coroner said that except for some evidence of tumor in her bowel, the bulk of the cancer was in her brain. We know she died from cancer-related seizures, Anthony. What I want to know now is why. And I want an answer that's more than simply saying it was genetic. I won't rest until I know what caused my baby to die. You'll help me, won't you?"

"Of course."

"Good. Why don't we start with Coach Drake? He might have the answer straight up."

Puzzled by Tanner's choice of words, Anthony said, "The answer?"

"I may be a naive father, Anthony. But I'm not deaf, dumb, or blind. I know Leah was doing something outside the rules to post those sudden record-breaking times of hers. I want to know what it was and if it killed her. You wouldn't happen to know the answer, would you?" he said, pausing to look Anthony squarely in the eye.

"She was training better," said Anthony, mustering a quick, rehearsed response. Until that moment he had never had the slightest reason to suspect that Tanner had any idea that Leah might have been involved in a performance-enhancing scam. Suddenly he had a sinking feeling that the ego-boosting game he had orchestrated for almost two years in order to gain the trust of an insecure, anorexic woman might come back to haunt him.

"Training, my ass, Anthony. It's possible that Leah was using drugs that may have killed her."

As they reached the asphalt roadway that led to the cemetery chapel, Anthony, who had driven to the cemetery in his car instead of riding in one of the funeral limos, said, "What makes you think that?"

"Just a hunch. And the fact that I found a packet of strange, waxy-looking beads in Leah's apartment the other night in a place that nobody but a distraught, overly suspicious father would've ever looked."

In a near panic, Anthony found himself running Sweets's emergency telephone number through his head. It was all he could do to keep from charging up the driveway for the cell phone in his car. Masking his anxiety as best he could, he said, "Where was that?"

"Stuffed inside a box of sanitary napkins beneath her bathroom sink." Tanner reached into the left-hand pocket of his suit coat. "Have a look," he said, thrusting a handful of the beads toward Anthony.

"Bizarre," said Anthony, taking one of the beads, examining it perfunctorily as he tried to keep his hand from shaking, and wondering how he had missed finding Leah's secret stash in two thorough sweeps of her apartment.

"It's a place to start, don't you think?" asked Tanner, taking the beads back from Anthony and slipping them into his pocket.

"As good as any. I'll help as much as I can," said Anthony, shivering in fear as he turned to leave.

"You cold?" said Tanner.

"No; it's just the events of the past few days catching up with me."

Tanner nodded understandingly. "I'm counting on you," he said, patting Anthony on the shoulder as he turned to head for the chapel and a waiting limo. Lost in grief, he never looked back at Anthony, nor did he hear Anthony mumbling, "Shit, shit, shit," as he broke into an all-out sprint, racing to call Sweets from the cell phone in his car.

Chapter 27

Dr. David Patterson's orthopedic practice sat in the heart of Denver's trendy Cherry Creek North shopping district, nestled on the top floor of a sixth-story doctor's office building and conveniently tucked among three general practitioners and a pediatrician who tossed Patterson enough orthopedic business to keep him in Rolex watches and tailor-made suits and on the society pages of the two Denver dailies.

Patterson's spacious, sparsely decorated waiting room had the faint smell of alcohol, wet plaster, and Betadine, and during the half hour that CJ had been sitting there waiting, he had had ample opportunity to run through the questions he was going to ask the orthopedist several times. The most central question was, could Patterson link Leah Tanner to Neil Cardashian?

His secretary, Flora Jean, had pulled together some sketchy background information on Patterson the day before. Patterson was from a Denver family of physicians that included his father, an uncle, and a brother; he was a cum laude graduate of a California medical school; and his Democratic political connections and longtime friendship with the dean of CU's medical school had secured him not only a part-time faculty position in the school's orthopedic department but also the position of physician to the women's swim team. One other fact that Flora Jean had verified from several sources was that Patterson was the real deal financially, old-Denver-money wealthy.

Three patients had been called from the waiting room back to the treatment area during CJ's wait, and he was left sharing the room with a sad-eyed, nervous-looking girl of about fifteen with a ring through her nose, baggy clothes, orange Day-Glo hair, and a plaster cast with dozens of multicolored signatures on her right arm. A pale-looking carbon copy of a woman, whom CJ assumed to be the girl's mother, sat at the girl's side. From time to time the woman would look up from the magazine she was reading to give CJ a look brimming with guilt that said, *I don't approve of the hair, the clothes, or the ring, mister.*

Agitated by the fact that he had been waiting for over a half hour, CJ had just risen from his chair to lodge a complaint with the receptionist when a woman in a starchy blue uniform, whom he took to be a nurse, appeared in the doorway between the waiting room and the treatment area and announced, "Mr. Floyd, Dr. Patterson can see you now."

CJ was ushered down a lengthy hallway dotted with

Ansel Adams photographs and through a set of swinging double doors to a slightly ajar oversized door with a brass name plate that read *David Patterson, M.D.* The nurse rapped lightly on the door before pushing it fully open and ushering CJ into the room.

The white-walled office was furnished with uncomfortable-looking chrome-and-leather chairs and smoked-glass-topped tables and desks that gave it a retro 1970s look. Motioning CJ up next to her, the nurse said, "Mr. Floyd to see you, Dr. Patterson." Then, flashing CJ a truant officer's look, she stepped back out into the hallway and closed the door behind her.

Patterson pushed aside the papers he was working on, stood up from behind his desk, and greeted CJ with a firm handshake and direct response. "I understand you're here about Leah Tanner and Neil Cardashian. Such tragedies." Patterson looked down at a notepad on his desk. "My staff assistant tells me you're an investigator. I take it you are working for Leah's father, Nate."

Surprised by Patterson's directness and his strange-sounding high-pitched, nasal voice, CJ wondered how the conversation between Flora Jean and Patterson's staff assistant had transformed him into being in the employ of Leah Tanner's father. Realizing that Flora Jean had probably bent the truth to grease the appointment, he said, "I am here about Leah Tanner. But I'm a bail bondsman, not an investigator, and I don't work for her father."

Patterson looked down at his notepad again and frowned. "What's this about, then?"

Sidestepping the Tanner issue, CJ said, "I understand you knew Neil Cardashian."

"I did. We shared season tickets to the CU football

189

games. I've heard about Neil. Bad news travels fast, Mr. Floyd. Especially in this age of electronic journalism." Then, pausing to collect his thoughts, Patterson sat back down in his chair, squinted at CJ, and said in a voice that almost squeaked, "Are you here about Leah Tanner or Neil Cardashian?"

"Both. And while we're at it, what's your news source saying about how Leah Tanner died?"

"My information is that Leah died from a series of seizures."

"I see. Well, I've got it on good authority that she and Cardashian died from the same thing."

Patterson eased his chair back from his desk, looking confused. "You must be kidding."

"Afraid I'm not," said CJ, eyeing Patterson intently to emphasize his point. "Mind if I have a seat?"

"Please."

CJ pulled one of Patterson's uncomfortable-looking chairs up to the edge of the desk and took a seat. Adjusting his weight in his seat, trying to get comfortable, he said, "Do you know whether Cardashian and the Tanner girl knew one another?"

"No, I don't."

CJ studied Patterson's face for signs that he might be lying. Unable to find a break in Patterson's expression, he told himself that Patterson was either one hell of a liar or he was telling the truth. "Who else besides you might know whether Cardashian and Leah Tanner knew one another?"

Patterson thought for a moment before answering, "Anthony Rontella."

"Who's he?"

"Leah's boyfriend. He's an athletic trainer at CU up in Boulder."

"I see," said CJ, pondering whether Leah's boyfriend could have served as a conduit between Leah and Cardashian.

"Know where I can find Rontella?"

"He has an office in the CU athletic department in Boulder. I can get the number if you want it."

"It would help."

"I'll tell my secretary to get it for you," said Patterson in a tone that told CJ he was wearing his welcome out.

"Before I leave, I'd appreciate it if you could answer a couple more questions," said CJ.

"Make it fast."

"You mentioned Leah Tanner's father earlier. What made you think I was working for him?"

"I don't know, to tell you the truth. Maybe it was the determined look on your face. I guess you just seemed like the kind of man Nate would hire to look into the death of his daughter—somebody intense like him. As a matter of fact, I always thought Nate wanted to see Leah draped in Olympic gold more than she did herself."

"So much so that he'd let her get involved in experimenting with a drug that might kill her?"

Patterson frowned at CJ's accusation. "I don't know about pushing her that far, but I can tell you this. Against my advice, he talked her into swimming injured more than once. And a couple of years ago he browbeat her into continuing to swim when she wanted to quit. Whenever he came to her practices, he always had the look of a racehorse owner in his eyes, never the look of a father. I don't buy your drug theory, but I do know that Nathan

Tanner is the kind of man who wants to win, and when it came to Leah, he never let up."

"Is he as easy to find as Rontella?"

Patterson paused before answering the question, clearly more concerned about passing on information about Tanner than Rontella. "He operates out of a 17th Street corporate tower downtown. He's the senior partner in one of those bloodsucking monster-vac law firms. His specialty is international law."

"Sounds like there's not a lot of love lost between you and the barrister crowd downtown." CJ cocked a half smile, thinking that he'd have Julie Madrid run a little law infraction profile on Patterson. "Any special reason you dislike lawyers?"

"None that I care to share with you."

"Any other link between Leah Tanner and Dr. Cardashian that I should know about? And since we're being honest with one another here, Doctor, any connections that might include you?"

The muscles in Patterson's jaw started to twitch. "I was team doctor to a swimmer who died and I shared football tickets with a colleague. That's the end of my connection. If you want to know more about Leah Tanner, I'd suggest you talk to her father, boyfriend, or coach. As for Neil Cardashian, try your luck at the Health Sciences Center."

"Got a name for Leah's coach?"

"Ellis Drake. And before you go browbeating him, you should know he's a good man."

"Any chance he might have wanted Olympic gold as badly as Leah's father?"

"I wouldn't know."

Considering the fact that Patterson had been so willing to toss Leah's boyfriend to the dogs and carve up Nathan Tanner, CJ was surprised at his soft-peddling of Drake. Adding Drake's name to his growing list of suspects, CJ looked around the room, scanning it for any hint of a tie-in to Cardashian—a photograph, a second cigar box, research contraptions similar to those in Cardashian's lab. Finding none, he turned back to Patterson. "What sparked your interest in orthopedics? Athletics?"

"Hardly. I never had a serious workout in my life until I was in my mid-forties and realized that I was overweight and out of shape, and my cholesterol was a tad over two-fifty. In fact, that's how I first met Neil Cardashian. He and some other people from the medical school came up to Boulder about a year ago and gave a half-day continuing education seminar to the athletic department, faculty, and staff on cardiopulmonary health and the longevity research that Neil was involved in."

"Telomerase research?" -

"Yes," said Patterson, surprised that a bail bondsman would know anything about telomerase. "I didn't realize that you were a scientist as well as a bail bondsman," he added sarcastically.

"It doesn't take a scientist to figure out that two people with identical autopsy findings probably died from the same thing."

"You're pretty cavalier about tossing around medical findings, Mr. Floyd. Let me toss you a few facts of my own. First, the final autopsy results on Leah Tanner aren't in. I know. I called about them earlier today. As for Neil Cardashian dying from the same thing as Leah, all I have is your say-so. Maybe you should save playing forensic pathologist for another day, Mr. Floyd, or at least until you have a degree."

CJ knew Patterson was right. His conclusions about how Leah Tanner and Neil Cardashian had died were based on the impressions of Vernon Lowe, a pathologist assistant who just happened to be a friend. Grudgingly accepting the premise that he might be jumping to conclusions, CJ decided that before he began chasing after a new trio of suspects, he'd call Henry Bales and find out whether he and Sandi had been able to tie the cigar-box gels directly to either Leah Tanner's or Neil Cardashian's death. Realizing that he had probably pushed Patterson as far as he could, he eased up out of his chair. "I'll stop by the front desk and get the addresses and phone numbers you mentioned."

"Fine. And Mr. Floyd, please don't come back."

"I won't, unless of course I find out that you killed the Tanner girl or Cardashian," said CJ, smiling as he angled his way across the room, leaving Patterson with his jaw agape and his face ashen.

A few minutes later, with the addresses of Ellis Drake and Anthony Rontella tucked into his vest pocket, CJ bounded down the building's stairway in an early-morning exercise mode he knew would make Mavis proud. All the way down the six flights of stairs, he kept asking himself the same question: Why had Patterson seemed so protective of Ellis Drake?

Slipping into the Bel Air a little winded, he pulled away from the curb still puzzled, popped a Muddy Waters tape into his tape deck, and eased back into his seat deep in thought as the old bluesman broke into a classic rendition of "Windy City Blues." Navigating his way through Cherry Creek shopping district traffic, he pulled onto Speer Boulevard and ran the Bel Air up to sixty, enjoying the guttural sound of the engine backing down when he finally eased off the gas. Before heading for Boulder, he pulled into a gas station to fill up and call Henry Bales to debrief him on his meeting with Patterson and tell him that he would be talking to Leah Tanner's coach, Ellis Drake.

"He's a big black man, Ellis, and he's sticking his nose where it doesn't belong." Pacing his office nervously, David Patterson was almost screaming into the phone. "His name's CJ Floyd. And he's on his way to see you."

"I've got nothing to hide," said Drake.

"But I do. I don't want him sniffing around my state medical board file."

"He's a bail bondsman, you say?"

"He said he is," said Patterson, nearly tripping over the phone cord.

"Then he's used to people stonewalling," said Drake.

"Meaning?"

"Meaning, I can stonewall with the best of them."

"Make sure you do."

"No problem," said Drake. "I'll do it for your sake, David, but like I said, I've got no reason to run and hide. Talk to you later." Drake cradled the phone and looked around his office at the photographs of the hundreds of athletes he had coached over the years. The walls were painted in warm earth tones, and sports souvenirs, memorabilia, and trophies filled every nook and cranny. It was an office that was in stark contrast to the sterile, whitewashed walls of David Patterson's and one in which Ellis Drake felt especially comfortable when it came to stonewalling.

Chapter 28

It was mid-morning by the time Henry and Sandi finished setting up their experiment to determine whether there were signs of telomerase in the brain tissue samples Vernon had delivered the previous evening. Sandi's short-cut assay relied on the principles described in the recent research paper she had given in Los Angeles. Although the technique for identifying telomerase was akin to dyeing an Easter egg, Sandi had never used it to identify human telomerase, employing it only for the detection of telomerase in the brewer's yeast she had been studying. She knew that tweaking her brewer's-yeast protocol to detect remnants of human telomerase catalytic protein in a sample of human brain was no more than a ten-thousand-to-one shot, but she and Henry had spent all night preparing to beat the odds.

Sandi had just finished passing several thin ribbons of brain tissue Henry had cut through an equilibration buffer when she noticed a pinhead-sized artifact in the center of several of the ribbons. "Strange," she said, holding one of the postage-stamp-sized tissue ribbons up to the light.

"What's that?" asked Henry, walking over to have a look.

"It probably wasn't visible until I prehybridized the samples." Sandi teased off one of the tissue sections with a pair of surgical tweezers.

"Think it could be our telomerase source?" said Henry, gently grasping Sandi's wrist and rotating it toward the light for a better look at the tissue artifact.

Surprised at how smooth Henry's hands were for a man who professed to be a cowboy, Sandi said, "Maybe, but one swallow doesn't make a spring." She glanced down at several remaining tissue sections that lacked the same artifact. "Odds are it's nothing."

"There's only one way to find out."

"Finish the assay?"

"You got it," said Henry, smiling.

"And if we find telomerase product?"

"I'd bet that our cigar box of magic bullets contains the stuff too, and based on Vernon Lowe's comments, I'd wager that Cardashian was using them as rectal suppositories on himself. He certainly wouldn't be the first scientist to turn guinea pig or kill himself testing some theory."

"It'll take me a little while to complete the assays."

"No problem. I'll go out and get us some coffee and rolls."

Henry checked his watch and realized that he had been working for nearly twenty-four hours. Then, looking at

Sandi and realizing that she appeared almost as fresh as she had when he had picked her up from DIA, he shook his head, amazed.

Catching Henry in an all-out stare, Sandi forced back a blush. "I'll take a cinnamon roll and decaf."

Thinking of his own quixotic, too often nutritionless eating habits, which bordered on those of a pubescent teen—potato chips for breakfast, half a dozen daily Cokes, and a fast food Golden Arches dinner, if he found the time—Henry said, "We can skip the cinnamon rolls and have a late lunch at Mae's. It's the restaurant over in Five Points that CJ's lady, Mavis Sundee, owns."

"Good food?"

"The best soul food in the state. But it's cholesterol city. Keeps CJ forever fighting the battle of the bulge."

"You're on," said Sandi, checking her probe concentrations and eyeing the hybridization chamber's digital temperature readout. "As soon as I finish this."

"Great," said Henry, finding himself wondering what made Sandi Artorio tick. After spending nearly a day working at her side and watching her take nothing more than a couple of thirty-minute breaks, he knew she was intense. She hadn't said so, but he had the feeling that she didn't like the fact that Cardashian may have beaten her to the punch with telomerase. There was also a hint of vulnerability about her that he couldn't quite put his finger on. Something akin to the fact that perhaps like him, when you came right down to it, she was really just a simple person at heart. He didn't know what passions lurked beneath Sandi Artorio's scholarly facade, but he found himself wanting to know as much about her as he could. "Let me check on the OR schedule and make sure I'm not up for frozen sections. If I'm not, after you finish your assay, we'll have the entire rest of the afternoon to relax."

"Fantastic," said Sandi, barely looking up from her work.

"While I'm at it, I'll fill Tess in on where we are with everything and check in with CJ."

"Okay." Sandi checked the concentration of her hybridization mixture to make certain that it was sufficient to avoid background staining problems, placed several of the tissue samples Henry had cut earlier into the hybridization chamber, and began her run, seemingly oblivious to Henry's presence.

"I'll be right back." Henry glanced back over his shoulder, hoping that by the time he returned, Sandi's competitive fast-forward gear would be back in neutral. Twenty minutes later he returned to find Tess Gilliam's wheelchair parked in one of the laboratory aisles. Sandi was standing next to her, arms behind her back at parade rest as they both stared out the window toward the Front Range skyline.

"Sorry for the delay," said Henry. "I got caught up in screening a bunch of thyroid cancer slides. Any answers?" he said to Sandi before walking over to Tess and affectionately patting her hand.

"We're not dealing with artifact." Sandi's voice was almost hollow. "The in situ findings are positive. Two of the tissue samples with the artifact showed telomerase catalytic protein."

Henry shook his head in disgust.

"Now all we have to do is match these brain-tissue findings up with what we eventually find in the gels from the cigar box, and we'll know for sure whether Cardashian was testing his product on himself."

"And marketing it to boot. Don't forget Leah Tanner."

Before Henry could respond, Tess, sad-faced and clutching the arms of her wheelchair, said, "I think Neil may have been targeting athletes. The problem is, I don't know why. That swimmer who died might just be the tip of the iceberg, Henry. And frankly, it's got me scared."

"Looks like CJ's already chipping away at your premise," said Henry.

"How's that?"

"I talked to him while I was out. He's on his way to Boulder to check on an athletic tie-in up at CU."

"Anything specific?" asked Sandi.

"No, but he said he has some leads."

"Good," said Sandi. "Because I'm beginning to think this whole telomerase thing has more than one face. There's certainly more to it than Cardashian attempting to develop some kind of human longevity pill."

"Mind clueing me in?" asked Henry.

"We can talk about it over lunch, if you're still up for it."

"Sure am."

Looking at Tess, Sandi said, "Want to come along?"

"No. I've already eaten. Besides, I've got my daily meeting with Dean Adler. I'll stay here and have another look at your assay results. It'll also give me time to look through some old electron photomicrographic results I shared with Neil right after we started working on telomerase together. The nuclear detail in them is amazing, and I think they just might shed some light on your athletic angle."

"Don't pop any fountain-of-youth pills while we're gone," said Henry, smiling at Tess and wondering what her 1970s-technology ultrastructural photographs of cells could possibly offer over Sandi's new-age recombinant DNA techniques.

"Wouldn't think of it."

Henry gave Sandi a sleepy-eyed look as they left the lab. "Let's take the stairs. Maybe the exercise will keep us awake."

"Fine by me."

By the time they reached Henry's pickup, Sandi was breathless.

"Looks like our mile-high altitude has finally caught up to you," said Henry, swinging back the truck's door for Sandi and thinking that for the first time since he had met her, Sandi Artorio seemed to be out of sync.

"That and no sleep."

"Don't worry. The coffee at Mae's will perk you up. CJ swears by it. I swear it's trail-ride java left over from the 1880s."

"That strong?"

"Stronger."

As they both slipped on their seat belts, another truck moved slowly past Henry's and into the parking lot. Jamie Lee Custus shot a quick look as she cruised past, patted the Bowie knife on the seat next to her, and eased into a parking space to await the call she was expecting from Sweets.

Chapter 29

Lieutenant Menton wasn't sure just how Neil Cardashian had died, but he knew from what the Denver coroner's office had told him that regardless of how he had discovered Cardashian's naked body, Cardashian's death wasn't shaping up as a homicide. He didn't have all the nitty-gritty details, but the coffee-stained preliminary autopsy report he was reading as he sat in University Hospital's Wall Street Deli stated that Cardashian had died from *undifferentiated carcinomatosis of undetermined origin*, and that wasn't murder.

Menton had reviewed enough autopsy reports to know that what the document was really saying was that Cardashian had died from cancer and the coroner's office had been unable to find the cancer's primary source. He also knew from having talked to Tess Gilliam two hours earlier about some strange suppository gels and from the follow-up meeting he had had with the dean of the medical school, Louise Adler, who struck him as more of a bureaucrat in charge of damage control than a physician, that Cardashian had been a rogue scientist out of control.

Menton nursed his coffee for another five minutes before moving to leave and meet Tess Gilliam. He had barged into her world once before and felt the sting of her lawyer, so he decided that this time around he'd have to be a little more friendly if he expected to persuade Dr. Gilliam to fill him in on what he suspected she knew about what might be missing from Cardashian's preliminary autopsy report.

Leaving the deli, he glanced back down at the checkerboard of tile, telling himself that for hospital food the fare wasn't half bad.

Ellis Drake's stocky and very determined redheaded secretary stood at Drake's office doorway, blocking CJ's path to her boss. The look on her face reminded CJ of the half scowl his own secretary, Flora Jean, flashed when she wanted people to take a hike.

Eyeball to eyeball with CJ, daring him to make another move, the secretary said, "I told you, Mr. Floyd, you need an appointment."

"I only need ten minutes of the coach's time."

Before they had a chance to escalate what was becoming a shouting match, Ellis Drake opened his office door, eyeing them both as if they were two of his recalcitrant swimmers.

"Is there a problem?" he asked, filling the doorway

with his 240-pound girth, looking at his secretary for an answer.

"Mr. Floyd insists on seeing you right now. I told him he needed an appointment."

Drake moved out of the doorway and back into his office, surprising CJ with his nimbleness. Beckoning CJ into the room, he pulled off the oversized baseball cap he was wearing and ran his fingers through his crew cut. "What's so important that it can't wait for an appointment, Mr. Floyd?"

"I'm looking into the death of one of your swimmers."

"Are you from the coroner's office?" added Drake, looking unperturbed.

"Nope. I'm a bail bondsman, and I'm hoping you can shed some light on why Leah Tanner and a CU research scientist named Neil Cardashian seem to have died from the same thing."

"Seizures?"

"No: brain cancer."

Drake's mouth dropped open. "What?"

"Brain cancer," repeated CJ. "Did you know Cardashian?"

"I'd met him."

"Where?"

"He was a friend of one of our team physicians, David Patterson." Then, frowning, he added, "Cancer? That doesn't make sense."

"It's possible that your swimmer and Cardashian were experimenting with some kind of drug that killed them."

Drake flashed CJ a skeptical look. "I see. And just why, Mr. Floyd, are you involved?"

"Because I've got a client who the police have decided is a suspect in Cardashian's death."

"I thought you said Cardashian died from taking a drug."

"I did, but I didn't say he or Leah took the drug willingly. Could be there's a little touch of murder going around."

Drake walked over to one of the two chairs in the room and sat down. "Have a seat," he said, motioning for CJ to follow suit.

CJ sat down and looked around the warmly lit room, dominated by glass-fronted cases overflowing with athletic trophies, testimonial plaques, and sports memorabilia. Photographs of athletes, mostly swimmers and divers, accented every wall.

"Are you into sports, Mr. Floyd?" said Drake, sensing CJ's fascination.

"I'm a fan of sorts."

Drake reached behind his chair and slipped a photograph off the wall behind him. "Then here's a photograph worthy of a fan," he said, handing CJ a color photo of five people with their arms over each other's shoulders. Drake was at the far right, grinning ear to ear, dressed in the same nylon sweatsuit he was currently wearing. His arm was draped over an attractive female swimmer decked out in a form-fitting, figure-flattering swimsuit. The two men flanking the swimmer on her other side were also grinning broadly. The photo's other bookend was a tall, slender, serious-faced man.

"That was taken about a month ago at the finals of the Big Twelve conference swimming trials. The woman's Leah Tanner. She knocked 'em dead. Took first in three events and shaved two seconds off the best times she'd ever posted. And there's me, of course. The man to Leah's right is her boyfriend, Anthony Rontella. The man next to him is Dr. Patterson."

"I've met Patterson," said CJ.

"Oh," said Drake, feigning surprise.

"Who's the sourpuss at the end?"

"Leah's father, Nathan Tanner."

CJ stared at the photograph, memorizing the faces. Rontella was only of medium build, but his neck size and muscular biceps told CJ that he was probably a lot stronger than he looked. The sandy-haired, unsmiling Nathan Tanner was deeply tanned and reminded CJ of more than a few of the criminal defense lawyers he knew.

Watching CJ drink in the photograph, Drake stood up and sucked in his gut. "If what you're saying's right, maybe I should have suspected something then. Leah's times were pretty phenomenal. Now I've got a dead athlete on my hands and a lifetime to think about it."

"It's a bad situation," CJ said sympathetically.

Drake didn't answer as CJ moved back from studying the photograph to examining the defeated look on Drake's face. "If you don't mind, I'd appreciate a little background on the folks in the photo, besides you and Leah."

Drake glanced at the photograph and sighed before spending the next five minutes telling CJ what he knew about Nathan Tanner, Patterson, and Rontella. His synopsis of Tanner dovetailed with what Patterson had told CJ. Drake's take on Anthony Rontella was unflattering; he pegged Rontella as an opportunistic schemer out for one big score, with Leah Tanner and her Olympic potential as his payoff. The only person Drake had nothing but positive things to say about was Patterson.

Drake had barely finished his glowing depiction when CJ, bored by the summary, decided to scan the photograph he was holding one last time. As he did, something on Anthony Rontella's bare arm beneath the sleeve of the drab gray CU athletic department T-shirt he was wearing caught his eye. CJ held the photo a little closer, trying to bring the fuzzy outline on Rontella's arm into focus. "What's that on Rontella's arm?" said CJ, pointing at the picture.

"Got me. Never really paid much attention to it. I'd say it's some kind of tattoo."

Nodding in agreement, CJ said, "Got a magnifying glass in here?"

"Everything but," said Drake. "Know where I can get one, though. Just down the hall. One of our emeritus professor types has one. He uses it to read the stock pages when he comes in in the morning."

"Think you could rustle it up?"

"If he's here." Drake left his office, shaking his head, and returned a couple of minutes later with the magnifying glass. He handed it to CJ and stepped back while CJ scanned the photo. Recognizing the out-of-focus outline on Rontella's arm as a tattoo of two crossed rowing oars, CJ raised the magnifying glass and said, "I'll be."

"Did the glass help?" asked Drake.

"It sure did. In fact, it puts a whole lot of things into perspective," he said, recalling the tattoo he had seen on Cardashian's arm in the photos he had found during his search of Cardashian's condo, and realizing that he now had a link between Rontella and Cardashian.

Chapter 30

It was the blood splatter on Henry's clothes and face that finally made Sandi sick to her stomach. So sick, in fact, that Henry, glassy-eyed and fighting back tears, barely had time to help her to a sink at the back of Tess Gilliam's lab before she threw up.

Sprawled on the floor several feet away, Tess was lying face up next to three lily-pad-sized pools of coagulated blood. Eyes closed and placid-faced, aside from a tendril of blood dangling from her left ear, she looked to be asleep.

Henry and Sandi had come back from lunch at Mae's to find Tess's laboratory ransacked and Lieutenant Menton kneeling over Tess's body feeling for a carotid pulse. Shoving Menton aside, shouting, "Get the hell out of the way," Henry had begun several minutes of CPR until

Menton had to pull him away, saying, "She's dead, Dr. Bales, she's dead."

Exhausted, his face dripping with sweat, Henry sat slumped against a chemical cabinet, holding Tess's head in his lap, tears streaming down his face, until paramedics and the first members of the crime-scene team Menton had called during Henry's futile resuscitation attempt showed up and Menton escorted Henry out of their way.

In his anguish, Henry had never noticed the pencil-eraser-sized bullet wound in the back of Tess's neck or the larger, ragged-edged exit wound just above her left clavicle. Nor did he realize as Menton walked him away that his hands, face, and shirt were speckled with blood.

Stepping back from the sink and looking sadly up at Henry, Sandi adjusted the compress of paper towels Henry held to her head and thought about the leisurely two hours they had spent at Mae's. She felt guilty about not forcing Tess to come along, guilt that was accentuated because she and Henry had had such fun sharing their fascination with and love of old-time radio, 1930s movies, and early rock and roll. As they were leaving Mae's, Henry had offered to take her horseback riding and fly-fishing at his ranch, "as soon as they settled Tess's telomerase problem." She had graciously accepted, trying not to sound too eager, and Henry had driven back to the university slowly, on side streets, as if he were trying to make their special time together linger. Now it appeared that the telomerase problem had more than likely cost Tess her life, and a day that two hours ago had been so promising had turned itself 180 degrees.

"Are you okay?" said Henry, preparing another cold compress.

"Yes. Are you?"

Henry nodded without answering.

"Your shirt's a mess."

Henry glanced down at the flecks of blood covering the front of his shirt and then at the bloodstains on his arms. "I'll change later," he said, gritting his teeth, forcing back tears, scanning the laboratory, now thick with police.

Menton had stationed a cherubic-faced plainclothes policewoman next to the door to challenge anyone attempting to enter. Working his way toward Henry and Sandi, Menton stopped to talk to a criminalist who was examining Tess's head. "Got anything for me yet?"

"Single shot to the base of the skull, Lieutenant. Real professional looking. We've already packaged the slug. I'd say it was a .32. Don't see many of those around these days. The shooter was real close. Obvious powder burns on the lady's neck. For the moment, that's it."

Menton nodded and kept moving. Easing up to the sink, he said, "Sorry about this, Dr. Bales, Dr. Artorio. Real tragic. I know you both wish I'd drop into a sinkhole about now, but I need your assistance if you expect me to put a face on this."

"Assistance? How?" said Henry, his voice barely audible.

"I'd like to see the suppository gels or beads, or whatever they are, that I spoke to Dr. Gilliam about by phone earlier today."

Henry brushed a patch of dried blood off the back of his hand without responding and shot Sandi a look that said, *Don't give him too much.*

"The beads?" said Sandi, taking Henry's cue.

"It's a place to start."

"I left them in a cabinet in the storage room in the

back. I'll get them for you." Sandi walked away, sidestepping broken laboratory glassware and shattered pieces of a hybridization chamber, toward the storage room.

"I'll come with you," said Menton.

Inventorying the countertops on her way, Sandi realized that the telomerase positive in situ hybridization slides she had left there were missing. Following in Sandi's footsteps, Menton said, "Please don't touch anything. Just point out the beads to me. I'll have someone handle things from there. And since Dr. Gilliam never got the chance, perhaps while you're at it, you can explain to me exactly why they're so important."

"I'll do my best," said Sandi, glancing back at Tess and then at a somber-faced Henry.

Years earlier Henry had ridden to the top of Mt. Evans with Tess shortly after she had hired him as a postdoctoral fellow. Tess had insisted on driving her recently purchased, specially equipped, fire-engine-red Buick, giving Henry a firsthand view of how a paraplegic operated a motor vehicle. He had been amazed at how skillfully Tess manipulated the complex hand controls, and a little nervous as they sped up I-70 with the Buick's speedometer pegged at just a notch above eighty for almost the entire trip. As he had unpacked Tess's wheelchair from the car's trunk in the cold mountain air of the Mt. Evans visitors' parking lot, he could feel Tess looking at him.

"I know what you're thinking," she had said, smiling broadly as Henry nosed the wheelchair up to the door of the Buick. "This lady drives too fast. You wouldn't think that if you had to coast around in one of these chariots for a while." She slapped the side of the wheelchair and slipped into it unassisted from the front seat. "Damn thing'll make you want to fly."

Henry hadn't considered the incident in years, but suddenly it had him thinking about Vietnam, and the death of his friend, Tommy Haskins. Pounding his fist on the countertop, swearing that he could hear the distant wind-whipping noise from the blades of medevac choppers as Tommy's life slipped away, he was close to screaming when Sandi snatched him back to reality, shouting from the back of the lab, "They're gone! They're gone!"

Startled, Henry headed for the storage room.

"They were here, half a cigar box of gels along with five I had sectioned ready to assay." Sandi looked from Menton to Henry, uncertain whether to tell Menton that the formalin-filled bottle with Cardashian's brain tissue was also missing.

"You're sure you left them here?" said Menton.

"Absolutely."

"In a cigar box and not some specialized laboratory container?" Menton said skeptically.

"That's what we found them in."

"And they're all gone?"

"Every one of them."

"Pills you claim are capable of extending life?"

"Possibly extending life, Lieutenant. Try not to turn what I said earlier into an absolute. But, regardless of whether I'm right or not, I think they're the reason that Cardashian and Tess are dead."

"Cardashian died from cancer. I've seen the autopsy report. Now you're telling me that a bunch of missing beads did him in."

"Very probably."

"I see," said Menton, realizing that he had a lot of homework to do at the coroner's office. "I'm not saying you're wrong, Doctor. I'd just appreciate it if you'd explain the link between cancer, the missing beads, and the bullet in the back of Dr. Gilliam's head."

Sandi frowned, angered by Menton's callous description. "I'm sure some people find your jagged edges charming, Lieutenant, but I don't. I just lost a dear friend, and I'd appreciate it if you'd put a damper on your sarcasm. As for your question, I can't explain the connection."

"Sorry," said Menton, eyeing an equally offended-looking Henry.

"Thank you."

"Let's start over. Earlier today Dr. Gilliam told me a little about the potential of those beads. I dropped by to get the rest of the story. If you want me to have any chance of finding her killer, I'll need you to fill in the blanks."

Eyeing Menton cautiously, Sandi summarized the results of her assays, postulating that the beads contained telomerase without mentioning one word about her assay of Cardashian's brain tissue. Finishing her summary, she glanced sympathetically at Henry, wondering how long it would be before the self-assured, witty cowboy masquerading as a doctor whom she had shared lunch with would surface again.

Deciding to ask one final question, Menton said, "How do you think the missing pills pack their punch?"

"My expertise is in the molecular biology of the enzyme, not its pathophysiology, Lieutenant. That would have been Dr. Gilliam's bailiwick."

"Meaning?"

"Meaning, Lieutenant, that I work on basic biological

mechanisms. What makes the watch tick, if you will. I don't investigate what it takes to knock the timepiece out of sync."

Smiling at Sandi's response and thinking that if Menton had led with a carrot instead of a stick when he started his questions, Sandi might have been more hospitable, Henry said, "Do you need any more from us now, Lieutenant?"

Menton scanned the laboratory as if he were searching for a reason to continue. Then, clearing his throat, he said, "I'll need your phone numbers."

"In case you've forgotten, Lieutenant, Dr. Artorio lives in Bethesda, Maryland. She's been staying with Dr. Gilliam."

"Funny. Somehow I got the impression that she was staying with you. Your phone number will do just fine, Dr. Bales."

Henry pulled out a pen and quickly jotted his phone number on a piece of nearby filter paper. Handing the paper to Menton, he glanced at Sandi. "Ready to get out of here?"

"I sure am."

"You know where to find us, Lieutenant," said Henry.

Threading their way back through the lab and around the gauntlet of cordoned-off evidence, they walked through the laboratory hand in hand. Near the doorway, Henry snatched a glance back at Menton, who was engaged in a conversation with another policeman, but Menton never looked up.

They hurried without speaking past a gaggle of dumbstruck faculty members lingering outside the laboratory, down the hall, into Henry's lab, and directly past Henry's wide-eyed senior research fellow. When the fellow asked,

"What happened?" Henry shrugged, pulled Sandi into his private office, and closed the door. Almost breathless, he said, "I need to call CJ."

"First tell me why you had me withhold information from Menton. I hope he didn't pick up on it," said Sandi, slumping into a nearby chair.

"As soon as I talk to CJ." Henry grabbed the phone and punched in CJ's number.

Flora Jean answered in her patented West Virginia coal-country drawl, "Floyd's Bail Bonds."

"It's Henry, Flora Jean. I need to speak to CJ; it's urgent."

Surprised at how desperate Henry's voice sounded, and disappointed that the man who usually chatted with her about her latest baking breakthrough or the night classes she was taking at Red Rocks Community College had brushed her aside so quickly, Flora Jean shouted across her cramped receptionist's alcove through the open doorway to CJ's office, "Henry Bales is on line one; says it's urgent."

CJ had just hung up from asking Julie Madrid to run background checks on Dr. David Patterson, Ellis Drake, and Nathan Tanner. It had taken some prodding, since Julie was preparing for a trial, but she had agreed, leaving CJ feeling like it was the old days and leaning back in his worn leather chair, smoking a cheroot and admiring his back-wall photo gallery of the hundreds of bond skippers he had brought to justice.

He hadn't been able to hook up with Anthony Rontella while he was in Boulder. According to Coach Drake, Rontella was on a trip to Fort Lewis College in Durango, and he'd be gone the rest of the week. Checking out Rontella was something he'd have to do later.

"You got me, cowboy," said CJ, responding the way he usually did to a call from Henry.

"Tess's dead, CJ. Someone killed her early this afternoon. I need your help."

"Shit." CJ stubbed his cheroot out in an ashtray. "I'll be right there."

"No need. What I really need to know is whether Sandi can stay with Mavis. She's pretty distraught over Tess."

"I'll call Mavis and hook it up as soon as we're off the phone."

"One last thing, CJ. Sometime later this evening I am going to need to drop by Rosie's, maybe pick up a gun."

Rosie's Garage was a Five Points gas station, garage, community watering hole, and hangout that CJ's best friend, Rosie Weaks, had operated for twenty-five years.

"Are you crazy, Henry?"

Henry looked over at Sandi, who had bolted out of her chair the instant he had said the word *gun*. "No. It's just that this little scientific skirmish we've been involved in has escalated into an all-out war. You know the kind, CJ, one where people you care about get killed."

"I'll go pick up Mavis. We'll meet you at her place in half an hour," said CJ. "And drop the gun shit, Henry. It's not your thing."

Henry walked over to Sandi and slipped his hand into hers. "I'll see you in half an hour," he said, cradling the phone.

Squeezing Henry's hand, Sandi said, "You can't . . ."

Henry squeezed back without answering, thinking as his eyes welled up with tears, *Sure I can. There aren't any rules in war.*

Chapter 31

After two days of fighting off vomiting, seizures, and bloody stools, Ernesto Salas drifted off into semiconsciousness. Burdened by her own anxious fatigue, Atina Salas sat back in her wobbly wicker chair, scooted up next to Ernesto's bed, and whispered, *"Al fin duerme, mi niño; dulces sueños."*

Determined not to have Ernesto hospitalized, where he might be killed like his grandfather by incompetent doctors, Atina had lied earlier in the day when Dr. Gómez called to check on Ernesto, telling Gómez that Ernesto was much better and that he had only a mild case of diarrhea. Busy attending to Castro's cold, Gómez had eagerly accepted Atina's assessment, knowing that disrupting the treatment of Cuba's number one patient, even briefly, could be a career-ending mistake. He welcomed the opportunity to diagnose Ernesto's malady as severe gastroenteritis brought on by a combination of tainted food, training in the hot sun, and Olympic-year stress.

Atina watched Ernesto breathe peacefully for several minutes, unaware of the seriousness of his condition. Then she kissed him on the forehead and rose from her chair, hoping that he would doze long enough for her to catch a few minutes of long-overdue sleep herself. Normally she could have counted on Rulon Mantero or her brother-in-law Manuel to spell her, but Rulon had died in a mysterious fire that had consumed his backwoods shanty, and Manuel was on another of his baffling trips to the United States.

Word had it that the police had found a cigar box chock-full of American hundred-dollar bills dug just barely into the earth beneath Rulon's house. The police had questioned her about the money, even showing her the singed box. She told them truthfully that she knew nothing about the money, stating, her arms gyrating in protest when they threatened to interrogate a confused, barely conscious Ernesto, that they should spend their time investigating thieves and not the premier's hand-picked heavyweight boxing champion. The police quickly folded their cards and left, unwilling to risk intimidating the well-connected grandmother of a potential Cuban Olympic champion.

Pleased that she had shaken the police, Atina nonetheless remained concerned about Rulon's death and the American money. Her concern hinged on the fact that the cigar box that had contained the money, although burned almost beyond recognition, was, nonetheless, immediately recognizable to her as one of her own handcrafted counterfeits, a knock-off whose existence should have been known only to her, a few trusted rollers, Anthony Rontella, and her brother-in-law Manuel Hernández.

Exhausted from tending to Ernesto, Atina's arms dropped to her sides as she drifted off to sleep, thinking that later in the day she would call Anthony in the United States and try her best to also locate Manuel.

Chapter 32

Sweets stood in the mammoth great room of the Golden, Colorado, mountaintop mansion that had been a family retreat for nearly seventy-five years. Eyeing the massive handhewn overhead beams and anxiously gripping a tumbler of scotch, Sweets growled into the telephone, "Your little foray into the world of Caribbean stogies could end up costing me money, Anthony. And, if it does, I'll be your settlement agent, you little con artist." Sweets adjusted the voice-altering device on the phone's mouthpiece and took a sip of scotch.

Anthony's cigar-importing scheme would never have come to light if Manuel Hernández hadn't passed along news of it to Sweets when he had checked in with Sweets to say that he was back stateside. Aware that Anthony had ventured off on his own when he should have been concentrating his full attention on Cardashian's experiment involving Ernesto Salas, it was all Sweets could do to refrain from slamming down the phone, calling Jamie Lee Custus, and have her settle up with Anthony right then.

The fact that Hernández had apparently felt no need to pass along the information about Anthony's freelancing until the Cuban police had questioned him about Rulon Mantero's death had Sweets worried. Millions, and in the long run maybe even billions, of dollars were at stake.

Sweets gazed out the room's picture windows toward a fifty-acre mountain meadow where a half-dozen palomino horses were grazing. The foothills retreat only twenty minutes from downtown Denver had always been the one place that Sweets could get away from the constant pressures of the telomerase scheme. It was a sanctuary where none of the game's players, including strong-arm types like Custus and Hernández, or even the brainchild of the project, Neil Cardashian, had ever set foot. Now Sweets felt as though the sanctuary had been violated. "Where are you?" said Sweets, grimacing and turning away from the pastoral scene outside.

Anthony thought about lying, but he knew Sweets was probably using caller ID. "In Durango."

"For what?"

Anthony's words came out haltingly, like those of an abused child who knew he was about to get a beating. "I'm trying to sell the telomerase concept to someone I know down here at Fort Lewis College." Defensively, he added, "It's the way to go; I know it."

"You're what?"

"Grooming another audience."

Sweets thumped the tumbler down on a nearby table,

sloshing scotch onto the table's immaculately restored antique finish. "That's it! You're done. I don't know what made me think you had the sense to carry out a team effort like this in the first place. I never should have listened to Neil. First cigars, and now you're planning to test the product ahead of schedule and outside our defined network. It takes time to develop a product and build demand, you idiot. How many people have you told about the gels?"

"A few coaches, some trainers I know," said Anthony, failing to mention that he had been lining up people on the West Coast for half a year. "No harm, no foul," he said, trying to defuse the tension.

Sweets paused and thought about Neil Cardashian, the common bond that had brought them together. "Do you have any of the gels with you?"

"Yes," said Anthony, thinking about how easy it had been to obtain the gels from Cardashian when he had baited the egomaniacal research scientist with the fact that they could increase their test sample size tenfold in a matter of months without Sweets ever finding out.

"Stay put in Durango, and don't let the gels out of your sight. I'm sending someone down there to pick them up."

"Not on your life. My name's not Sitting Duck. I know what happened to Rulon Mantero," said Anthony, noting how strange Sweets's mechanically altered voice sounded when Sweets became excited.

"That was Cuba; this is here. If you want the rest of the ten thousand you're expecting for supplying the Cuban boxer, you'd better give the gels to the person I'm sending to Durango, take your money, and disappear."

Fearful of losing his nest egg and perhaps his life, Anthony said, "Are you sending Hernández?"

"No, someone else. A woman named Jamie Lee Custus."

"I want cash," said Anthony, relieved that he would be dealing with a woman rather than Hernández.

"You'll get it. Where do I have Custus come?"

"The Coventry Motel."

"She'll be there by tomorrow evening. And Anthony, don't hold back anything. I want what's left of all the gels, not just the remnants of the stash you were doling out to Leah Tanner."

"You'll get them," said Anthony, smiling like someone who knew he had a decided edge. "How will I recognize the woman?"

"She'll have ID, but since you asked, she sounds like a Texan and walks with a limp."

"No funny stuff, Sweets. I'd hate to have to send your handicapped bag lady back to Denver with two bad legs."

"Save your chest-thumping, Anthony. Just give her the gels."

"Tell her to meet me at eight P.M. in the motel lobby, where people can see us, and not before."

"Eight it is."

"Anything else?"

"Don't spend all your money in one place," said Sweets.

Anthony thought about the hundreds of telomerase gels he had pilfered from Cardashian, the ones he had held back from Leah, and the scores of gels he had kept for himself while supplying Ernesto Salas. "I won't," he said, smiling as he contemplated the cash stream he expected from trainers and coaches once word about his product was out. "And you do the same," he said, thinking as he hung up, *Screw you, Sweets!*

Sweets was back on the phone with Jamie Lee within minutes. "Handle Rontella with kid gloves," said Sweets, after explaining the situation.

Perplexed by Sweets's restraint, Jamie Lee said, "All right."

With a fresh tumbler of scotch in hand, Sweets walked over to the window to admire the now frolicking horses. "That is, until you have the gels. After that, solve our problem permanently."

"Got you."

"One other thing. Take a cell phone with you. We'll need to stay in touch."

"Easy enough."

"Anything else I should know?" asked Sweets.

"Just that there's a mess over at the Health Sciences Center involving the Gilliam woman."

"You have anything to do with it?"

"Don't ask, don't tell," said Jamie Lee. "Either way, Gilliam's dead."

"Too bad."

"Yeah. You should know this, though. I've been keeping tabs on those friends of Gilliam's, like you asked. The doctor from D.C. and that pathologist, Bales."

"And?" said Sweets.

"I'd settle up with them, if I were you. They're trouble."

"Good observation. Do what you have to do to make us both happy. Just don't make a mess, and don't leave a trail."

"I never do."

Watching a determined stallion mount an uncoopera-
tive palomino mare, Sweets thought about Rontella's in-
sipidness, reflecting on how difficult it often was to
impose one's will on a clear intellectual inferior. "I'll give
you the rest of your agenda later." Then, as if not to
spook the horses, Sweets took another sip of scotch and
whispered into the phone, "Good-bye."

Nathan Tanner had Ellis Drake sweating, cross-examining
him in Drake's Boulder office as if he were in court on
the witness stand.

"Then you've never seen these before?" Tanner shoved
a handful of the waxy beads he had found in Leah's apartment in Drake's face.

"No, I haven't."

"They're suppositories. I'm having them checked by a
lab. I think they're laced with some substance that's
lethal. I don't know what, but I intend to find out. Any
chance they came from you?"

Eyeing Tanner as if he had taken leave of his senses,
Drake said, "Get serious, Nathan. Do you know what
you're implying?"

"Yes. That you were supplying my daughter with some
kind of performance-altering substance and it killed her."

"I'd never do anything so cruel. You know that."

"What about your staff?"

"I don't hire lunatics."

"Then explain to me why my baby died," said Tanner,
glassy-eyed, his right eye darting in every direction.

"I don't know. But for what it's worth, you're the second person to come in here asking me the same kinds of

questions. A black bail bondsman out of Denver named CJ Floyd was in here, standing right where you are, claiming that someone else died from the same thing as Leah. In fact, at first I thought he was working for you."

"Never heard of him."

"I found that out. Anyway, he said that Leah and one of our medical school faculty, Dr. Neil Cardashian, died from the same kind of cancer."

"What!" said Tanner.

"Cancer. Floyd sounded real sure of himself too. Like he had some kind of inside dope."

"What did he want from you?"

"Not much. He asked me a few questions about Dave Patterson and Anthony Rontella, and of course you. And then he took a real fancy to that picture right behind you." Drake pointed to the photograph he had shown CJ.

Bolting out of his seat, Tanner rushed over to the photograph. "I remember when this was taken," he said, teary-eyed.

"Floyd seemed real interested in it. In fact, I dug up a magnifying glass for him so he could get a better look at the tattoo on Anthony's right arm."

His left eye suddenly twitching, Tanner slipped the photograph off the wall, examining it more closely. "Did he say why he was interested in the tattoo?"

"No. But when he left he seemed satisfied that he had found what he had come after."

"Think you can round up that magnifying glass again?" said Tanner, focusing on Anthony's arm.

"No need. It's still here." Drake retrieved the magnifying glass from his desktop. "Think the tattoo means anything?" he said, handing it to Tanner.

Scanning the photo, with both eyes now twitching in anger and the muscles in his neck visibly rigid, Tanner said, "I don't know. But if it helps me even the score with whoever killed my Leah, I'll track down Floyd and ask him myself."

Chapter 33

The silver-haired University of Colorado PR man looked beleaguered as he stood at the microphone in a room full of people, preparing to put a plausible spin on why a prominent University of Colorado Health Sciences Center doctor had been murdered. Although used to speaking to the press, Ryan Sanger felt uncomfortable being a spin doctor to a murder. He had been fielding questions from reporters, faculty members, and police for more than two hours, and now he was set to do a six o'clock news remote that would air in minutes. To make matters worse, the medical school's dean, Louise Adler, had arrived moments before, sidled up next to him, and shot him the kind of stare that said, *Don't make a mistake.*

Staring out into the crowd, he caught a glimpse of the

police lieutenant who had briefed him on what, if asked, he could and couldn't say about the crime scene.

Sanger glanced over at Adler with a smile, determined to mask the fact he and Adler had never seen eye-to-eye. Pondering how he would hold up once the cameras started rolling and he began talking about his dear friend Tess Gilliam, Sanger cleared his throat, pulled a notepad from his coat pocket, and surveyed it nervously.

Sensing his trepidation, Adler brushed several errant wisps of hair off her forehead and gave Sanger a hang-in-there look that caught him by surprise. "Are you up to this, Ryan?"

"I'm fine."

"Good. Be caring but firm. Present things the way we discussed them earlier, and above all, don't give this university a black eye."

"I'll do my best."

"I know you will," said Adler, patting Sanger on the shoulder.

Interrupting the conversation, a sleepy-eyed man whom Sanger recognized as a Channel 4 news director walked up to the microphone, tapped it to make certain it was on, and held up two fingers. "Two minutes, Mr. Sanger."

Sanger nodded at the man and rechecked his notes.

"Forty-five seconds," said the news director, disappearing behind a bank of television lights.

All too quickly, the room turned quiet, and all Sanger could hear was the news director's voice. "Thirty seconds. Twenty. Ten, and . . ."

*   *   *

Henry Bales's stomach sank and his eyes glazed over as he watched the breaking news story from home at the top of the hour. Stretched across the bed in clothes still splattered with blood, and listless from a fitful thirty-minute nap, he listened as Ryan Sanger detailed the facts surrounding Tess Gilliam's death.

Henry had left the Health Sciences Center in agony after twenty-four hours without any sleep and dropped Sandi at her safe haven with Mavis. From there he had gone back home to change clothes and wash off Tess's blood, only to fall asleep and awaken to a new stab of pain.

After staring blankly at the TV screen for another few minutes, he switched his television off and called Mavis to check on Sandi. Assured that Sandi was safe and asleep, Henry phoned CJ to remind him not to forget their eight o'clock meeting at Rosie's Garage, a meeting CJ had agreed to only after sensing that if he didn't, Henry might very well make the mistake of his life. Hoping to shake his sluggishness, Henry set the alarm clock next to him for seven-thirty, lay back on the bed, and tossed and turned for another fifteen minutes before finally drifting off to sleep.

Chapter 34

Rosie's Garage had been located in Five Points at the corner of 26th and Welton Streets since Rosie Weaks and his wife, Etta Lee, had first started the business twenty-seven years earlier, three months after Rosie finished Denver Diesel Mechanics school. Beginning with nothing more than two aging Conoco gas pumps, an unpaved gravel drive, and a lean-to service hut for oil changes and lubes, Rosie's had grown from a run-down eyesore to a Five Points business success.

The now spotless concrete drive sported three service islands with six pumps, all of them topped by the same 1940s-vintage white enamel globes that had been there when Rosie and Etta Lee had signed on. The original service hut with its grease-monkey pit had been replaced by a modern garage with three service bays, a small business office, and a huge storage room in the back. Whenever Denver politicians wanted to catalogue the black community's successes, they never failed to single out Rosie's Garage.

Like Mae's Louisiana Kitchen a half block down the street, Rosie's was a long-established community gathering place, but over the years the garage had become much more. Rosie's mammoth back storage room, known to locals as "the den," was also a watering hole for gambling, playing the numbers, and buying liquor on Sundays, still against Colorado law. The same politicians who touted Rosie's success as a small business never seemed to get around to mentioning what went on in the back room.

The third Friday night of the month always meant gambling at the den, and third Fridays always managed to produce, in addition to their share of winners and losers, several tussles and at least one serious fight. There were too many people full of liquor packed into too confined a space with too much money on the table for fisticuffs not to occur.

Although no more than a white-walled cinder block storage room on most days, on third Fridays the den sported one of the most elegant portable bars in the state, a bar that, years earlier, Rosie and CJ had rescued from a turn-of-the-century Kansas City stockman's saloon. They had moved the three-piece, forty-foot, semicircular solid-mahogany bar the seven hundred miles from Missouri on a flatbed truck in a near blizzard just one month after CJ had returned from his second tour of Vietnam. During the move Rosie had almost rolled the truck in eastern Colorado after hitting a sheet of black ice outside the town of Limon at two A.M. When the truck finally ended its spin, stalled, and angled across both westbound lanes of I-70, leaving Rosie catatonic in his seat, all CJ could think of were the times he had sat on the deck of his patrol boat, the *Cape Star*, strapped to a machine gun, shirtless in ninety-degree heat. The first words out of CJ's mouth when Rosie restarted the flatbed had been, *I knew I wasn't meant to buy it in a fuckin' Colorado blizzard.*

On gambling nights, the first thing CJ always did on entering the den was to scan the room for the nearest exit. He adhered to this habit because he could never be certain whether it would be a night that Rosie might be visited by District 3 cops, who had orders to shut him down and jail a few patrons at least twice a year. The infractions for which Rosie usually got cited, fire-code violations or disorderly conduct, never illegal gambling, resulted in no more than a $500 fine and an occasional night in jail. The raids kept the white community, Denver's two dailies, the black churches, and legal Colorado gaming interests appeased, secure in the knowledge that "the gangsters and thugs" of Five Points were being kept in check.

In truth, the unlawful mob of black folks involved in the illegal pursuit of trying to win twenty bucks were mostly hardworking brick masons, teachers, custodians, and meter maids looking for a release from their daily grind and finding it in three hours of freedom at the den.

Entering with an eye out for an exit, CJ was amazed to find the room only half full. Surprised by the lack of customers, he headed for the bar, where Rosie's chief mechanic, Monroe Garrett, was busy tending bar.

"What'll it be?" asked Monroe, wiping his hands on a

fraying automotive shop towel, then slapping the damp towel onto the bar with a loud whack.

"Negra Modelo."

Monroe reached beneath the bar into a washtub filled with ice, pulled out CJ's favorite Mexican beer, popped the top, and slid the bottle and a mug across the bar.

"Quiet tonight, wouldn't you say, Monroe?"

"It's a Nuggets night. Ain't you heard? Basketball's the great Denver pastime. That and screwin' my man. Besides, last week Rosie had a run-in with Councilman Deavers over his monthly kickback fee. Word on the street has it that ten to one it's our night to get a visit from the cops."

CJ nodded understandingly and took a sip of beer from the bottle before pouring the rest into the mug. "Where's Rosie?"

"Last I saw of him, he was sittin' at one of the high-stakes poker tables in the back, yammerin' with that half-breed-lookin' doctor friend of yours, Bales. Surprised to see Bales down here in the Points on his own. He's usually stuck to you like glue." Then, looking philosophical and stroking his chin, Monroe added, "He's got a strange look in his eyes tonight, if you ask me, though, CJ. And on top of it, poor son of a bitch looks like he slept in his clothes."

Surprised that Monroe had recognized Henry, much less recalled his name, since he could remember Henry setting foot in the den only rarely, CJ eyed the back of the room.

Squinting into the room's cloud of smoke for Henry, CJ slipped out his wallet, extracted three one-dollar bills, and slapped them down on the bar. Then, beer mug in hand, he headed for the back of the room, nodding quick greetings to people on the way.

Rosie and Henry were seated at a rickety card table next to a fire exit. Thumping his mug down on the table, CJ eyed the fire door and exchanged a high-five with Rosie, the six-foot-three-inch, thick-necked, 250-pound, redheaded behemoth of a man who had been his closest friend since first grade. Rosie shot back an infectious smile. "How's it hanging, CJ?"

"Loose." Moving toward Henry, CJ knotted his fist and tapped the top of Henry's extended fist lightly, the same patented greeting they had exchanged since Vietnam. Then, squeezing Henry's shoulder, CJ said, "I'm sorry about Tess."

"Thanks," said Henry, staring blank-faced out into the room.

Realizing that Henry wasn't quite ready to talk about Tess, CJ sat down, his back to the wall. "Slow tonight, isn't it, Red?" said CJ, calling Rosie by the high school nickname he allowed only his wife and a handful of close friends to use.

"Gotta learn to take the heat with the cold, CJ. Especially when you're dealing with sin."

"And the bitter with the sweet," added Henry, sounding defeated.

Thinking he had never heard Henry sound so down, CJ said, "How are you holding up?"

"Better than earlier. Guess blabbering on to Rosie about Tess and the whole telomerase scheme for the past twenty minutes has helped."

"Helped my ass." Rosie rolled his eyes. "Henry's been trying to get me to hook him up with a piece. I've been telling him to stick to curing disease. Let the police handle this Gilliam situation. Maybe you can set him straight, CJ. All a gun's ever done for anybody in situations like this is turn a page of trouble into a whole damn book."

"And maybe cost some fool their medical license," said CJ, looking Henry directly in the eye.

"I'm a big boy, CJ. I understand the risks."

"Good, because I'd hate to see you pulling the midnight shift at Denver General emptying bedpans for a living, wishing you'd thought this thing through before you did something stupid enough to make you lose your meal ticket. Who the hell you planning to shoot, anyway?"

Henry shrugged without answering.

"Glad to see you've thought everything through. Now, before you run off playing vigilante, why don't we take a minute to consider things for real? Maybe we can piece the puzzle together well enough to drop it in that cop Menton's lap and save me ever having to bond your irrational ass out of jail."

Henry shook his head. "This can't be CJ Floyd the bounty hunter giving advice. Not the same man who once chained a bond-skipping wife beater to the bed of a pickup, drove him back from Cheyenne to Denver, and dumped him in the lobby of a police substation, threatening, if I remember right, 'to circumcise his ass' if he ever beat his wife again."

CJ gave Henry a deadpan look. "No, it's just CJ Floyd, your friend."

Henry took a sip of beer, plunked down his glass, and again stared blankly off into space.

Hoping to defuse the tension, Rosie said, "I vote for reexamining that puzzle you mentioned, CJ."

"You up for some straight talk, Henry?" asked CJ, realizing that rehashing the details surrounding Tess's death would be painful.

Henry nodded, offering a weak "Yes."

"Okay," said CJ, easing back in his chair. "Here's my take on the whole thing. And most of it hinges on what I found out on my trip to Boulder. Somehow your boy Cardashian stumbled onto a potential fountain of youth that he packaged in the form of a suppository that looks something like a bath-oil bead. He tries the shit on himself and a swimmer who's an odds-on favorite to take a gold medal at the Olympics. Turns out this stuff's a hell of a lot more potent than Cardashian thinks, and he ends up killing them both." CJ glanced at Rosie, who was taking in his comments wide-eyed.

"Problem is, there's a little speed bump in Cardashian's scheme. Tess Gilliam also knows the lay of the land. Before Cardashian dies, Tess calls in Sandi Artorio to help her unravel the scheme. Next thing we know, Tess is dead.

"The way I see it, we've got three probable killers, maybe four. David Patterson, that CU swimming-team doctor. I know he's hiding something. I've got Julie trying to find out what. There's the Tanner girl's father. A real piece of work. Reactionary, demanding, just the kind of daddy every girl wants. Could be he wanted Olympic gold bad enough to sacrifice his daughter. Julie's on his case too. There's the swimming coach, Ellis Drake. He didn't strike me as a killer, but for some reason he's sure protecting Patterson. And finally, there's the Tanner girl's boyfriend, an athletic trainer named Anthony Rontella who's conveniently out of town. According to Drake, he's down in your neck of the woods, Henry, visiting with coaches at Fort Lewis College over on the Western Slope."

"Is there any way the four of them fit?" asked Henry, deep in thought.

"Don't know how yet. Maybe Julie will dig up some connections. I plan to check on Drake myself. He's been coaching around here for thirty years; should be able to turn up something on him. To tell you the truth, though, I'd lay money on Rontella being the common thread."

"Why's that?"

"Believe it or not, because of a tattoo. While I was in Boulder, Drake showed me a group photo of him, Patterson, Rontella, the Tanner girl, and her father. In the photo Rontella had an unusual tattoo on his right arm. A couple of crossed rowing oars. The exact same tattoo Cardashian had."

"That's the connection," said Henry, suddenly animated. "Has to be. Cardashian was supplying telomerase gels to Rontella, and Rontella was supplying Leah Tanner. Rontella's the one we want, CJ. I'd bet on it."

"Sounds good to me," said Rosie, nodding in agreement.

"Maybe so. But right now Rontella's six hours away."

"Six hours by car, CJ. It's only an hour by plane. Rontella could've killed Tess and been back in Durango in the time it takes to see a movie," said Henry.

"Okay, let's say Rontella's our key. There're still some things that don't fit. One has to do with the way Tess was killed. I checked with Menton. I had to drag it out of him, but he finally told me that Tess died from a single gunshot to the base of the skull. Real professional-sounding, not like some lucky shot from a gofer middle-man athletic trainer."

Henry frowned. "He's an experienced athletic trainer, CJ. He'd know where to put a bullet if he had to. Rontella's the tag line in this. Mark my words."

"What's in it for him?" asked CJ.

"Cardashian probably paid him to supply the Tanner girl."

"Too short-term a profit," countered CJ. "One score and Rontella's done."

"Then he's got more athletes to supply?"

Nodding in agreement, CJ said, "Certainly would give him a reason for visiting colleges over on the Western Slope, wouldn't it?"

"Sure would. Especially since we don't know how many cigar boxes full of telomerase gels there are floating around."

"Damn," said Rosie. "You mean to tell me you're after some kind of steroid bagman?"

"I wish," said Henry. "What this guy's peddling makes steroids look like sugar cubes."

Whistling loudly, Rosie said, "Shit."

"So do we go after Rontella first?" asked Henry.

"Slow down, Henry. We'll need more than my tattoo theory and a hunch that Rontella's peddling pills to athletes to pin this whole thing on him. I still want to hear what Julie digs up on Patterson and old Daddy Dearest Nathan Tanner before I cast my vote."

"Suit yourself, but I still think Rontella's our man."

Rosie nodded in agreement.

"If so, where'd he get the magic telomerase pills?"

"From Cardashian," said Henry.

"Don't think so. Cardashian wouldn't have been stupid enough to give his bagman enough magic beads to set himself up in business."

"He could have stolen them."

"Then why kill Tess?"

"I'm not sure."

"Me either." CJ wrapped his hands around his beer mug. "But I've got a hunch. I think Tess may have understood more about what was going on with this whole fountain-of-youth scam than any of us think."

"CJ, please!"

"Not in the way you're thinking, Henry. I know Tess wouldn't have been involved in anything unethical. But think about this for a moment. Before I visited Coach Drake and stumbled across the Cardashian-Rontella tattoo connection, we didn't know that athletes were being targeted. In fact, until Vernon clued us in, we didn't even know that Cardashian and Leah Tanner had died from the same thing. Your focus and Sandi's has been to try and zero in on the longevity aspect of Cardashian and Tess's research, prove that Cardashian's gels are some kind of superhighway to everlasting life, right?"

"Yes."

"Well, what if you're on the wrong interstate?"

"What?"

"Consider this. There's no way you can convince me that a bunch of college kids hoping to swim faster, shoot better hoops, or run the hundred-yard dash in nothing flat are looking for some kind of longevity pill. They'd want a quick fix, not some pie-in-the-sky magic pill designed to make them live forever. Winning now would be their goal. Any reason to think our missing gels could give an athlete that kind of boost?"

"I'm not sure. Sandi would be the one to ask."

"Then let's ask her. It might be the key to why Tess was killed. Could be she unraveled Cardashian's scam just enough to figure out who was pulling his strings. I want you and Sandi to dig though Tess's research files and see if you can't come up with something about the missing telomerase gels that could have cost her her life."

"I'm not sure what we'll be looking for."

"Shit, Henry, you're the scientist. Look for whatever the hell you look for when you're trying to solve one of your research problems."

Frowning, Henry said, "I still think we ought to be going after Rontella."

"He'll keep."

"Backing off him might end up costing more people their lives. Hope you haven't forgotten about what killed Cardashian and the Tanner girl?"

"I haven't forgotten. But pissing up a rope's a lot harder than aiming for the stool. I understand how upset you are about Tess, and I know that right now it looks like Rontella's the perfect person to land on. But give my idea a shot, at least for the short run, Henry. Maybe Tess came up with something she didn't have a chance to discuss with you and Sandi. It could be the person we need to put the squeeze on is right here in Denver."

CJ was about to begin another round of persuasion when Monroe Garrett eased up next to Rosie, and whispered loudly enough for CJ to hear, "We've got cops on the way."

Easing up from his chair and moving toward the exit,

Rosie nodded for CJ to do the same. "Time to move it, homes."

CJ grabbed Henry by the arm, nearly jerking him out of his seat.

"What the—?"

"Pretend we're back in country and VC are on the way," said CJ, nudging Henry toward the exit. "It's haul-ass time."

By the time they stepped out into the alley, a half-dozen people were on their heels. Suddenly the garage-side entrance to the den exploded off its hinges from the force of a battering ram, and four mule-faced policemen rushed inside.

"Run," shouted CJ, streaking down the alley as a platoon of cops swarmed into the den, guns drawn, knocking over card tables, slamming roulette wheels with their billy clubs, and screaming, "Everyone against the wall!" By then Rosie slammed the fire door shut.

Thirty yards down the alley, CJ slowed and looked back toward the den.

"What about Rosie?" said Henry, pulling up next to him, out of breath and panting.

Bending over, hands on his knees, CJ said, "He'll be fine. It's just the cost of doing business down in the Points. His lawyer's probably already downtown waiting to post his bond. Tomorrow Rosie and one of our full-of-shit city councilmen will renegotiate their monthly contract, and everything will turn out hunky-dory."

"You mean the cops are just playing games?"

"They're just poker chips, Henry. Used to up the ante."

"And Rosie? What's he anteing up?"

CJ straightened, looking back over his shoulder to make sure they were safely out of danger, and smiled. "Cash, Henry, cold, hard cash," he said as they moved from the alley into the glow of a flickering corner street-light. "The same thing that's driving Cardashian's telomerase scam. The only difference is that for Cardashian the payoff was bigger and his project could end up costing a lot of people their lives."

Henry found himself thinking about Tess once again as he considered whether CJ's game plan was the correct way to settle a very personal score. Debating whether to spend the next few days digging through Tess's research files on the off chance that something might be there to help them, as CJ suspected, or to head after Rontella, he followed CJ out of the streetlight's glow still haunted by the fact that by jet Anthony Rontella and Colorado's Western Slope were only an hour away.

Chapter 35

"There hasn't been any activity since Floyd came home last night." Manuel Hernández sat up from his slouch in the front seat of the rental car he had parked two houses north of CJ's office and took a sip of lukewarm coffee, silently cursing Sweets and a sinus-splitting migraine while he talked to Jamie Lee Custus on a cell phone. Bondsman's Row was strangely quiet except for the throaty engine noise of an idling RTD bus sitting at the corner of Delaware Street and 14th, half a block away.

Parked across the street from Mavis Sundee's Five Points home, Jamie Lee was several hours into her own stakeout. Her dashboard ashtray was brimming with stubbed-out cigarettes and an empty 7-Eleven Big Gulp container, and a pair of shopworn binoculars rested next to her on the front seat. It was just past eight A.M. and she was suffering through a painful cramp in her bad leg that had kept her up most of the night.

"Wait a minute." Hernández uncoiled from his slouch and tried unsuccessfully to shake off his migraine as he watched the front door of the building next to CJ's swing open. Julie Madrid darted off her porch, glanced in his direction, cut across CJ's lawn, and sprinted up the steps onto CJ's porch and into the house.

Hernández inched back down in his seat as a car sped past. "It's somebody from the building next door. A woman." Hernández slipped a pair of stubby Russian-made binoculars up to his eyes. "What a set of tits. Wait a minute, a car just pulled off the street into the driveway between the two buildings. Damn. Must be a fuckin' female convention. Got another one getting out of the car. Son of a bitch," said Hernández, his Spanish accent suddenly turning thick. "This one's a goddamn Amazon, and she's black. Six-one if she's an inch. Plain-faced and no tits, but she's got a set of legs on her like you see on those pantyhose commercials on TV. Bet she could crack your walnut give her half a chance."

"Do you ever think with your brain instead of your pecker, Hernández?"

"*Bete a la chinqada,* Custus."

"No, you kiss mine, you little worm. Try concentrating on what you're supposed to for a change instead of every piece of ass that strolls by. Have you seen any sign of the Artorio woman?"

"No. I'd recognize that sweet little ass for sure. Nobody's approached the building all morning except for the Amazon and her friend with the trophy rack. The first one looked Latina, but she's definitely not the Artorio woman." Hernández refocused his binoculars. "Hold on, the front door's opening. A big black guy just stepped out onto the porch with the first woman. Fucker's a couple of inches taller than the Amazon. Has to be our boy Floyd. Now they're going back inside."

"Damn. I hope the Artorio woman hasn't given us the slip. I can't spend all day chasing her down. I've got a two o'clock flight to Durango."

"What about the doctor Sweets said you might have to take out?"

"Bales?" Jamie Lee smiled securely. "His truck was still parked at the university and the lights in the lab were on when I pulled the plug on my parking-lot surveillance around five. Can't be in two fuckin' places at once. Besides, Sweets said the Artorio woman is more important. So I'm sticking to her. I sort of figured she or Bales would show up at that bondsman's office sooner or later. Sweets claims that Floyd's their muscle. Guess I was wrong."

"Want me to stick around here?"

"Yeah. I'll stay put here for a while. If one of them shows up on your end before I head for Durango, let me know. And Hernández, don't forget your job's to keep up with them while I'm gone."

"Not a problem. What does Sweets want us to do about them, anyway?"

"Whatever it takes. They know too much about the gels. Sweets thinks they may have even kept a few samples for themselves. I want them as a pair if it comes down to it. Always makes things easier and a lot less messy."

"Then it's your problem. Settling scores for Sweets

back in Cuba's one thing. It's a whole different deal here in the States."

"What's the matter, Hernández? Got cold feet?"

"No. I just don't like the wet-dog smell of your American prisons. Besides, killing women is more your line of work. Does the name Gilliam ring a bell?"

Checking her temper, Jamie Lee took a deep breath. "Let me clue you in on a couple of things, you little rodent. First, until you see me pop somebody with your own fucking eyes, don't start pinning murders on me, and second, you're in this until Sweets says you're not."

"Whatever you say." Hernández adjusted the phone in one hand and gave Custus the finger with the other.

Agitated, Jamie Lee picked up her binoculars from the console and scanned the perimeter of Mavis's house one more time. "Nothin' shakin' here," she said finally, watching a squirrel scamper up a nearby tree and onto one of the eaves of Mavis's house. The quaint Queen Anne reminded her of the house she'd lived in as a child before her father left and her mother remarried a long-haul trucker who had constantly threatened and beaten them both as if they were loading-dock scabs.

"Here either," said Hernández.

"I'll stick another half hour. You do the same. And Hernández, remember, if you fuck this up, I've got something for you."

"I'm shakin' in my boots," said Hernández, laughing. "I'll call you if I need to," he added, pushing the end button on his cell phone.

Shaking her head and wondering how she had ever been stupid enough to hook up with Hernández, Jamie Lee glanced down at her leg. Her ankle was tingling and more than double its normal size. Swinging her leg up onto the transmission hump, she reached down and felt along her calf, aware that the last time her leg had gone totally numb, she had ended up needing more surgery.

Unable to elicit any feeling, she scratched at her leg until it started to bleed, stopping only when rivulets of blood streamed down her calf and the leg erupted in pain. Satisfied that she still had at least some feeling, she pulled a wad of Handi Wipes out of a backpack on the floor and dabbed away the blood. Then, slipping the tissues back, she teased her Bowie knife out of the backpack and admired it briefly before stuffing it back in.

Chapter 36

CJ savored the nutty-sweet flavor of the last of the pumpkin-walnut muffins Flora Jean had baked earlier in the week, washed it down with a slug of bitter coffee, and frowned at Flora Jean.

"I've told him to wait for me to get to work to start the coffee," said Flora Jean, looking up at Julie from her perch on the arm of one of the two squat-legged leather chairs that had occupied opposite corners of CJ's office since his uncle had started the bail-bonding business in 1946.

Julie, who avoided the chairs at all costs because they smelled too musty, sat in the room's bay-window seat, craning to see through the glass. Turning toward CJ, Julie shook her head in disgust. "That car was out here when I came to work at six. It's been there almost three hours. Somebody's doing surveillance, CJ, and you're the goldfish."

CJ set his coffee aside. "There's no way you can see who's in that car from where you're sitting, Julie, unless you can see around corners. Let me check it out from up-stairs."

"Go ahead, and while you're up there, maybe you should try your hand at figuring out how to brew coffee," said Flora Jean, turning up her nose at the cup of coffee CJ had poured for her earlier and pushing it aside. "I don't want any more of this foul-tastin' syrup interfering with the taste of my muffins."

CJ eyed Flora Jean apologetically. Rising quickly from his chair, he was across the room, down the hallway, and halfway up the steps to the apartment above his office where he lived before Flora Jean had the opportunity to hit him with a second barrage.

A few minutes later he returned, smiling. "Cream-colored Taurus. Last year's model. One occupant. Couldn't tell if it was a man or a woman, but they're wearing a green windbreaker and they're checking us out, all right. Your place and mine," he said, looking at Julie. "Here's the plate number." CJ slipped a piece of paper out of his vest pocket and handed it to Flora Jean. "How about call-ing your girlfriend at Motor Vehicles, the one who always demands her money up front, and find out who owns that car?"

"Sadie's upped her price," said Flora Jean. "Says that with her new supervisor and the fancy new security log-on rules they've got down at DMV, pulling ownership data on people can be damn risky. Claims it could cost her her job."

"What's her new price?"

"Forty bucks."

"That's almost double!"

"I'll spot you the difference," said Julie, interrupting. "I don't like being tailed."

"No need," said CJ. "I like it even less. Tell Sadie we need the info in a hurry," he said to Flora Jean.

"I'll get her on the phone right now." Flora Jean was across the room and out of CJ's office in three quick strides.

"Who do you think it is?" asked Julie, glancing back out the window.

"One thing for sure. It's not the people from Publisher's Clearing House here to give us our million bucks."

"Quit joking, CJ. Or have you forgotten about Tess?"

"No, I haven't, and I'd wager that our friend out there in the Taurus hasn't either."

"Then why don't we turn the tables and dog his butt for a while?"

"As soon as I get an ID from Motor Vehicles, that's what I had in mind."

"Think we should tell Menton?"

"And have him scare our spotter off, or better yet collar him and then let him slip through the revolving door of the law? No, I don't want Menton in on this until I've worked my way a little further up from that bottom feeder out there to the top. In the meantime, how about filling me in on what you found out about Patterson, Tanner, and Coach Drake."

"Thought you'd never ask." Julie reached across the window seat and slipped a small spiral notepad out of the leatherbound organizer CJ had given her the day she opened her law practice. "Dug up the most on Patterson."

"Shoot."

"Socially he runs with the big boys. Comes from old-time Denver money, and he's well connected politically. Has a condo in Vail and a cattle ranch in Walden. He and his wife are perennial charity-ball boosters, and he's been a mover and shaker in the local American Cancer Society and the Colorado Historical Society for decades."

"Sounds like Dudley Doright sniffing for a cushy place to land in the Colorado history books."

"Until you check out his driving record. Three DUIs in the past three years. One DWI. But he still has a license. You and I wouldn't be moving anything up and down the streets but a shopping cart with that kind of record."

"Sounds like he knows whose palms to cross when it comes to driving. Unfortunately, that doesn't make him a killer. That Cancer Society thing's intriguing, though, especially considering the fact that cancer did in both Cardashian and Leah Tanner. There could be a connection. How about doing a little more digging in that direction?"

"Easy enough."

"What else have you got on him?"

"The state board of medical examiners hasn't catered too well to his drinking problem. A silk-stocking 17th Street lawyer I know claims that Patterson has a couple of reprimand letters in his file down at the state medical association. Word has it that if he screws up negotiating the roads again, the state board's primed to force him into a rehab program for impaired physicians."

CJ stroked his chin thoughtfully. "Rehab for impaired

physicians. Has a nice ring to it; sounds a whole lot better than a program for drunks. What about Patterson's background in the world of serious science? Any telomerase kind of fit?"

Julie checked her notes. "He did a research fellowship year following his orthopedic residency at Stanford. Studied metabolic bone diseases."

"I'll be. Maybe the good doctor's foray into science got him to thinking about manufacturing some kind of superman pill."

"What?" said Julie, frowning at CJ's assessment. "I thought this whole mess was about cooking up a potion that guarantees everlasting life, not cloning a bunch of John Elways."

"It is. But I've got a hunch it's also about giving athletes some kind of extra boost. I tried to sell Henry on the idea last night."

"Did he buy it?"

"Not totally, but at least I've got him thinking."

"CJ Floyd, scientist-at-large. Sounds impressive to me."

"Lighten up, would you? I'm just thinking out loud."

"Okay. By the way, how's Henry holding up?" Julie added, recalling how CJ had described Henry's out-of-character vengeful behavior at the den when he had called her the previous night to make certain that she knew about Tess and inform her that Henry would now be paying her attorney's fees.

"Not good, but at least I think I talked him out of trying to mete out justice himself." Relaxing back in his chair, CJ pulled a cheroot from the top drawer of his desk and lit up.

Julie pinched her nose as the smell of the cigar smoke filled the room. "You need to quit those things, CJ."

"I'm cutting back. Down to three a day. Cut me a little slack and tell me what you've found out on Drake and Tanner."

Julie shook her head. "Everyone I talked to about Drake said he's just a sweet old man, but I did tumble a couple of interesting tidbits. He's shrewd when it comes to money, and he's made a killing in the stock market the past few years. I also found out that Coach Drake's the one who got Patterson his job as the swim team's physician. And by the way, my source on all this is golden."

"Drake's good with money and looks out for his friends. Can't give the coach any jail time for that," said CJ, suspecting that Julie's source was a *Denver Post* sports writer she had been seeing.

"Sure can't. But considering the problem we're dealing with here, Drake's investment portfolio sure draws your attention."

"What's he betting his money on? Athletic gear?"

"Nope. Pharmaceutical stocks."

"My, my," said CJ, taking a lengthy drag on his cheroot. "Kiss your inside trader for me. Could be I may have missed the boat on our sweet old coach. What about Tanner?"

"Couldn't get much on him. He keeps his activities pretty close to the vest. One thing I did find out, though, is that he was taking plenty of bows for his daughter's swimming success."

"How's that?"

"The same person who gave me the scoop on Drake's investments told me that Tanner spent the last six months telling anyone who would listen that he personally rejuvenated his daughter's swimming career."

CJ frowned. "Programmed her death might be closer to the truth if Tanner's actually our man."

"Anyway, sports scene scuttlebutt has it that a year ago Leah was about to be cut from the swim team. Drake kept her on the squad only after a barrage of heavy lobbying from her father, and a miraculous out-of-nowhere improvement in her times."

"Cardashian's gels working their magic?"

"That would be my guess," said Julie, nodding. "Especially considering the curve you just threw me about the gels being custom-designed for athletes. Problem is, how do we square that with the fact that Henry and Sandi claim the gels should have transformed Leah Tanner into an ageless sea turtle, not a jackrabbit?"

"I don't know. Like I said, I'm going to have to ask them."

"Let's try Henry at work."

"I will as soon as you tell me whether your sports scene source mentioned anything to you about Leah Tanner's boyfriend, an athletic trainer named Anthony Rontella."

"No. Do I need to add him to my list?"

"Sure do. Henry's already pegged him as Tess's murderer. See if you can tie him to Drake and the pharmaceutical angle."

"I can't get around to him until this afternoon. Remember, I've got a trial pending. By the way—"

Flora Jean rushed into the room, cutting Julie off. "Sorry. Mavis is on the line for you, CJ. Says it's important."

CJ set his cheroot aside in an ashtray and picked up the phone. "Hey, good-lookin'. What's on your mind?"

Clearing her throat, Mavis adjusted the phone to her ear. "Hope this isn't an overreaction, but we might have a problem."

CJ frowned, knowing Mavis rarely overreacted to anything. "Go ahead."

"Sandi's gone. So's her luggage."

"What?"

"It gets worse, CJ. I can't reach Henry. I've tried to get him on his beeper, but he's not answering his pages. All I get is voice mail at his house, and his secretary at the medical school says he hasn't shown up for work. After what happened yesterday with Tess, I thought I'd better call you."

"Son of a bitch," said CJ, slipping the receiver away from his ear, looking up at Julie and Flora Jean. "It's Mavis. She says Henry and Sandi are AWOL."

Julie smiled. "I've heard about the body language between those two. Could be they just connected."

"Connected, my butt. Nope, this isn't about connecting. It's about Tess Gilliam and the ghost of a kid named Tommy Haskins. I should have known it. Henry's out chasing his past and blaming himself once again for not being able to protect a friend." Realizing that he'd left Mavis hanging, CJ slipped the phone back up to his ear. "I'm back."

"Who were you talking to?"

"Julie and Flora Jean."

"Oh. Any chance they know where Henry and Sandi are?"

"No. But I do. Henry's home base."

"Where?"

"Durango. To find an athletic trainer named Anthony Rontella. Henry's convinced the guy killed Tess. I can understand Henry taking off. What doesn't make sense is why Sandi would tag along."

"Maybe she wants to keep Henry from doing something stupid. She and I talked for a long time yesterday after Henry dropped her off at my place. Henry's stopped the woman in her tracks. She thinks he's Dr. Kildare and Tom Mix rolled into one."

CJ glanced back at his cheroot, picked it up, and took one last drag before stubbing it out. "I'm gonna run over to the medical school and try to track down Henry. Maybe someone over there will know where he is. If he and Sandi show up, let me know. And Mavis, good take. It may make a difference."

"Difference in what?" said Mavis, noting a hint of alarm in CJ's voice.

"If Henry's right about Rontella, the difference between Rontella staying alive and Henry killing him."

"Henry's not capable of things like that, CJ, and you know it."

CJ suddenly found himself thinking about Tess Gilliam, Tommy Haskins, a distant Vietnam jungle treeline, and the sounds of machine-gun fire. "I hope you're right. God, I hope you're right. I'll talk to you later, and don't forget, call me if either one of them turns up."

"CJ, watch yourself."

"Always do." CJ cradled the telephone and stared up at the ceiling momentarily before turning back to Julie. "Something made Henry bolt out of here in a hurry."

"Revenge?" asked Julie.

"No, it's more than that. Henry wouldn't act so impulsively without a reason, and he wouldn't go charging off after Rontella unless he had proof that Rontella killed Tess or knew who did. I wonder if it's something about the tattoos I told him about."

"Tattoos?"

"Yeah, Cardashian and Rontella had identical-looking crossed-oar tattoos on their right arms. Maybe there's a third tattoo out there, and Henry's found it."

Stroking his chin, CJ said, "When you cross-examine Coach Drake, see if you can get anything more out of him about Rontella's tattoo. When I questioned him in Boulder, he swore he'd never really paid much attention to it."

"I'll do my best."

"Good. Now back to our friend out there with the binoculars." CJ felt his belt for his pager. "When you find out who our bird dog is, page me. And Flora Jean, while I'm gone, why don't you check out the flights to Durango? I may end up needing a seat."

"Done."

Rising out of his chair, CJ said, "I'm going upstairs to check and see if our friend's still out there."

"Want me to handle him?" asked Flora Jean.

"Yes," said CJ, suspecting that their spotter was going to rue the day that he drew the task of keeping tabs on the workplace of Flora Jean Benson.

Nathan Tanner had drawn a blank with Anthony Rontella's tattoo, unable to determine how the tattoo connected Rontella to Cardashian. Looking out the windows of his thirty-second-floor office north toward Coors Field, he kept telling himself that he had wasted too much time trying to uncover what he thought for certain would turn out to be a Cardashian-inspired steroid-peddling scheme. He had paid $750 for a rapid chemical assay of one of the gels he had found in Leah's apartment, and all the outlay had gotten him was a worthless two-page printout stating that the principal ingredient in the gels was a eugenol-based vehicle commonly used in rectal suppositories and that the gel contained no evidence of steroids. Frustrated, he had sent a second gel to a research laboratory in Boston that specialized in unusual chemical assays, but it would be a week before he received any results.

Tanner turned away from the early-morning light and thought about his brief, unpleasant, and unproductive meeting with Lieutenant Clifford Menton, the cop he had learned was investigating Cardashian's death. It had taken him an hour of what lawyers disparagingly called *blueline time*, time spent suffering through the sights, sounds, and smells of an overheated police station, to decide that he was wasting his efforts trying to get anything about Cardashian out of Menton. He had left Menton's office, temples pulsating, convinced that it was time to seek another route to justice.

Rethinking his strategy and eyeing the first rush of I-25 traffic headed into the city from his perch, he decided to pursue the only remaining leads he had: Anthony Rontella and CJ Floyd.

He knew that Anthony, whom he hadn't heard from since Leah's funeral, was out of town somewhere on the Western Slope. Anthony's disappearance made him suspicious that Anthony knew more about what had happened to Leah than he had let on. Rontella he could find and deal with; Floyd was a different matter.

Walking over to his desk, he thumbed through a Rolodex, extracted a business card that said "Leland Blanding," and dialed the number at the bottom. Two secretarial transfers later he was talking to Blanding, an investigator he had used before. "It's Nate Tanner. I need you to follow a man for me, and I want you to locate another."

"Got a reason?" said Blanding without even the pretext of a return greeting.

"Is one hundred seventy-five dollars an hour reason enough?"

"Got names?"

"CJ Floyd and Anthony Rontella."

"Floyd? I've heard of him. A bail bondsman, right?"

"Yes."

"What's your beef with Floyd?"

"It's personal," said Tanner, positive that a man like Blanding didn't really care why he wanted Floyd followed.

"What do you want on him, then?"

"Not much. Where he's been, where he goes, and who he sees."

"And Rontella?"

"Find out where he is. If I have to I'll charter a plane to go talk to him. He has an office at the CU athletic department in Boulder. It's a place to start."

"How soon do you need the info?"

"ASAP."

"Fine. But I hear that Floyd's a tough SOB. It'll cost a little extra for me to shadow him."

"Whatever. Just send me the bill."

"I'm on it this minute. One question though, Mr. T. Why the cloak-and-dagger tactics? That's not like you."

Tanner found himself thinking about Leah's lifelong bout with anorexia, his selfish parental pushiness, and his lack of insight into his daughter. "Let's just say I've got a score to settle. Get back to me when you have something you think I can use."

"I will," said Blanding. "And before the day's out. You can count on it."

"Great." Tanner cradled the phone, wondering whether his strategy of trailing a worker bee like Floyd and pegging Rontella's whereabouts would pay bigger dividends than the two laboratory assays and his encounter with Lieutenant Menton.

Chapter 37

The great Western watershed known as the Continental Divide traverses Colorado for over six hundred miles as it forms the headwaters of some of America's most famous rivers, including the Platte, Colorado, and Rio Grande. Trekking its way across southwestern Colorado, the Divide snakes through the largest mountain range in the U.S. Rockies, the San Juans, as it cuts through dense forests of Engelmann spruce and subalpine fir before lumbering across the nearly 500,000-acre Weminuche Wilderness and finally streaking for the New Mexico border.

The most spectacular drive along the Divide and through the San Juans is over eleven-thousand-foot Red Mountain Pass by way of Colorado's famed U.S. Highway 550, the state's historic million-dollar highway, built in the days when a million dollars could still buy fifty miles of road blasted through mountainsides, Precambrian quartzite, black slate, and schist.

Henry Bales had been driving for six nonstop hours when he crested the pass, accelerated, fishtailing his pickup on the road's mid-morning glaze, and glanced over at Sandi, who was asleep in the seat next to him, her lips puckered into a sensual pout.

They had left Denver for Durango at five A.M, and Henry was determined to make the Flying Diamond by noon. Negotiating his way down the pass he knew like the back of his hand, he reached over and tapped Sandi lightly on the shoulder.

"Wake up, I want you to see this," he said, pointing ahead toward a staggeringly beautiful alpine valley known as Mineral Creek, bordered by red and yellow talus slides and the scores of avalanche chutes he had explored and given his own names to as a child.

Unbuckling her seat belt to stretch, Sandi peered sleepy-eyed through the windshield.

"See that silver-and-black mass off in the distance?" asked Henry, watching Sandi stretch and thinking that even after a morning of being corseted into the front seat of a pickup, she still looked beautiful. "The one that looks like a catcher's mitt between the two mountains," he added, pointing toward a range of snow-capped mountains in the distance.

Squinting into the sun, Sandi said, "Yes."

"It's a rock glacier that's been creeping down the ravine between the Grand Turk and Sultan Mountains since I was a kid. When I was growing up in these mountains, I used to swear that I could see the thing move."

Noting a nostalgic look on Henry's face, Sandi stared at the glacier for a while before asking, "Why'd you leave?"

Henry draped his hand over the steering wheel and smiled, focusing momentarily on the Needle Mountains to the southwest. "A year of studying soil conservation biology at Fort Lewis College told me that that wasn't what I wanted to do. So I left school just before my sophomore year, joined the navy, and ended up a corpsman in Vietnam. Like most nineteen-year-old country yokels looking for adventure back then, I didn't know what I was getting myself into. When I came back from the war, I knew two things. It would be a cold day in hell before I'd ever leave the shores of the U.S. again, and after seeing the human misery that was Vietnam I knew I wanted to be a doctor. Turns out the kind of doctor I became doesn't lend itself to making a living down here. Guess I traded off a way of life for a career."

"Any regrets?"

"Some. But everybody's got a few. Don't you?"

"A few," said Sandi, smiling at Henry and wondering how she could be drawn so intensely to someone she had known for such a short time. Eyeing the hard set of his jaw and the slightly cocked, sweat-stained Stetson he was wearing, she asked herself why she had agreed to break into Tess's lab the previous night, ignoring the crime-scene tape, and dig through mounds of Tess's research papers, searching for what Henry kept calling a new telomerase angle. An angle that CJ Floyd, of all people, had pitched to him. A cockeyed take that linked Tess's murder and the missing telomerase gels to enhancing the performance of athletes, not the flame of everlasting life.

After two hours of searching they had stumbled onto what Henry thought might be the answer to their riddle: a batch of twelve photographs taken through an electron microscope and stuffed in a tattered X-ray folder Velcroed to the underside of the seat of Tess's wheelchair. They had found the folder only after Henry stood in the middle of the lab in frustration, gyrating in circles and asking himself out loud, *Where would Tess hide a key?* One side of the folder sported a perfectly drawn circle with the Roman numeral two in the center. The word *telomerase* had been neatly printed beneath the circle.

After poring over the high-resolution photographs of cells magnified a hundred thousand times, convinced that they were somehow the answer to the telomerase puzzle but not fully understanding how or why, Henry had slammed the photos down on a countertop, looked pleadingly at Sandi, and said, "There's an athletic connection in these photos somewhere. You'll have to help me find it." Until that moment she had felt like an interloper, someone to stand at Henry's side while he exorcised his guilt over not being there when Tess needed him.

Taking the folder from Henry, she scrutinized the photomicrographs, examining them closely using magnifying lenses, looking for a tie-in between Tess, athletes, and telomerase. She was almost as frustrated as Henry when she finally noticed a tiny out-of-focus ellipse in the upper-left-hand corner of one of the photos. Examining the photo more closely, she had turned to Henry and said, "Check out the upper-left-hand corner, at ten o'clock, and tell me what you think."

Henry, who had been busy wiping down Tess's wheelchair and the adjacent countertop to remove any telltale evidence that he and Sandi had been there, stepped over to examine the photo. The ultrastructural detail of the organelles inside the cells suddenly jumped out at him as he wondered how he had missed their now obvious pathology. There, floating in a sea of cells, were a host of cell nuclei bursting with mitochondria, the cell organelles that served as the oxygen-carrying switch engines for the body.

"Oxygen mills," said Henry, almost shouting. "The cells in these photos are pregnant with them."

"O_2" said Sandi, recognizing Tess's coded periodic-table shorthand for oxygen, O and the Roman numeral II that had been written on the outside of the X-ray jacket. "How could we have missed it?"

"By thinking too much," said Henry, still staring at the photomicrograph. "Looks like while Cardashian was busy trying to crack the immortality code, he stumbled across a telomerase outlier that has more to do with telomerase giving our bodies' cells a heck of a mitochondrial boost than with programming them for everlasting life."

"And if someone needed it, an exponential shot of oxygen to take along for the ride," said Sandi. "Sure would be helpful if, say, you happened to be a world-class athlete streaking for the finish line at the end of a race."

"I'd say, and I'd wager that in the right athletic circles, Cardashian's unexpected finding would be worth its weight in gold. Ever run across a quirk like that in your own telomerase research?"

"No. I never thought to look," said Sandi, her voice quivering with guilt. "Maybe if I had, Tess would still be alive."

"No need to beat yourself up." Henry draped his arm over Sandi's shoulder and pulled her toward him. "I can do enough of that for both of us." Pulling Sandi closer, he tried to think of something else reassuring to say. Instead he found himself bending down toward her, tilting her head toward his, caressing her cheek, and kissing her soft, warm lips.

The embrace and sensuous kiss that followed seemed to linger for much longer than either of them remembered. They had left the lab hand in hand, joking about it several minutes later, convinced that, like college kids on a weekend lark, a trip to Durango would enable them to not only solve Cardashian's puzzle but put a face on Tess's killer.

Slipping her seat belt off, Sandi moved up onto her knees, leaned over, and gave Henry three quick kisses on the cheek. "Tired?" she asked, stroking his earlobe, drinking in the scenic backdrop of the Mineral Creek valley.

"Yes," said Henry, realizing that the two hours of restless tossing they had squeezed in on research cots normally reserved for overworked postdoctoral research fellows to crash on in the back of his lab could hardly count as sleep.

"Maybe we should have waited and caught a plane?"

"And risk letting whoever's in this with Rontella know not only where we were headed but what time we'd be there? No. We can catch up on our sleep when we get to the ranch. Rontella's here through tonight. CJ verified it yesterday afternoon with a cooperative CU athletic department secretary in Boulder who keeps tabs on the whereabouts of the athletic faculty and staff. He told me so on our way home from the den the other night. She even told CJ where Rontella was staying."

Sandi slipped her arm behind Henry's neck, inching up to him until he could feel the fullness of her breasts. "I thought you said Rontella was just an overzealous athletic trainer who probably linked up with Cardashian as a way to line his pockets."

Henry tapped his brakes, easing into place behind three semi trailers loaded down with cattle. "He also may have killed Tess. One thing for certain, he's not operating this telomerase scam all alone."

"Then who's giving him directions?"

"I don't know—Dr. Patterson, Nathan Tanner, his buddy the coach, Ellis Drake. I just wanted to make sure that we had good separation between us and whoever it is before I started pressuring Rontella for an answer."

"Separation? Sounds like some kind of quarterback-to-wide-receiver football speak to me."

"No, just navy lingo left over from Vietnam. It's military parlance for the distance between you and your objective."

"Or the enemy? Sounds too much like war," said Sandi, watching the cow-dung-splattered bumper of the cattle truck ahead of them rock from side to side.

Flooring the accelerator, Henry shot out into the passing lane as Sandi grabbed on to him tightly. The truck's speedometer eased upward, pegging out at ninety-two as Henry passed the last cattle truck, slipped back into his own lane, looked at a startled Sandi, and said, "Objective, enemy; sometimes they're both the same."

Chapter 38

Julie's heart was thumping as Flora Jean locked the front door to CJ's office, handed her the keys, and glanced toward the cream Taurus. "Just do exactly what we talked about inside," said Flora Jean, starting down the steps.

After learning from her source at DMV that the Taurus outside the office was an Avis rental and realizing that the only sure way of finding out who was in the car would be to take aggressive action, Flora Jean, who didn't take being stalked lightly, had devised a plan. She and Julie would leave the office, walk toward the car, and separate. Flora Jean would then continue across Delaware Street toward the jail while Julie headed for her office. Flora Jean knew that for the plan to work, the person in the car, who they now knew from repeated second-floor observations was a man, had to be distracted and the car's driver's-side door had to be unlocked. "Best way I know to attract a bee is still with a little honey," Flora Jean had said as they worked out the plan. Then, looking at Julie, she added, "And, sugar, you're the bait."

Before leaving the office Julie discarded her bra and Flora Jean pinned her blouse in back until it fit exhibitionist tight. "Here's hoping that Peeping Tom's third leg does most of his thinking," Flora Jean said, adjusting Julie's blouse one last time before leaving. "But in case it don't, I've got somethin' that'll help." Reaching into the top drawer of her desk, Flora Jean pulled out the derringer she had carried through boot camp, two years in the marines, and Desert Storm and palmed it with a smile.

Tripping on a sidewalk crack as they headed toward the car, Julie forced a tentative smile, looked straight ahead, and continued walking until Flora Jean cleared the Taurus's front bumper. Then, turning swiftly, she started jogging toward her office.

Hernández's eyes were locked on Julie's jiggling breasts when Flora Jean snatched open the door, grabbed a handful of shirt collar and windbreaker, and pulled him from the car. Hernández was on the ground with Flora Jean's knee across his throat and the stubby barrel of the derringer up his nose so quickly that all he could say was, "Shit."

"I don't like being spied on, mister. Neither does my friend." Flora Jean glanced toward Julie. "We can walk back up to the office or across the street to the jail; it's your choice," said Flora Jean, hoping that she had a few seconds more before the light at the end of Delaware Street changed and cars started moving up the street.

"Your office," said Hernández, looking cross-eyed at the gun barrel.

"Funny, I thought that's what you'd say. Let's move." Flora Jean helped the much smaller five-foot-seven Hernández to his feet. "And no funny shit, unless of course you want to swallow your own snot."

Draping her arm over Hernández's shoulder and slipping her derringer into his ear, Flora Jean said, "Just pretend we're sweethearts," as they headed back toward the office. Then, eyeing Julie, who was now at her side, she added, "As soon as we get inside, I think you'd better call that cop Menton."

Atina Salas had reached the point of exasperation. She had given up trying to reach Anthony after calling him in Denver all morning without success. Her efforts to contact her brother-in-law Manuel had also proved fruitless.

With nowhere to turn and with hundreds of thousands of tobacco scam dollars at risk because of Anthony's sudden disappearance, the only reason she had been able to maintain her composure was because of Ernesto's rapid recovery from his illness. The previous evening he had awakened from days of semicomatose sleep, immediately consumed nearly a quart of water, and asked her to prepare his favorite meal of *moros y cristianos* and *fufu*. Ernesto had wolfed down the black beans and rice and highly seasoned mashed green bananas without looking up even once.

Although he still appeared a bit disoriented as he moved around her apartment for the first time in days, at least she had the peace of mind of knowing that for the jewel of her life, the obvious danger had passed. Now what she had to do was hook up with Anthony to finalize their shipment plans or watch years of preparation and a lifetime of savings wash away.

Lieutenant Menton loosened his tie and stared across his desktop at Julie. It had been an hour and a half since Julie Madrid's frantic phone call had interrupted his coffee break. Armed with a fresh cup of coffee, he now sat in a musty room at the city jail surrounded by Julie, Flora Jean, and CJ. "I can't detain the man any longer, Ms. Madrid. Your stalking charge is as flimsy as wet tissue paper. His papers are in order, and his travel visa's good, looking at it frontways, sideways, and upside down. I'm afraid I'm going to have to let Mr. Hernández go." Then, looking at Flora Jean, he added, "In the future, Ms. Benson, I'd be a little less reckless with that derringer if I were you."

"What did he say about knowing Neil Cardashian?" asked Julie as she and Flora Jean frowned at Menton's counsel.

"Says he never heard of him."

"And Anthony Rontella?" asked CJ, who had returned from his fruitless trek to the medical school to try to locate Henry to find Menton, two squad cars, and Flora Jean in Desert Storm mode waiting for him.

"Same story."

"Damn," said Julie. "Isn't there something else we can get you to hold him for? The man's in this telomerase mess up to his eyeballs, I'm certain of it. What about the Cuban cigar box full of those gels we told you about?"

"What about it?" asked Menton, looking confused.

"He's Cuban," said CJ.

"And I'm part Greek," said Menton. "It's not a crime."

"He's working for someone. Count on it," said CJ.

"Aren't we all?" Menton shook his head. "Listen, Floyd, we've gone as far with Hernández as we can. We've got a local address on him and all the particulars concerning his return trip to Cuba. His travel documents say he represents a South American distributing firm, and according to people we called in Chicago, his business here's legit. We can't hold the man forever."

"Then why was he casing my office?"

"He says he wasn't. And he's pretty damn convincing. Speaks near perfect English."

CJ cocked an eyebrow. "Perfect?"

"Better than most of what I hear on the Denver streets."

"Damn," said CJ, giving Julie a look that said, *Menton just rang a bell.* "How old's Hernández?"

"His international driving permit says he's fifty-eight."

"Fits," said CJ, smiling.

"What fits?" asked Julie.

"His age and his command of English," said CJ, leaving Julie confused. "Did you ask him if he ever lived in the U.S.?" said CJ, directing his question to Menton.

"Yes."

"What was his answer?"

"Claims he never has."

"I'd say he's lying."

"Unfortunately, just like being parked outside your office, lying's not against the law."

"It is if it links you to a murder."

"Or to someone giving orders from higher up," Julie

281

chimed in. "How about Nathan Tanner? He practices international law. Have you taken a look at him?"

"We're doing our job, Ms. Madrid. Why don't you stick to yours? I'm getting enough pressure from above me to kiss Tanner's rear. I don't need yours. As for Hernández, he gets to go."

"Can you check one last thing for me before he leaves?" asked CJ, noting Menton's annoyance at Tanner's obvious interference in his investigation.

"Depends."

"Nothing big. I'm just curious about whether Hernández has a tattoo."

"What?"

"Indulge me for a minute, Lieutenant, and see if Hernández has a tattoo of crossed rowing oars on one of his arms."

A hint of recognition spread across Menton's face as he remembered his city dump experience and recalled the tattoo he had seen on Neil Cardashian's arm.

"Can't hurt." Menton stood up, said, "Excuse me," and left the room.

Several minutes later Menton returned smiling. "Seems as though Hernández and Cardashian share the same tattoo. And suddenly, Hernández doesn't feel like talking. I think I can arrange for him to visit us a little longer. As for you, Floyd, I want every speck of information you have on those tattoos."

CJ looked at Julie for guidance. Catching their exchange, Menton said, "Tell Mr. Floyd what I can do in the event he decides not to cooperate in a murder investigation, counselor."

"The rules favor the lieutenant, CJ."

"Guess I'd better cooperate, then," said CJ, prepared to tell Menton what he had found out during his own investigation and hoping that when he finished, he'd still have time to track down Henry Bales before he did something foolish.

Three hours of sleep were better than none, Henry told himself as he stood on his ranch house porch thinking about how to take on Rontella. Looking down the lane, he watched Sandi head back toward him with a handful of spruce cones and several small spruce branches tucked under one arm.

"Thought these would make a wonderful table spray. I found them lying on the ground beneath a huge blue spruce." Ascending the porch steps, Sandi held the branches out toward Henry.

"Fresh," said Henry, inhaling deeply, noting the burdened expression on Sandi's face and realizing that her scavenging was meant to take her mind off Tess.

"Everything is around here. How do you ever convince yourself to return to Denver?"

"Force of habit."

"Habits change." Sandi placed her cache on a nearby table and slipped her arm into Henry's. Her hair was still damp from a recent shower, and its freshness lingered as he pushed a lock off her forehead and kissed her. Relaxing into Henry's arms, Sandi slipped her hands around his neck and closed her eyes. Then, teasing Henry with a series of playful kisses, she retrieved her cones and branches, grabbed his hand, and pulled him toward the house.

Several minutes later, Sandi was arranging her spray on a dining room table that had been in the Bales family for over a hundred years. "Do you think Rontella killed Tess?" she asked Henry, who was nursing a Coke.

"I don't know. On the way down here I was certain he had. Now I'm not so sure."

"Maybe he was just a middleman."

"No. He's more than that. There's a connection we're overlooking. I'm sure of it, and I'd bet this ranch the connection's tied to those tattoos CJ spotted on Rontella and Cardashian. If I hadn't been in such a flameout over Tess, I would have investigated the link a little further before we left Denver."

"Why don't you call CJ and ask him to do it?"

"I will after I talk to Rontella myself. I want to hear his version first."

"Henry, don't you think perhaps it's time to turn this whole thing over to the police?"

Setting his Coke aside, Henry looked at Sandi thoughtfully and smiled. Then, taking her hand and squeezing it, he said, "Ever heard of the LORAN navigational system?"

"No," said Sandi, surprised by the question.

"It's navy speak, an acronym for the electronic navigational traffic cop the world uses to make sure every ship that sails stays headed in the right direction. Tess's murder damaged what I like to think of as my own internal LORAN, and I'm going to have to repair the damage my way."

"What about another guidance system?" said Sandi, walking behind Henry, slipping her hands over his shoulders, and hugging him to her. "We can work on developing one."

Smiling up at Sandi, Henry said, "I'm ready, but I still have to deal with Rontella."

Realizing that Henry's mind was made up, Sandi said, "I'm coming with you."

"Okay, but I deal with Rontella on my terms, and alone."

"Fine."

"Good." Henry gave Sandi's hand a quick squeeze, thinking as he did that his guidance systems could ill afford another hit.

Chapter 39

The Coventry Motel sat at the edge of a grove of hundred-year-old cottonwoods along the bank of the Animas River. Laid out in the shape of a boomerang, the Coventry hadn't seen an upgrade in forty years. The driveway leading up the registration area was a puzzle of crumbled asphalt, and the building's paint, once an inviting shade of white, had turned putty gray.

It was just past five P.M. when Henry nosed his truck up to the registration area's front door, looked at Sandi, and said, "Stay put."

Although the cottonwoods hadn't yet budded, the woodsy aroma and the earthy smell from the river below reminded Henry of the smells from the early springtimes of his boyhood.

"Take your jacket," said Sandi as Henry slipped out of the cab into the crisp March air.

"I won't need it."

Laying Henry's threadbare Filson jacket across her lap, Sandi let out a nervous sigh and watched Henry disappear inside the building. Beyond the cottonwoods she could hear the rush of the river. Anxious to see the waters that Henry claimed to have pulled thirty-inch trout from as a child, she was about to ignore Henry's orders to stay put in the truck when Henry reappeared, smiling.

"Eight B," he said, slipping into the cab. "Last room on the end next to the river."

"No Rontella?"

"The clerk rang his room for me, but no one answered. Figured I might as well check it out for myself."

"Henry, please don't do anything foolish," said Sandi, noting the determined look on Henry's face.

"Can't. I've got you here to make sure I don't."

Recalling that she had seen a gun case at the ranch, Sandi thought about asking Henry if he was armed but decided against it when she remembered that the case was filled only with shotguns and rifles.

The noise from the river increased as they headed toward the far end of the motel. "The river's really loud," she said as Henry pulled up in front of 8B and switched off the truck's engine.

"That's because there's a twenty-foot dropoff just upstream from here. You ought to hear it during peak runoff. Sounds like a locomotive." Patting Sandi's hand, he moved to leave the truck. "If Rontella's here, I'll try and make it quick. If he's not, I'll be right back." Henry was out of the pickup and standing at the door to 8B before Sandi could respond.

The flimsy weathered door wobbled in the jamb as Henry knocked. After several unanswered knocks, he looked around at Sandi and shrugged. Then, grasping the doorknob on the off chance that the door might be unlocked, he turned the knob. The unstable knob jiggled in his hand as he opened the door and stepped into a dingy stale-aired, mustard-carpeted room with cinder block walls, a single overhead light, and twin beds without headboards. One bed was unmade, and a pair of faded blue running shorts lay balled up on the floor at the foot of the other. A doorless bathroom, neon vanity light flickering, sat immediately to his right.

Flipping on an overhead light, Henry canvassed the room, checking beneath the beds and behind the bathroom shower curtain for any sign of Rontella. Ending his search in frustration, he sat down on the unmade bed and looked toward the doorway disappointedly just as Sandi entered the room. "You weren't supposed to budge from the truck!"

"You were taking too long. I got nervous."

"Damn it, Sandi! Rontella could have been in here with a gun."

"Sorry," said Sandi, scanning the depressing excuse for a room. "What did you find?" she said, hoping to ease the tension.

"He was here. But it looks like all he left behind is an unmade bed and a pair of jogging shorts." Henry leaned down and picked up the knotted-up shorts. As he turned them inside out to examine them, his eyes widened in astonishment. The waistband was wet with blood. "Looks like whoever was wearing these babies had themselves a bleeding problem," said Henry, wiping his bloodstained fingers on the legs of the shorts.

"Rontella?"

"It's his room."

"Think someone beat us to him?"

"It's a safe bet."

"Why would they leave behind bloody shorts?"

"Beats me. But if I had to guess, I'd say someone was in a real hurry." Henry folded the shorts into a compact square.

"You're not going to take them?"

"Sure am. They're evidence."

"Suppose he comes back?"

"Then I'll give him back his shorts. But judging from the amount of blood absorbed into the waistband, I'd say that whoever was wearing them probably isn't coming back." Slipping the shorts under his arm, Henry looked around the room one last time. "Let's get out of here," he said, shaking his head as he grabbed Sandi's hand and moved to leave the room, worried that he was starting to take murder a little too much in stride.

She was cold, wet, and bruised, and her bad leg was throbbing, but she had solved her Rontella problem, and she had the gels. She hadn't expected to find such a small man when she surprised Rontella in his motel room at three o'clock in the afternoon instead of waiting for their appointed meeting at eight.

Shivering as she struggled up the riverbank toward the highway, Jamie Lee wondered what she would do with Rontella's duffel bag full of clothes. She could always burn them or bury them, she told herself, adjusting the bag's strap on her shoulder as she reached the highway to a rush of diesel fumes from a passing semi.

From her perch on the highway's shoulder, the river noise below was less deafening, and for the first time since she had surprised Rontella, she had a chance to rethink what she had done and consider whether she had made any mistakes. She had dragged a dazed and bleeding Rontella from his motel room down to the river, pleased that the belly stick she had given him had taken all the fight out of him. But she had misjudged Rontella's will, and when she reached the river fall, where she planned to let the Animas current solve her problem forever, Rontella had summoned a burst of energy and pulled her into the river with him seconds after she had set aside his clothes and the precious gels. They had bumped downstream grasping one another for almost thirty yards, rebounding off jagged rocks and boulders, before she had been able to free herself from Rontella's grip, grab a tree limb, and watch the river sweep Rontella away.

Now, shivering and with her teeth chattering loudly, Jamie Lee looked up the highway and thought about the mile-and-a-half trek back to her car. Stepping back from the shoulder into a thicket of willows, she dropped Rontella's duffel bag to the ground, knelt, unzipped it, and poked around, finally pulling out a University of Colorado sweatshirt. Slipping on the sweatshirt and enjoying its warmth, she continued rummaging through the duffel in hopes of finding a pair of sweatpants as well. But all she found were T-shirts, soiled underclothes, and the twelve giant ziplock bags chock-full of the telomerase gels that she had gotten Rontella to admit he was carrying before she stabbed him.

She was rezipping the duffel when she spotted a badly faded T-shirt. An arrow of fear shot straight through her as she remembered the faded blue jogging shorts she had used to plug up Rontella's stab wound and keep him from bleeding all over the motel room. The shorts weren't in the bag, and she couldn't remember what she had done with them. Panic-stricken over the possibility that she had left behind something that could tie her to Rontella's death, she swung the duffel bag over her shoulder, mouthed, "Fuck!" and started her trek back toward her car. She really didn't have a problem, she told herself, increasing her gait. Once she got to the car, it wouldn't take her more than a couple of minutes to swing back by the motel and police Rontella's room a final time.

Suddenly the wind kicked up and a cold rush of air sent her into a series of new shivers. Glancing across the highway toward miles of sagebrush prairie and rolling hills, she told herself that soon she'd be warm and safe and that once she delivered the gels to Sweets, she would never do another crazy person's bidding again.

Chapter 40

The thirty-two-seat turboprop was on its second bumpy approach to the Durango airport after aborting its first due to wind turbulence and snow. The plane's white-knuckled passengers were fearfully quiet, and except for a baby crying softly in a front-row seat and the suddenly talkative old cowboy occupying the seat next to CJ, only the plane's droning engines and the rush of air over the wings filled the cabin. CJ's seat partner, a weathered man wearing cowboy boots and worn jeans, had that close-to-the-earth look and the hard, lean body of a man who had worked the land all his life.

"Headed for Durango on business or pleasure?" said the man, whose thinning hair was pressed pancake flat against his head, courtesy of the sweat-stained Resistol cowboy hat he had tucked into the overhead compartment as they boarded.

"Business," said CJ. Aggravated at having made half a dozen calls to the Flying Diamond and never connecting with Henry, he shot the man a brief glance and stared out the window.

"Won't see nothin' out there today; too stormy. Folks around here call it March madness. Just like that college basketball tourney you see on TV. Snow one day, sunshine the next." Staring across CJ and out the window, the man smiled. "Looks like today came up snow."

Ignoring the man, CJ's thoughts turned back to his city jail encounter with Lieutenant Menton and Manuel Hernández. It had been Menton who had put the fear of God into Hernández—an easy task, according to Menton, once he pieced together the tattoo connection among Hernández, Cardashian, and Rontella. CJ had no idea exactly what Menton had told Hernández to get him to cooperate, but he knew it involved convincing Hernández that he was going to take the fall for Tess Gilliam's murder and likely spend the rest of his life in an American jail if he didn't play ball.

In an attempt to gain a fuller measure of cooperation from CJ, Menton had confided that Hernández, Cardashian, and Rontella's tattoos were symbols of their cross-generational ties to the sport of rowing. CJ had no way of knowing Hernández had also told Menton that he and Cardashian had spent two years in college together prior to the Castro revolution as members of the University of Pennsylvania's varsity crew. Beyond that, Hernández wasn't talking, especially about who might be pulling his strings.

Suspecting that Menton had told him only selected bits of what he and Hernández had discussed, CJ thanked Menton for his diligence in pursuing Tess Gilliam's murderer and hastily left Menton's office with Flora Jean and Julie, keeping his own hole card—the information he had on Anthony Rontella—to himself.

Bumping down through five thousand feet with the plane pitching and squeaking, CJ wondered how Julie was doing with her background checks on Dr. David Patterson, Nathan Tanner, and Coach Ellis Drake.

"Won't be much longer," said CJ's cowboy companion, stretching his legs. "Where you headed in Durango?"

"The Flying Diamond Ranch."

The man nodded. "Good outfit. Been run by the Bales family for over a hundred years. The foreman's a close friend of mine."

"Scotty MacCallum?" said CJ, wondering why in all the years he had been helping Henry with springtime branding he had never met the man seated next to him.

"You know Scotty?"

"Sure do."

The old cowman beamed. "I'll be damned. Ain't that a coincidence. How do you know him?"

"By way of Henry Bales. Henry and I've been friends since Vietnam."

Every muscle in the old man's face suddenly went slack, and his eyes turned cloudy. "Lost my son in that war," he said, his voice barely a whisper.

CJ said, "Sorry," sensing that he had inadvertently pulled a scab off an old wound.

"Thanks," said the man as the plane pitched sideways,

buffeting headwinds as it broke through the airport's seven-hundred-foot ceiling.

"By the way, name's William Haskins," the man added. "Friends call me Will. Do a little ranching around here myself."

CJ swallowed hard as he reached across the seat to shake hands. "CJ Floyd," he said, almost afraid to ask what was on his mind. Finally he asked tentatively, "Your son's name wouldn't have been Tommy, would it?"

"It was," said the man, looking at CJ thoughtfully as he relaxed his grip.

"I knew your son," said CJ, watching the old man's reticent expression flicker into a smile.

"He was a good boy," said Haskins, relaxing back in his seat as the plane touched down. They were halfway to the gate before Haskins spoke up again. "Got a ride to the Flying Diamond?"

"No."

"You got one now. And maybe when you and Henry get your business settled, you can drop by my place, have yourself a drink. Don't stock anything but Coors and Jack Daniel's. But they seem to work for most folks."

"Thanks, we'll make it a point to come by," said CJ, barely able to keep from telling Haskins that in a sense it had been his son's spirit that had driven Henry back home.

CJ glanced out the plane's window one last time. The glow from the plane's running lights beaming into the falling snow reminded him of the streaming pattern of anti-aircraft fire. Caught in a momentary trance, he sat motionless.

"You comin'?" said Haskins, finally tapping CJ on the shoulder.

"Yeah," said CJ, turning away from the window, rising, and stepping into the aisle.

"Good. For a moment there, I thought you were considering staying behind."

"Not on your life," said CJ, following Haskins down the aisle, wondering whether Henry had ever told the old man the impact his son's death had had on him.

Chapter 41

Sounds like a personal problem," said Sweets, pacing the entryway of the family retreat, speaking into a cell phone. "Just deliver my gels."

"Didn't you hear me? I used the shorts to plug up a stab wound in Rontella's belly. And they're gone." Jamie Lee adjusted the cell phone to her ear with a scowl and leaned back against the headboard of her rock-hard motel room bed. "Who knows, the way they can type DNA these days, my calling card's probably all over the damn things."

"Then you'd better find those jogging shorts, hadn't you? You're the one who decided to pay Rontella a surprise visit instead of waiting until you were supposed to meet with him. You should have stuck with the plan."

"Don't lecture, Sweets. I had my reasons. And don't

forget, I also have your gels. Help me with this, or I'll dump the damn things off a mountaintop. They don't mean a fucking thing to me."

"Hold on," said Sweets, aware that Jamie Lee usually meant what she said. "You're positive it was Bales and the Artorio woman who searched Rontella's motel room?"

"Of course I am. Who else would be down here snooping around? Besides, when I called the motel reception clerk, told him I was Rontella's girlfriend, and asked whether the friends we had been expecting had shown up, the clerk described Bales and his truck to a T. Even told me that the woman who waited for him in the truck when he was there looked Spanish."

"You do have a problem."

"Consider this for a moment, Sweets. If I do, then so do you."

"Meaning?"

"Meaning I've done some checking on you, my friend. I can hit you where you live."

"That wouldn't be wise."

"Neither is spending your money on dozens of phone numbers that you think can't be traced, gadgets that disguise your voice, or talkative couriers. You should know that for the right price in America, you can find out about anything and anyone."

Taken by surprise, Sweets grimaced. "Give me a for instance."

"Sure. I know you're talking to me from Golden. Cost me five hundred to find that out. I know those precious gels of yours took out a swimmer named Leah Tanner as well as Cardashian. And I know that the contraption you're using to disguise your voice is an electrolarynx, you schizoid freak. I finally pegged the Robby-the-Robot sound when I realized it was the same one I heard coming from throat cancer rehabs while I was rehabing my leg."

"What do you want?" said Sweets, more concerned about Custus knowing where the call was coming from than anything else.

"Simple. A little more money. The kind I'm going to need to vanish for a while after I deal with Bales and Artorio."

"Give me a number."

"Fifty thousand."

"Too steep."

"The price isn't negotiable, Sweets. Especially if you don't want to end up kissing off your precious gels."

"Fucker," said Sweets, cupping a hand over the phone's mouthpiece.

"Now, now. No need to be rude. Just tell me when I get my fifty."

"I can have it to you by tomorrow afternoon."

"Come on, we both know the electronic world we live in can deliver cash faster than that."

"But airlines can't. I'll be in Durango by noon tomorrow to pick up the gels."

"And the money?" said Jamie Lee.

"I'll have it for you; don't wet your pants. I'll call you with a place we can meet once I'm there."

"No. I'll meet you at the airport. A nice safe public place where everyone can see us. After we hook up there we can finish our business wherever you like."

"Not very trusting, are you, Custus?"

"Certainly I am. I just wouldn't appreciate being set up. By the way, how will I recognize you?"

Sweets paused and looked thoughtfully around the entryway before walking over to an elephant's-foot cane rack, extracting a cane, and slipping off the handle that doubled as a .32. "I'll be carrying a cane."

"Better bring a coat and boots with you too. It's snowing like hell down here."

"I'll have a coat draped over my arm. The coat and cane will be your cue."

"Nice and tidy. I like that. Got a flight number?"

"No. But United Express has a flight that'll have me there by noon. I've taken it before. And Custus, as for your other problem with Bales and Artorio, you'll have to solve that one on your own."

"Any more advice?"

"No."

"Then we'll settle up tomorrow." Jamie Lee cradled the phone and glanced out her window at the snow. Sitting up in bed she picked up her Bowie knife from the nightstand beside her, preparing herself for the task and freezing temperatures she was about to face and reminding herself that if Sweets stepped too far out of line, it would be just as easy to kill him as the Artorio woman and Bales. Then, laying the knife aside, she picked the phone back up and dialed a Denver number Anthony Rontella had given her before she stabbed him, certain that the call would solve her problem with Sweets once and for all.

Chapter 42

Except for the intermittent fits of wind and the muted bawling of a few cows, the Flying Diamond, covered in a fresh blanket of heavy wet snow, was backwoods quiet.

Sandi tossed a couple of pieces of cherrywood on the fire Henry had built and sat back down next to him on the overstuffed leather couch he had pulled up in front of the fireplace.

Henry gave her a puzzled half smile. "Now that we're settled in, maybe we can reason through this telomerase thing one more time."

"Okay by me," said Sandi, relaxing back and kicking off her shoes. "Why don't we start with that message Julie left on your answering machine for CJ?"

"Speaking of CJ, he should've been here by now. Julie said he left at four."

"Snowstorms slow things down, Henry, especially airplanes."

"Yeah. Okay, let's replay the message." Leaning toward an end table, Henry tapped the play button on his answering machine and listened to Julie's message once again.

"Henry, it's Julie. CJ's on his way to Durango. He's on a United Express flight and should be there by seven. Said he'd get a ride to the ranch on his own. By the way, you should know he's ticked about you running off half-cocked. When he gets there, tell him I made a few additional athletic connections that might be of some help. Rontella and Cardashian were big-time collegiate rowers in their day, more than a generation apart, but they were both crew captains during their days at Pennsylvania schools. I also did some checking on a lowlife named Manuel Hernández. He's a new fly in the ointment you don't know about. CJ can fill you in on him. Anyway, I found out that he was Cardashian's coxswain when Cardashian was chalking up rowing honors at Penn. Three strange bedfellows if you ask me. Anyway, that's it for now. I'll call you back if I get any more. Stay warm. I hear one of our springtime-in-the-Rockies snowstorms is headed your way."

The message clicked off to a loud beep, leaving Henry stroking his chin and Sandi looking perplexed.

"Let's see," said Henry, leaning forward, one hand on his knee. "We've got a bunch of missing and potentially lethal telomerase gels, two dead scientists, at least two people somehow connected to their deaths by the sport of rowing, some clown named Hernández who until a couple of hours ago we'd never heard of, a missing athletic trainer, and a pair of bloody jogging shorts." Thumping his forehead disgustedly, Henry added, "Did I leave anything out?"

"No."

"Maybe we should've just left this whole mess for Lieutenant Menton to resolve," said Henry, sounding overwhelmed.

"And have me miss out on a trip to the Flying Diamond? No way," said Sandi, smiling, hoping to keep Henry upbeat, and his mind off Tess.

"Maybe this Hernández guy Julie mentioned is the key."

"Could be. A coxswain, though? I thought a coxswain's job was to scream at the crew to get them to row harder. Never really considered them athletes," said Henry.

"I think they have some responsibility for steering the scull as well. I've never been into rowing myself."

"Think Hernández may have been orchestrating this whole thing?"

"No. It's coming from higher up than some cheerleading coxswain."

"Then where do we go from here?"

"We wait for CJ, see if three heads are better than one."

"And if not?" asked Sandi, snuggling up to Henry. "What are our marching orders then?"

"Then I guess we let Menton do his job." Henry slipped his arm around Sandi and stared into the roaring fire.

"Let's not worry about it right now."

"I won't if you won't," said Henry, reclining and pulling Sandi down onto him.

Relaxing into Henry's arms, tingling from the touch of his fingers slowly working their way down her spine, Sandi met Henry's eager kiss. "Pull me into you," she said, breaking the kiss.

"Is that a new marching order?"

Rolling her body into Henry's to punctuate her message, she said, "Yes."

"Then I guess I'd better comply," said Henry, entwining Sandi's left leg in his and ending the conversation with a deep, passionate kiss.

Stoking the fire, shirtless and spent from lovemaking, Henry flinched and mumbled, "What the . . . ?" as the jingle of his antique doorbell interrupted his and Sandi's interlude.

"Company?" asked Sandi, hastily slipping on her blouse and jeans and patting the floor with her feet for her shoes.

"CJ," said Henry, shaking his head, donning his shirt and pants, padding toward the door shoeless and thinking, *Guess he's just paying me back.*

"Hold your horses, CJ," said Henry, swinging open the door.

Dressed in coveralls and wearing a ski mask, Jamie Lee exploded into the entryway, jammed the edge of her Bowie knife against Henry's throat, smiled, and began backing him into the room. "You have a pair of jogging shorts I'd like back, Dr. Bales. Just hand them over and we'll be done with our business real quick."

It hadn't been difficult for Jamie Lee to get directions to the Flying Diamond or to case its corrals and barns while Henry and Sandi had been making love. And it had been child's play to rifle Henry's truck in a failed effort to find the jogging shorts. But deciding to take on Bales and the Artorio woman together, knowing that a two-on-one confrontation would be risky, had been a headier decision.

Unaware of what was happening until Henry nearly backed into the couch, Sandi looked up and forced back a scream. "Stay put," said Henry.

"Better do as he says," said Jamie Lee, nudging Henry toward the fireplace until he was facing Sandi. "If you don't mind, the shorts," she said matter-of-factly, tweaking the knife blade against Henry's neck and breaking the skin.

"They're in my truck," said Henry, watching the fear in Sandi's face, trying his best to remain calm.

"Already searched it. Didn't find a thing. It's truth time, Dr. Bales. Not time to stall."

"Did you look beneath the lip of the bed liner behind the cab?"

"No."

"Then you missed them," said Henry, feeling a stream of blood work its way down his neck.

"We'll find out soon enough." Eyeing Sandi, Jamie Lee smiled. "Hope your loverboy here isn't lying, sweet pea. Think it's time you got up off that couch."

Never taking her eyes off Henry's, Sandi stood up.

"We're gonna take a walk to the barn, sweet pea. You'll be leading the way; we'll be right behind. If you so much as flinch from a snowflake, you can bet I'll slit loverboy's throat." Pressing her blade against Henry's neck to reinforce the message, Jamie Lee nodded for Sandi to move toward the door. "Move it out."

"He doesn't have any shoes on," said Sandi, her voice cracking as she headed toward the front door.

"And you're not wearing a bra. I caught the tail end of your screwing session. Sweet, real sweet. Just keep moving. We won't be outside long enough for anyone's feet to freeze off."

Sandi stepped onto the porch into a twenty-mile-per-hour headwind and a rush of blowing snow. Staring out across the meadows, trying to accommodate to near whiteout conditions, she shivered, wrapped her arms around herself, and walked down the front steps.

The Flying Diamond's original barn, long transformed into a garage and shop for Henry's automotive tinkering, sat catty-corner from the house across thirty yards of graveled drive. Hugging herself and crunching across the snow-covered gravel into the wind, Sandi clenched her teeth, hoping to keep her emotions under control. Recalling her father's stubborn toughness, she checked her fear and continued toward the barn.

When she reached the open barn door, Jamie Lee called out, "Step inside, turn on the lights, and don't look back."

"I don't know where the light switch is," said Sandi.

"Just inside the door on the wall to your right," said Henry, feeling the knife blade vibrate against his Adam's apple, realizing he was shivering uncontrollably and that the soles of his feet had started to go numb.

Flipping on the lights, Sandi moved inside the barn, stopping just short of the front bumper of Henry's pickup when Jamie Lee said, "Hold it. Get the shorts and bring them back over here to me."

Moving around the pickup, feeling along the side rail, Sandi located the jogging shorts, slipped them from beneath the truck's bed liner, and turned to face their assailant.

"Turn the hell back around and step backward until I say stop, then hand the shorts to me," said Jamie Lee.

Walking backward, Sandi retraced her steps.

"Stop." Jamie Lee grabbed the shorts, tucking them into one of her coverall pockets. Satisfied that she had what she had come for, she slipped her knife across the angle of Henry's chin, drawing a rush of blood. "Just so you know I mean business. A message before the madness, Dr. Bales." Jamie Lee smiled as Henry grabbed his jaw, groaning in pain. Rapping Henry's hand with the butt of her knife, she felt a sudden rush of pleasure. The same kind she experienced just before she snapped the logging foreman's neck and plunged her knife into Anthony Rontella's belly. Pleasure that escalated until the engine noise from a vehicle heading up the lane toward the ranch house snatched her attention. Momentarily flustered, her eyes darted around the barn as she realized that the vehicle was getting closer. "Where are the keys to your truck?"

"Try the ignition," said Henry sarcastically, as a stab of pain from a new neck wound touched off a chorus of self-preservation he hadn't felt since Vietnam. Grunting, he shot both elbows into Jamie Lee's midsection, doubling her over and sending her staggering forward into a startled Sandi.

Regaining her balance and grabbing Sandi around the

neck, Jamie Lee jammed the point of her knife into Sandi's ear.

"Stop! I'll kill her. I promise," screamed Jamie Lee, freezing Henry in his tracks as the lights from the approaching vehicle flooded the barn.

Shoving Sandi aside, Jamie Lee ran for Henry's pickup, jumped in, and started the engine. Flooring the accelerator, she kicked up a trail of dirt and gravel, barely missing Sandi's outstretched legs and creasing Henry's right hip with a fender as she cleared the barn door.

The rack of floodlights mounted on the roof of Will Haskins's truck had been designed to deliver enough backwoods candlepower to bathe a fifty-square-foot campsite in light. Blinded by the light, Jamie Lee was on top of Haskins's one-ton flatbed before she had a chance to steer clear of his truck. The impact from the crash sent her flying head first into the windshield and snapped CJ and Will against their seat belt harnesses so hard that for days afterward they both complained of shoulder pain.

The blare from the horn of Henry's truck echoed down the Cedar Creek valley for what seemed to Henry like much longer than the seconds it took for him and CJ to reach the pickup and find Jamie Lee slumped against the steering wheel, moaning, blood streaming from her mouth and soaking her ski mask.

"What the shit?" said CJ, leaning into the cab and shaking his head as Henry slipped off Jamie Lee's ski mask and checked to see if she was breathing. Satisfied that she was, Henry said, "We better make sure she didn't snap her neck."

"What the hell are you talking about, Henry?" said CJ, looking at Henry's bare feet and bloodstained shirt.

"You're bleeding like a stuck pig your damn self. We'd better tend to that first."

Henry ran his hands across his chin and checked his bloody fingers. "I'll be fine," he said, ripping off a shirt cuff and pressing it to his jaw.

"What the hell happened?"

"I'll tell you in a bit." Henry turned and headed for the barn. "Just stay with her a second while I check on Sandi."

Finding a confused and shivering Sandi standing in the barn's doorway, Henry embraced her so tightly that she finally said, "Henry, I can't breathe; let me come up for air."

Realizing only then that Henry was wounded and bleeding, Sandi pulled a wad of tissues from her pocket, and pressed them to Henry's jaw as they walked back into the floodlights toward CJ.

"Now will you tell us what happened?" said CJ, looking at Henry and Sandi as a startled Will Haskins stood beside him shaking his head.

"Jungle water, pure and simple," said Henry, knowing CJ would get his drift.

Chapter 43

The lanky country-boy-looking paramedic attending to his wounds barely looked eighteen to Henry, and except for the blond hair and the hint of a goatee just below the cleft in his chin, the man reminded Henry a little of himself years earlier.

"There you are," said the paramedic, placing a final strip of tape along the bottom edge of Henry's dressing. "That should hold you until we get to the hospital. Why don't you go on and hop in the ambulance? We'll head out in a couple of minutes."

"Sorry, friend, I'll be staying here." Henry leaned forward on the battered old sawhorse he was seated on, adjusted the range duster Sandi had brought out of the house for him, and gazed around the barn.

"You can't. That one cut you've got is pretty wicked. It'll require some suturing."

"It can wait." Henry glanced down at his horse-blanket-wrapped feet, more concerned about frostbite than knife wounds. Looking beyond the barn door, he realized for the first time since La Plata County Sheriff Booker Reardon had arrived with his slow-talking deputy in tow that the snow had stopped. The sky was partially clear, and the fresh-fallen snow resembled the placid surface of a glimmering moonlit lake.

The barn, now Reardon's base of operation, had finally lost its chill, thanks to CJ's firing up the barn's old coal stoker. Earlier the sheriff and a second paramedic had walked a dazed, belligerent, cursing Jamie Lee Custus to a waiting ambulance, where she had been attended to and fielded a barrage of questions from Reardon without ever giving him more than her name.

Sandi stood next to Henry, draped in one of Henry's heavy canvas winter range dusters. Finally warm enough to stop shivering, she looked for all the world to Henry like some Old West version of a female desperado.

Shaking his head, Reardon returned from the ambulance past the leaking radiator of Henry's pickup, which remained embedded in the cow catcher on the front of Will Haskins's truck, and reentered the barn.

"Woman's name's Jamie Lee Custus," said Reardon, striding up to Henry. "Says she's not talking to anyone, especially me, until she sees a doctor and a lawyer. I'm gonna have 'em run her on over to the hospital and make sure her brains aren't scrambled before I try to question her again." Eyeing Henry's dressing, Reardon said, "Suggest you let the folks at the hospital give you the once-over as well."

"No need. I'm all right."

Reardon, who had been a close friend and hunting buddy of Henry's father and had known Henry since he was born, smiled at Sandi before responding. "Save your macho act for the city, Henry Bales. You're getting in the ambulance and riding back down to Durango. Consider it an order."

Curtailing his bravado, Henry looked at Sandi and mumbled, "Okay."

"You can ride up front with Ethridge here," said Reardon, glancing at the paramedic who had dressed Henry's wounds. "I'll ride in back and try to get more than grunts and profanity out of the Custus woman." Reardon slipped the jogging shorts he had taken from Jamie Lee out of his coat pocket and examined them curiously. "Maybe I can convince her that she needs to cooperate, especially since you claim these shorts connect her to a dead man. Not to mention the fact that she's staring at more than a little jail time for her shenanigans out here."

"Do what you can to loosen her up," said Henry.

"Oh, she'll have a chance to get loose," said Reardon with a grin. "And so will you, and Dr. Artorio and Mr. Floyd. Believe me, before this is over, everyone will have a chance to tell their tale."

"Tonight?" asked Henry.

"Yeah, tonight," said Reardon, his tone of voice acutely serious. "But first I wanna find out why our friend in the ambulance was two ticks away from cutting your throat and why she was carrying around those gels you told me about. My deputy found a dozen baggies full of 'em in a duffel in the trunk of her car just up the road. The quicker I know the whole story, the quicker we all go home. Someone will bring you back here when we're finished. And Henry, just for starters, how about telling me again why a woman wielding a Bowie knife would want to drop by the Flying Diamond and kill you."

"Like I said before, it's a long story, Sheriff, one that gets real convoluted."

"No problem, I've heard long stories before. Besides, we've got the whole rest of the night."

Chapter 44

It was two A.M. when Henry, arm in arm with Sandi and a trailing CJ, arrived back at the Flying Diamond to a dark, chilly house and a cold fireplace full of ashes.

Before leaving Sheriff Reardon's office, Henry had popped a couple of Motrin, hoping to take the edge off his jaw pain. But the pills weren't working and the twenty-five stitches running just beneath his jawline and tugging at his swollen skin only intensified the pain.

"I'm ready to call it a night," said Sandi, slipping her arm out of Henry's and stretching as Henry flipped on the entryway lights.

"Me too," said CJ.

"Think I'll have a glass of orange juice before I hit the sack," said Henry, heading for the kitchen. "Anyone else up for refreshments?" he added sarcastically.

Sandi shook her head. "No way. One more shot of acid and my stomach will dissolve." Giving Henry a kiss on the cheek, she turned and headed down the hallway toward Henry's bedroom.

"CJ?" asked Henry, swinging open the refrigerator door, taking out a quart of orange juice, and placing it on the kitchen table.

"If you cut it with a shot of vodka."

Henry walked across the room and slipped a dusty, unopened bottle of vodka from an overhead wine rack. "Stuff's been slumbering there for years," he said, uncapping the bottle and handing it to CJ. Then, grabbing two glasses from a nearby cabinet, he took a seat across the table from CJ, poured himself a glass of juice, and stared at it intently. "What's your take on the person Sheriff Reardon's calling Sweets?"

CJ filled his glass half full of orange juice, capped the pour with a generous splash of vodka, twirled the mixture around slowly, and took a drink. He wanted to say, *Tess's dead, Henry, let go of it,* but instead he found himself rethinking their past few hours with the sheriff.

Reardon had turned out to be a sly old cuss. After leaving the hospital with Custus in handcuffs and hearing their full telomerase story in his Durango office, including the details of how Cardashian, Leah Tanner, and Tess Gilliam had died as well as accounts of their sparring matches with Lieutenant Menton, Reardon had escorted them to a drafty room, where they spent the next half hour exchanging notes on everything from rowing tattoos to Bowie knives.

Although according to Reardon, the Custus woman was claiming that some mythical person named Sweets had orchestrated the entire telomerase deal, none of them had taken her claims seriously. At least not until Reardon, as serious-faced as Henry had ever seen him, had pointed out that Sweets supposedly lived in a Denver suburb, spat out orders to Custus using some voice-altering device, thought nothing of having people killed, and planned to meet Jamie Lee at noon the next day in the Durango airport.

When Henry asked the sheriff how he had been able to swing the Custus woman from belligerent to cooperative, the sheriff had thought a second, smiled, and said, "I offered her a deal. Told her that if she tossed me a bone I'd make sure the boys in blue up in Denver didn't go after her for killing Tess Gilliam, and that I'd convince the prosecutor down here to consider her story that she acted in self-defense should that guy Anthony Rontella's body ever turn up."

When Henry jumped from his chair screaming, "But she killed them both!" the sheriff had calmly eased him back down, saying, "Don't think so, Henry. Her expertise is with a knife, not a gun. From what she says, I'd wager your friend Tess was more than likely killed by this person Sweets." The sheriff's assessment had caught Henry off guard, sending him into a silent funk that lasted until they were almost back to the Flying Diamond.

Pouring himself a second glass of orange juice, this time cutting it with vodka, Henry glanced at CJ and said, "Let's run over the list of probable killers once again. Maybe we can turn one of them into Sweets."

"Okay," said CJ, sitting back in his chair and taking a long sip of his drink.

"Tanner," said Henry.

CJ shook his head. "Kill his own daughter? Nope. Be-sides, there's no tattoo tie-in, and as far as we know he doesn't have the scientific background."

"Patterson, then."

"I'd put him at the top of my list. He's a doctor, he knew Cardashian, and Julie said that he had research ex-perience. Strange, though, when I questioned him in his office he damn near bragged about his lack of athletic skills. If rowing's our link, he sure didn't strike me as any kind of rowing jock."

"He could've been trying to throw you a curve."

"Maybe, but somehow he doesn't totally fit the bill. That leaves Coach Drake," said CJ.

"Or Hernández, that Cuban you told me about."

"Nah, he's a flunky. Besides, Flora Jean kicked his ass and took his gun."

"That doesn't mean he's not our key. You said yourself he had a tattoo. We know from what Julie dug up that he was a coxswain at Penn, and unlike the Custus woman, he prefers guns to knives."

"You're stretching, Henry. Let's get back to Dr. Pat-terson and Coach Drake."

"Fine."

"Is there anything either one of them told you that we might have overlooked?"

CJ took another long swallow from his drink. "Let's see. Julie did tell me that Coach Drake made a killing in pharmaceuticals. As for Patterson—he did mention that Cardashian and Tess gave the athletic department an in-service cardiopulmonary review and an update on telo-merase last year, and come to think of it—"

"Hold it, CJ. Back up a sec. Patterson told you that

Cardashian ran an in-service for the athletic department? And Tess was involved? That doesn't make sense. Sports physiology would have been way out of Tess's league."

CJ thought for a minute. "Actually, he didn't say Tess was involved in the in-service. Guess I just assumed that since they were discussing telomerase, their dog-and-pony show included Tess."

"I'd bet against it," said Henry. "If anyone else was involved, my money would be on Dr. Patterson."

"Think Patterson slipped up by mentioning the in-service to me and that's why Drake's covering his ass so tight?"

"That, or he's covering his own," said Henry.

"Think one of them's our man Sweets?" asked CJ.

"We'll find out tomorrow at noon."

"Unless the sheriff reneges on his promise," said CJ.

"He can't," said Henry with a smile. "You can bet Sweets isn't traveling using his real name. The sheriff's going to need us to point Sweets out."

"Remember that tomorrow, Henry. Finger pointing, that's our job; nothing else."

"I'll remember," said Henry, swirling his drink around in his glass as he thought about the fact that he was finally going to have the chance to settle up for Tess.

Chapter 45

Lieutenant Menton never liked plans in which private citizens became involved in police work. But he was in Durango, operating outside his jurisdiction, working with Sheriff Reardon to detain and hopefully arrest the person thought to be responsible for what Denver's two daily newspapers were touting as the "Fountain-of-Youth Murders."

After receiving a lengthy three A.M. explanatory phone call from Reardon at home, Menton had tried his best to convince Reardon to come up with a better plan for dealing with the person he was calling Sweets than to involve CJ Floyd and Henry Bales in a possible on-site airport identification. He had even spent the early-morning hours before his flight to Durango unsuccessfully trying to locate each of the three suspects he thought might be

Sweets: Dr. David Patterson, Nate Tanner, and Coach Ellis Drake.

According to Patterson's wife, Patterson had left late the previous evening to drive to Arizona for a week-long fly-fishing trip. Menton had arrived at Tanner's $750,000 Cherry Creek condo unannounced at four-thirty A.M. to find that Tanner wasn't home. During a follow-up seven A.M. phone call to Tanner's office, he had learned that Tanner was on a business trip and hadn't shared his plans with anyone. After also failing in his bid to contact Coach Drake, Menton had had his people check the passenger manifests for all three daily flights to Durango to find, not surprisingly, that the names Nate Tanner, David Patterson, or Ellis Drake didn't appear on any of them.

Menton and his partner had arrived in snow-covered Durango on a smooth flight from Denver at nine A.M. They had been debriefed by Sheriff Reardon, and together Menton and Reardon had counseled CJ and Henry about their critical role in identifying the person known as Sweets. When Menton had complained one last time that he could identify the suspect himself, Reardon had snapped, "But I can't, Lieutenant, and since you're a guest in my house, let's say for the time being, you play by my rules."

Now Menton and the sheriff stood with CJ and Henry several feet beyond the doorway where deplaning passengers entered the small-town terminal. Sheriff's deputies had been strategically placed throughout the terminal, and for the past half hour everyone had been nervously awaiting the arrival of Flight 964. From where they were standing, CJ and Henry had a clear view of passengers as they made their way from the planes to the terminal.

Checking his watch and eyeing CJ, Henry, and Menton, the sheriff decided to rehash their procedure one last time. "Security will make sure that the passengers coming through the door and into the terminal do so one at a time. The flight's only half full, so there won't be but eighteen passengers." Then, looking at Henry, he said, "I'm bending the rules for you, Henry. Don't screw up. Once you ID the suspect, you and CJ move back into the secured area behind us, and don't move back out till the lieutenant or I tell you it's okay. Got it?"

"Loud and clear," said CJ, nodding, along with Henry.

Flight 964 arrived at the gate twenty minutes behind schedule. During the delay, Henry's two trips to the airport coffee shop to assure Sandi that everything was still all right only served to reinforce Lieutenant Menton's theory that law enforcement should be left to the police.

The first passenger off the plane, a tubby, balding, ruddy-looking man, jiggled his way down the plane's exit stairs, smiling and clutching a shopping bag to his stomach. He was followed down the stairway by half a dozen children and their parents, most of them loaded down with Denver Broncos paraphernalia. A couple of ranchers from nearby Cortez whom Henry recognized made their way down the stairway just behind the last straggling child.

Thirteen people were strung out across the tarmac when the next passenger appeared in the exit doorway, paused, cane in hand, coat draped over one arm, looked around, and started down the stairs.

Henry and Menton looked at one another, wide-eyed. "I'll be damned," said Henry, realizing that the person walking down the stairway was Sweets. Suddenly things

325

made sense. The clues had been there all along. He'd just overlooked them.

Picking up on the signals between Henry and Menton, CJ asked, "Who is she?" watching the smallish, stately-looking woman leave the stairway and start across the tarmac.

"Louise Adler, dean of CU's medical school," said Henry, his voice a mix of surprise and disgust as the disjointed facets of Cardashian's telomerase gambit started to tumble into place. An alliance between Cardashian and Adler made sense. Adler had the financial wherewithal to keep Cardashian's unethical project moving, and she had the medical know-how and ancillary research expertise to help Cardashian mastermind the deal. Even the athletic department in-service that CJ had mentioned now fit. Adler, not Patterson, had been the other in-service doctor. What didn't make sense to Henry was why.

Although seeing Adler had Henry momentarily shocked, CJ remained focused on carrying out their assignment. Grasping Henry by the arm, he began moving back toward their preassigned position when a series of shots he recognized as coming from a semiautomatic weapon rang out, and Louise Adler slumped to the ground.

The high-pitched screams of children, the immediate wave of hysteria, and the rush of people away from the entry doorway and into the terminal sent Lieutenant Menton sprawling to the floor. CJ shoved Henry backward as the ghost of Vietnam and the tightly wired survival reflex of a former patrol boat machine-gunner had him scanning the area for the source of the sniper's fire.

He never saw the person's face or the gun—only the quick glimpse of a profile as the shooter turned to run.

Bounding across an X-ray scanner in an adrenaline rush, knocking over screaming passengers, CJ was on the shooter in seconds. Tackling the man from behind and slamming him to the floor, he felt the weight of another body crashing down on top of him. Looking around, CJ found both his legs and the shooter's locked in Henry Bales's arms as Lieutenant Menton's partner came sliding toward them on his knees, his service revolver aimed point-blank at the gunman's head. The only words CJ was certain he heard in the mass of confusion were those of Menton's lanky partner shouting, "Don't move a fucking muscle!"

A mixture of fear and exhilaration rushed through CJ as he eased his weight off the gunman. Henry released his grip on CJ's legs as Menton's partner, still kneeling with his gun barrel only inches from the shooter's head, snapped the man's arms behind his back and slammed a pair of handcuffs on his wrists.

"Just keep kissing the floor," he said as Lieutenant Menton rushed up, his hands and shirt splattered with blood. Looking at Henry in desperation, Menton said, "Adler's injured bad. She needs a doctor." Then, bending down and grabbing the gunman by the hair, he jerked the man's head back for a look at his face. "Tanner," he said, relaxing his grip. "Son of a bitch."

Shaking his head in disbelief, Henry nudged his way past Sheriff Reardon, who was shouting into his walkie-talkie for an ambulance, and crossed the room full of terrified people to the doorway onto the tarmac. It wasn't until he reached the doorway that he realized that CJ was right behind him. "What the hell are you doing?" screamed Henry, pausing in the doorway.

"Same thing I was doing twenty-seven years ago. Covering your ass," said CJ as they both raced across the tarmac toward Louise Adler.

Lying on her back in a pool of blood and laboring to breathe, Adler forced out a bloody gurgle of unintelligible words as Henry knelt beside her.

"Louise, it's Henry Bales."

"Henry," she mumbled. Then, inhaling deeply, she fixed her eyes on his and said desperately, "I can't move my arms or legs."

For a split second, Henry's thoughts turned to Tess, and he considered getting up and walking away. But when he heard ambulance sirens approaching, he instinctively returned to the task at hand.

"She's stopped breathing," said Henry, looking at Adler, then glancing in the direction of the sirens. "Still remember the routine?"

"How could I forget?" said CJ, bending down, lifting Adler's chin with his hand, and forcing a breath into her mouth as Henry, hands cupped across Adler's upper sternum, counted off, "One and two and three and four and . . ." as they resurrected a CPR drill from their days in Vietnam.

Chapter 46

The moisture from the snowstorm that CJ had buf-feted through by airplane two days earlier had greened up most of Will Haskins's Three Forks Ranch. The sun was shining brightly, and the forecast called for clear skies for the Animas Valley for the remainder of the week.

Henry, Sandi, and CJ were seated at Haskins's dining room table, an ornate eighteenth-century Spanish heir-loom capable of accommodating twelve, enjoying a breakfast of cowboy biscuits, poorboy sausage, grits, and red-eye gravy that Will had insisted on preparing before dropping them at the airport for their flight back to Den-ver. Since losing his wife two years earlier, Haskins had decided to try his hand at mastering the art of cooking, and he never missed a chance to show off his skills.

"More sausage, Henry?" asked Haskins, looking across the table at Henry's empty plate.

"No, but I'll take some more coffee."

Haskins eased his chair back from the table. "It'll take me a minute or two to make some more, but I'll have it in a shake. Can I get anything for anyone else?" said Haskins, heading for the kitchen.

"Just coffee," said CJ.

"Nothing for me," said Sandi. "I'm stuffed." Looking at Henry and patting her stomach, she added, "I could get used to this ranching life."

"You will, sweetheart, you will," said Henry, cocking his head and giving Sandi his best Humphrey Bogart impression.

Sandi smiled, knowing that in spite of all good intentions, long-distance romances had a way of withering on the vine. "Make him keep his promises, CJ. He's made some whoppers."

"You can count on it. Mavis will hold him to it too."

"Good," said Sandi, watching Henry ease his chair back from the table and stare out toward the meadows. "A penny for your thoughts."

"Just thinking about Tess. Guess I'm back to rehashing this telomerase thing all over again."

"You're gonna have to let it go, Henry," said CJ. "The scam's over; Adler's lying in a hospital, probably paralyzed for life. The cops found the voice-altering gizmo that Hernández told them about, the one Adler used to play Sweets from her family home in Golden. And, on top of that, they confiscated a stash of telomerase gels packed away in twenty colostomy bags in her basement. Each bag contained a different handwritten note from Adler congratulating herself on forever changing the face of medical science. Sounds to me like Adler has enough deviant personality quirks going for her to make her some prison psychologist's career."

"The woman had more behavorial pathology than that," said Henry, still thinking about Tess. "Shrinks call it a diety complex. Knowing her, I'd say her problem was closer to wanting to be than to play God. Maybe that's why she thought she could succeed with Cardashian's telomerase plan." Henry took a final sip of coffee and set his cup down hard on the table to punctuate his point. "Any news about the college coaches and trainers Menton claims Anthony Rontella had recruited? The ones who were going to try out Cardashian's telomerase gels on their athletes?"

"Menton has their names. He found a list of them tucked inside the duffel bag of Rontella's that Custus was lugging around. Good thing too. Menton said that from what he could piece together, Rontella was planning on having his scheme up and running within weeks," said CJ.

"Sounds like we could have had a string of dead athletes down the line," said Sandi.

"Or a bunch of supermen," said Henry, who still wasn't so sure that Cardashian's scheme inevitably produced cancer.

"Not according to Menton. Now that he has what he thinks are all the gels, he says this is a done deal—no dead athletes and no pool of athletic supermen. What more could you want?"

"I want Adler to admit she killed Tess."

"You won't like this, Henry, but I doubt that her lawyers are going to let Adler own up to that right now."

"How long can she stonewall?" asked Henry.

"One sure thing, she can't do it forever. That cane-headed .32 she was carrying, the one Menton found in her luggage, is probably the gun she used to kill Tess. Sooner or later the cops will nail the connection, and once they do, you'll have your answer. Not to mention that Menton reluctantly told me that they found Rontella's, Hernández's, and the Custus woman's home phone numbers jotted on a prescription pad in Adler's study. Hell, with what the cops have on her, if she lives they'll slam-dunk her for life."

"And Nathan Tanner?" asked Henry, looking back at CJ. "What about him?"

"He's a nut case, if you ask me—whacked out with grief. I don't know exactly how he found out about Adler but he admitted to Menton that he was having me tailed."

"That explains why he was in Durango. It doesn't explain how he knew when Adler was arriving or that she was responsible for killing his daughter," said Henry.

"Maybe Rontella clued him in," said CJ.

Henry shook his head. "I doubt it."

"Custus, then?"

"She'd be my guess," said Henry. "With both Rontella and Adler out of the way, Custus knew that nothing could come back to bite her. All she'd have to do would be to make a phone call or two and convince a loose screw like Tanner that Adler killed his daughter."

"Think the cops can prove it?" asked CJ.

"Maybe with the right phone record or two. But it

would be one hell of a neat fit and nothing in life works out quite that perfectly," said Henry.

"Then quit dissecting everything, Henry. We don't know what lead Tanner was following. All we know for now is that he was tailing me and he was at the airport."

"All we have are theories, then," said Henry skeptically.

"That's all. Remember when we started this deal and I told you that mucking around in my world was a whole lot different from operating in yours?"

"Yes," said Henry.

"Still is."

Henry shrugged and shook his head.

"Have they found Rontella's body yet?" asked Sandi.

"No. But trust me, it'll turn up, and then it will be Custus's turn to twist in the wind. That's probably when all your answers will finally turn up, Henry," said CJ, glancing up as Will Haskins returned, a freshly brewed pot of coffee in his hand.

"Hot off the burner." Haskins poured CJ the first cup.

Inhaling the coffee's rich aroma, CJ looked out toward Haskins's rolling pastures and then back at Sandi and Henry. "Guess this ranching life really could capture you," he said, taking a sip of coffee.

"That it could," said Henry as Haskins filled his cup to the brim. Then, looking at Sandi, he added, "Like a lover, or the dream of becoming an athletic superstar, or the idea of discovering a fountain of youth."

Chapter 47

Few people ever told Fidel Castro no, so when Cuba's premier requested the pleasure of seeing his country's number one heavyweight put through his pre-Olympic paces, Atina Salas had little choice but to go along.

Security for the premier was surprisingly low-key on the evening Castro picked to watch Ernesto Salas display his boxing skills. The swamp-cooled Quonset hut that had been steaming and teeming with spectators the day Ernesto had become ill now echoed with the noise of fewer than thirty people.

Dr. Gómez was present, head bobbing, grinning like a carnival doll, along with Atina, Ernesto's trainers and coaches, and several handpicked Pinar del Río citizens. The Quonset hut's center ring was the only one standing, its two companions having been temporarily dismantled in the name of security.

It was almost eight P.M. when Ernesto entered the ring to a hearty round of cheers. All day long he had felt a renewed sense of energy. He was convinced that in honor of the premier's visit, the "vitamin-laced" suppositories that he had never stopped taking, even when he was sick—the ones that his dead friend Rulon Mantero had assured him would make him invincible—had finally kicked in. Before leaving his dressing room, he had even mentioned the fact to Atina. "I'm back to myself," he had told her. "Even stronger." He was glad he had saved a stash of the suppositories for occasions like this.

Seated on a sagging bleacher, two people down from the comandante, Atina felt a special sense of nervousness as she watched Ernesto warm up, trepidation brought on by the fact that Anthony Rontella had disappeared, her cigar scam was in the throes of final collapse, and four feet away from her sat a man who could have her shot with the snap of a finger should he ever get wind of what she had done.

Ernesto looked as fit as ever, without even the hint of a side effect from his mysterious illness. Dr. Gómez had pronounced him ready to fight, and now all that mattered was the fact that for five rounds Ernesto would have to put on his very best show.

Ernesto's sparring partner for the evening, in a rare boxing match that only the premier could command, was a man considered by many, at least in terms of technique, to be Ernesto's equal. Atina crossed her fingers, realizing that should Ernesto falter in front of the premier he could easily be replaced by his challenger, and her dream of attending the Olympics, like her tobacco scam, would turn to dust.

As the fighters met at center ring to take their instructions, the premier leaned over to Atina. "Good luck to your grandson," he said, smiling and flashing a row of badly stained teeth.

"Thank you," said Atina, taking a deep breath and crossing herself.

The two boxers circled one another in a game of cat-and-mouse for most of round one, neither man landing any serious punches, and except for a few more jabs and flurries, round two was more of the same.

Rounds three and four were won by Ernesto's opponent as it appeared that for some reason Ernesto had faded. Worried, afraid to turn her head and look at the premier, Atina was prepared to watch Ernesto's boxing career evaporate when, twenty seconds into the final round, Ernesto seemed to find a new source of energy, energy that appeared out of nowhere as if someone had slipped him an invisible supply of oxygen.

Realizing that indeed the mysterious suppositories had done their job, Ernesto peppered the other boxer with left jabs until the man wobbled into the ropes. Then capping his boxing display with a series of fierce punches and a lumbering right hook, he sent his opponent sprawling face first into the canvas.

Rising to his feet and applauding as everyone else in the stands followed suit, Castro looked at Atina and asked in an excited, piercing voice that soared beyond his beard, "He is an amazing Cuban son. Does his second wind always come exactly when he needs it?"

Stumped for an answer, Atina watched as Ernesto,

buoyed by victory, pranced around the ring, kissing his gloves, waving them up to her.

Realizing that the premier expected a response, Atina turned slowly in his direction. Staring him squarely in the eye and watching the accommodating yet determined expression on his face, she said, "His skills are from our past, comandante. Handed down to him by the *cabildos*. They are, in a way, everlasting, a gift as precious as life itself."